The Money Run

P. R. Steele

* A caper, as in the time of Shakespeare, is a trick, a prank, and in some instances, a gambol or a cavort.

DEDICATION

This book is dedicated to my family. To my wife Gail, Troy, Jennifer and Mike, David and Leigh, and Jason. And very importantly our grandchildren, Little Bit, Hankster, Charley, Mae, the big Fella, Moe, Cameron and Nathan.

ACKNOWLEDGMENTS

Cover design: P. R. Steele
Interior design: Amy Ruiz Fritz
Editor: Sue Clark

NOTE

Thieves find any and every reason to justify theft. You name it, and it's already been pulled. But you already knew that. During the Vietnam War, the over twenty-million-dollar military, bi-monthly payroll on Okinawa was in cash, delivered from base to base ... on a single helicopter. That payday flight was called the money run. You probably didn't know that.

IN THE BEGINNING

Near Khe Sanh, South Vietnam   April 7, 1971

The Viet Cong sniper checked the sun's position. He didn't need the sun to tell him what he already knew. He'd been hiding for more than a couple of hours. He searched through the scope because he wanted a pilot, but in a flight suit for the crewmembers, they all looked the same.

There—three standing beside one of the two helicopters. He watched the Marines walk inside one of the helicopters. One was got into the cockpit. The sniper held back his excitement. A pilot for sure. Three shots and three dead Marines.

He wiped his brow and pushed off the safety. He ignored the sweat burning his eyes, his cramped legs, and the insects feeding on him. Then he put his finger on the trigger.

The mortar attack would commence as soon as he fired. If they could destroy one of the huge helicopters, it would be a great victory. He closed his eyes, inhaled, relaxed, and opened his eye on the scope.

He placed the crosshairs on the Marine in the cockpit.

CHAPTER ONE

"Smile. You can do it. Relax." Jack Higgins winked at the kid in the copilot's seat as he held the guy's Kodak Instamatic camera. The lance corporal had just arrived in 1971 fresh out of aviation mechanics school. He looked like a FNG, a friggin' new guy, asking too many questions. Jack knew it wouldn't take long for the kid to discover the war wasn't about protecting anything American. This war was all about survival and not letting some incompetent senior officer get you killed.

"Hey, Thompson. Come on, man. Smile. You could even tell your girlfriend you're thinking about becoming a pilot." Jack cleared his mind, took the kid's picture, handed the Kodak back to Thompson, and walked outside.

In the shade of the huge helo, Todd Emmitt, his copilot, sat in front of the stub-wing fuel sponson reading a letter. He held up a picture.

A cute blonde smiled back at Jack.

"This tour, she stays right here." Todd pointed to his left upper pocket. "My good luck charm right by my heart. I'll never fly without her."

Jack could tell she gave Todd hope, because, among

other things on this tour, Todd always waited for the mail call.

Jack wished he'd found the right one. "You know, you're one lucky bastard."

Todd looked beyond him, to the hills. "Yeah, I know it. But, those slimy bastards are out there. Probably scoping us out."

"Screw this war," Sergeant Charles Pogany, the crew chief said as he hustled outside and around the back of the aircraft.

"Hey, Pogy, what's the matter?" Jack called to him as the left the cockpit for outside..

"This war sucks. Being stuck in the Corps sucks." Pog stuffed a letter in his pocket, and leaned against the stub wing fuel tank. "My mom's taking out a mortgage on the house. Ever since Pop's death, well, she needs to pay off all his business loans. This lousy two hundred bucks a month I get now. . ."

"Hey, Pogy, I've saved a few bucks. . ."

"Thanks, Jack, but I need a bunch." Pog cleared his throat and looked away.

A cold chill shot down Jack's spine. He felt the impact before he heard the sniper from the hills. The first round went into the cockpit. Jack hit the ground, and rolled. His left shoulder burned. The second round exploded next to where he'd been standing.

Both he and Todd ran for the cockpit. Pog lifted the injured kid out of the co-pilot seat.

"Stay back here with Pog. I'll get it turning." Jack yelled as he jumped into the right seat.

"Bullshit," Todd said. He hustled into the bloody left seat. Now they were both easy marks.

A mortar exploded nearby. "Jeez. That's way too close," Todd yelled. "As per the brief, let's beat feet."

Jack's hands flew as he went into the emergency mode, heart pounding as he hurried through the start check list.

Then he turned on the ignition and shoved the start T-handle forward to the auxiliary power plant. The helo's small jet whined as it lit off and accelerated to a hundred percent.

At the same time, Todd flipped on the generator switches as Jack depressed the number one engine start button. To Jack, it seemed forever as the big GE turbine spooled up to twenty percent. He shoved the engine-control handle forward to the on position. Fuel flowed, and at last the engine began to accelerate. After the number one engine starter dropped out, he depressed the number two engine start button.

"Come on, baby," he begged. At a hundred percent, and with the helo's rotor head spinning, they were good to go. Another mortar impacted the ground. Too close. Dirt and dust hit Todd's window.

The big airframe shook as the next mortar exploded on Jack's side. He depressed the radio transmit button and said, "Dimmer Six, the double deuce is ready to lift, and. . ."

All the debris from the close impacts mixed in the rotor wash and obscured everything. The dust cleared. The lead helo in front of them, took off, lifting out of the zone leaving two crewmen wounded on the ground. Jack noticed about six or seven Marines running across the field toward the commanding officer's departing helo. A mortar exploded, knocking several of them down as their commanding officer's aircraft became airborne. Another mortar exploded, blowing two of the abandoned Marines into the air as if they were rag dolls.

God damn it. There's a couple more to add to Bedford's list of dead Marines. You God damn chicken shit.

"Pog, when we get over to those guys Bedford deserted, get all of them on board. I'll be damned if we're leaving anybody behind." Jack wasted no time as he taxied to the wounded Marines. The red clay, pulverized by the mortars,

4

made a fine powdery dust that smelled like gun-smoke as it filled the cockpit.

Pog and the two crewmen on Jack's helo helped the wounded. Jack glanced down at a wounded Marine with a missing leg being carried toward his helicopter. Jack's throat burned. His eyes watered behind his sunglasses, because the wounded Marine looked just like Jack's brother. Those poor Marines were slaughtered. Wasted for nothing. *Bedford, you bastard, you're going to pay for this.*

"Alright, Jack, we got 'em all. You're good to lift," Pog shouted as their helo shook from a mortar exploding too close for comfort.

Jack added power and departed the zone as he transmitted, "Dimmer Six, this is the double deuce. Come in. Over."

"Dimmer two two, I've warned you for the last time not to use that call sign," Bedford yelled over the radio.

Jack raised his sunglasses, looked at Todd and mouthed, *I don't care.*

"Ah-h-h, Roger. . .six. We've cleared the zone. You left several wounded Marines behind," Jack yelled.

"Two two, come up squadron common. Over," Bedford barked.

Jack double-clicked the mic, acknowledging the last transmission. That radio frequency was for their squadron only, not for the public to hear.

"Two two, are you up?" Bedford demanded.

"Jack, cool it. Be careful," Todd said.

Jack just shook his head. "Yes, sir, we're up." Jack took a deep breath. "As I said, you left several wounded behind."

"Two two, that'll be enough. Do you hear me?"

"Yes, sir, but we stayed. . .until we 'evacked all of them."

"Captain, are you questioning my loyalty to the troops?"

"Loyalty? Fact remains, we have two KIAs from your crew, seven wounded, three severely. They were running

5

toward your aircraft. You took off without them."

"That's enough, Higgins," Bedford yelled. "Not another word. Join up and follow me back to the base."

"Sir, be advised, we're going direct to the Sanctuary with the causalities. Over," Jack snapped his words, flipping Bedford the bird, even though there was no way Bedford could see it.

The silence lasted a forever five seconds. "Dimmer two two, this is the end of your insubordinations. When you get back to the Marbles, you and Captain Emmitt will immediately report to my office. Do you understand me?"

"Sir, we understand. As soon as we return to Marble Mountain Air Station, we are to report to your office, suh," Jack slurred.

Todd glared in disbelief at Jack. He raised his visor, saying, "Jack, you didn't have to go there. He knows what he did. He ran."

"I don't give a damn, Toddy. This time it's too much. We both know what he did in sixty-eight."

"Jesus Christ, Jack. That son of a bitch did the same shit back then. He'll lie, dance his way around, but we'll be the ones to get screwed. Just like he did before. And anybody on squadron common heard you and Bedford." Todd jabbed his finger at Jack.

"We've got KIA's and wounded. He flat-assed ran. He can go to hell. This is the proverbial straw."

The aircraft shuddered and bounced around from air turbulence, causing Todd to grab the dash. "Hang on," he said. "Listen, Jack. I'm on your side. But we've got to think this one through. We can't go off half-cocked."

Jack exhaled through pursed lips and shook his head. "But, he killed Herb, and damn near killed John and Dennis. We both know their monthly military disability checks are a disgrace. Shit, nobody can get by on those piddley-ass checks. And," Jack nodded toward the cabin, "what about today? What will we say to their families?"

"I'm with you a hundred percent, Jack, but Cathy and I are getting married. Plus, I've been accepted to fly for American Air. I'm just saying there's nothing we can do. Jack, come on. It won't be just you. He'll screw both of us, and I've got a future."

"Man, don't worry. It won't involve you. This'll be just me. I'll contact Da Nang." Jack pointed to his chest then turned away. "Hey, Pog," he said over the mic. "How are they doing?"

"They're hangin' in there, but our new guy, Thompson, he's lost a lot of blood."

"I've got her redlined." Jack noted the airspeed hovered over the limit.

"Hey, Jack, you're bleeding." Todd said.

"Damn it, Jack," Pog said, as he entered the cockpit. "I saw we took a hit in the fuel sponson where you were standing. Shit, the sniper must've nicked you on your shoulder." He leaned closer and smiled, "Just grazed you. My hero. You'll get another Purple Heart."

"Who cares?" Jack sighed. "Toddy, you got her."

Todd took over the controls as Jack called Da Nang, and got clearance direct to the helo pad on the U.S.S. Sanctuary. Not before long, they landed on the deck and the medics unloaded the wounded Marines.

Todd lifted. They were less than three minutes from the runway at Marble Mountain Air Station, Da Nang.

The cards were stacked against them, and Jack knew it.

CHAPTER TWO

After they landed, Jack and Todd hurried to the line shack to fill out the post flight paperwork called the yellow sheets. Captain Henry "Hank" Jacobs, the squadron legal officer, walked in. He wasn't smiling.

"I need to speak to you all outside. Colonel Bedford sent me to escort you to his office."

"How bad is it?" Todd said, as they walked out.

"Guys, cut me some slack." Hank looked down. "I've tried to get him to listen to reason and simmer down, but you know how he is. I told him he didn't have enough to court martial you or Todd, and he told me to get out of his office."

"Hank, I was the aircraft commander, end of statement. And for the record, Todd didn't say a word."

Artillery going outbound in the distance, and multiple helos taking off and landing, were common-place background noise. Jack blocked it all out. "And as a matter of fact, Hankster, I've got witnesses this time, because the grunts saw it all."

"Did you question his departing the landing zone without the wounded?" Hank looked at Jack.

"Damned straight. And, man, they deserted those poor bastards. The guys on the ground saw what he did. Hell, we all saw him, and there's three KIAs to show for what he did, so far." Jack shrugged his shoulders.

Hank shook his head. "I believe you, but Bedford's crew say they were saving lives."

They entered the squadron's office area. Jack squinted from the bright skylights. Huge vibrating fans stirred the air above the clerks as they worked. The three stopped outside Bedford's office.

"Hank, he's a coward. Lives were lost. And he hauled ass to save his." Jack poked his finger toward Hank.

"Come on, we all know how he is. It's time someone called him on it, but I can't do anything to help you. You all wait here." Hank pointed toward Jack's feet.

Jack saluted an okay.

"I'll come out when the colonel is ready to see you." Hank sighed and straightened his shirt collar. He raised his chin, inhaled, and knocked on Bedford's door.

"Enter," Bedford bellowed. Hank walked in, leaving Jack and Todd in the hallway. Jack stared at the pale gray walls, then turned to watch the Marines as they walked past, carrying what looked like heavy file boxes, paying no attention to him or Todd.

"I think we're screwed." Todd folded his arms and leaned against the wall.

"He's probably just blowing a gasket." Jack frowned. "You keep quiet and let me take the heat."

"Nawh, I've been thinking. You're right. And I'm with you. I don't care. What's he going to do now? Make us shave off all our hair? Fly helicopters in combat in Vietnam? Shit, really and truly. We're bulletproof."

"That's the Toddy that got us through the Tet back in sixty-eight. But, seriously, stay out of this one. I was the aircraft commander."

"I love your Steve McQueen half-ass smirk. You can

kiss my rosy red ass while you're at it."

"You know. I love you, too, man."

"Okay, cut the mushy shit." Todd began to laugh.

Hank opened the door. "Captains Higgins and Emmitt, the CO will see you now.

The five-foot-six-inch Bedford sat behind his oversized metal desk in his leather executive chair, his back toward them, reading some papers. Jack knew Bedford's elevated boots were hanging above the floor from where he sat. His longer-than-regulation, gray-orange tuff bobbed from side to side, just below his bald spot, as he spun around on his throne.

Standing in front of the folding chairs, to Jack and Todd's right, stood the executive officer, Major W. R. "Spit" Hosier, with a fresh chew that distorted his lower lip. Spit held an empty Coke can in his hand for a spittoon. The tobacco stench made Jack work hard to stifle a gag reflex. Captain Jacobs stared straight ahead at the blank wall opposite him. The window air conditioner hummed over the constant rotor noise from the helo operations outside.

With his beady black eyes still on the paperwork, Bedford said, "You two can stand at ease."

He leaned over his desk as he appeared to still study a batch of papers. His lips moved as he read. Without looking up, he snarled, "Didn't I just tell you to stand at attention? Get your asses to attention before I throw both of you in the brig for insubordination." He looked up and pointed toward Jack and Todd, the papers still in his hand.

The two snapped to.

"That's better."

Captain Jacobs cleared his throat, coughed, and then said, "Sir, you just told them to stand at ease."

Bedford glared at Hank, and wiped the spittle from the corner of his mouth. "If I did, I meant at attention. Captain Jacobs, you're excused."

After the door closed, Bedford said, "The Huey

squadron needs two volunteer replacement pilots. Do you want to volunteer or stay here?"

"Sir, stay here, sir," Jack shouted.

"Good. Stay and you'll get the next Forward Air Controller quotas." Bedford's pen was poised above the papers.

A FAC tour was the kiss of death. No pilot wanted that three-month stint.

"Sir, considering everything, I'll gladly volunteer to fly Hueys." Jack forced a half grin.

Todd exaggerated his nod. "Yes, sir. My sentiments exactly."

Bedford moved from behind his desk and stood in front them. "Good. Lieutenant Colonel Tanner will be waiting for you. I wonder how long you'll last flying medevacs. Here, I've got your checkout sheets." He tossed them at Jack and they fell on the floor. "Do you have anything to say for yourself, Captain Higgins?"

Jack picked up the papers. He'd like to strangle Bedford, but too much was at stake.

"Higgins, you're a piss-poor excuse of a Marine Corps officer. Pick up those checkout sheets and get the hell out of my sight."

Jack shook the sheets at Bedford. "If that'll be all. . . "

"No, god damn it, that won't be all, you shithead. What you did today was inexcusable, unprofessional, and really pisses me off. Thankfully, Major Hosier was my copilot today and can attest to our actions. As for your radio tirade. . .typical and predictable, the same as your last tour. Showboating, grand-standing, risking anything to further yourself."

"Everyone saw you depart, Colonel, turn tail, and run."

"Two career field grade. . .officers' word against yours. Huh?"

"You ran."

"Bullshit. I was thinking about saving the onboard crew

11

and the aircraft, unlike you and your last tour. Wanna know something, hotshot?"

"Not really."

"Well, Slick, here's a tidbit for you. You, Emmitt here, and your roommate Hegidio, along with that half-breed Burton in Okinawa, all put in for augmentation to stay in the Marine Corps last fall. Remember?'

Jack half nodded but continued to glare at Bedford who sat down on the corner of his desk. "And I've got pull, something you never appreciated, you moron. The head of the selection board and I go back a long way. I put the word out to shit-can the four of you. I'm so far ahead of you, you never saw that coming."

Jack looked from Hosier to Bedford. "So you admit to this?"

"Sure. Like I said, two senior officers' word against yours? Ha. You make me laugh." Bedford wagged his head as he stood and moved in front of Jack, smiling. "What's the matter? You look like you want to hit someone. Go on. . .you know you want to."

"No, not really," Jack chuckled waiting to call him 3M, the code name they all called Bedford on their first tour— "mentally midgeted major."

"I'm giving you a direct order. Shut up. Not another word. Do you hear me?"

Gotcha. "Ah, am I supposed to say, yes sir, or nod my head?"

"I said shut the hell up."

Jack grinned and nodded.

Okay, you got him to lose it, now cool it. Just smile and be cool. Stare him straight in the eye. Stay calm. But, Bedford, your ass is mine.

"You moron." Bedford wiped the spittle from the corner of his mouth again. "Back in sixty-eight, Major Hosier, Lieutenant Colonel Tanner and I all wrote the schedules. We were trying to rid the Marine Corps of the likes of you and your ilk. Too bad we didn't get all of you at that time."

Jack shook his head. You slimy bastards.

"Ha. I thought so. No balls. Here, I've admitted everything you've been pissed off about from back then, and. . .nothing from you, except your stupid Higgins' grin."

Todd drew back his fist.

Jack stepped in front of him and grabbed Todd's arm. He whispered, "Toddy, cool it. I've got it covered." Jack turned to Bedford, "If that'll be all, sir, we'll start checking out." Jack held up their checkout sheets. He and Todd turned and marched out. Jack bent forward, and swung his arms, marching like Groucho Marx.

Checking out took less than fifteen minutes as they went from office to office, then collected their flight gear. The gray Dodge, four-door pickup for transporting flight crews, waited to take them to their hooch.

Jack jumped into the back and waved his arm in a grand gesture. "For our last tango, how about a ride back here? Once around the park and home, James." Jack banged the roof of the cab with his fist. Someone had mounted handholds on the roof. He and Todd each grabbed one.

"Yes, sir, Cap'n Jack," the driver in good-nature hollered out the window and let out the clutch.

The two Captains stood in the back of the pickup truck on the way back to their quarters. Jack tried to enjoy the cool breeze off the South China Sea, ignoring the sand dunes, the guard towers, and the chain link fence with the looped razor wire.

"Hey, Toddy."

"Yeah."

"Seeing's how we're in between commands, I'm going to the group CO tomorrow and request mast. The grunts will verify what those two did today. I'm not letting it go, anymore."

"Jack, Jack, I'm with you a hundred percent, but they'll

13

find a way out and you'll just get screwed."

"Man, today was just one toke over the line, and sweet Jesus, it's not going to end here. I don't care, and if that doesn't work. . .I'll do it another way"

CHAPTER THREE

The pick-up stopped in front of their hooch. Getting out, Jack thanked the driver for the ride. "Toddney, check out your six. Bedford's coming down the road."

Jack noticed the little tyrant was alone in his Jeep. Jack clicked his heels, snapped a Nazi salute, and just as quick, acted like he was waving to some imaginary person. Bedford skidded to a stop, almost hitting Jack. Jack didn't salute. Instead, he rubbed his eye, giving the finger.

"Captain Higgins, I saw that."

"Sir, saw what?" Jack walked around the Jeep and got in Bedford's face.

"You know what I'm talking about. Keep it up, loser."

"You look like you want to hit somebody." Jack began to chuckle. "Chicken shit, you're not so brave without all your faggot buddies around you."

"Go to hell." Bedford tried to spin the tires as he sped away.

Jack walked toward Todd.

"You just had to do that, didn't you? You keep stirring the pot, and what did it accomplish?" Todd held the door to the hooch open for Jack as an Arctic blast greeted them.

Their air conditioner rocked around the clock.

"Made me feel good." Jack glanced at Todd who closed his eyes and shook his head.

In the damp, darkness of the Quonset hut, the walls, floor, and sparse furniture were flat black. A painted set of red fluorescent bulbs gave the dark room the desired effect. Their roommate belched, loud enough to be heard over the air conditioner. Joe Hegidio, also known as Roadhawg, and often mistaken for mischievousness, continued to smile. As a well-built, above-average tall Marine, nobody ever crossed him. Innocent-looking enough, Roadhawg took pride in burping more than anyone else.

"Turn on the TV. Scuttlebutt travels fast." Roadhawg rubbed his hands together. "I want every last detail. I was up on squadron common and caught everything between you and Bedford."

Television didn't exist in country, so they "watched TV" by talking.

Todd and Jack took turns telling about the fiasco with the Khe Sanh mortar attack and Bedford's farewell address in his office. Jack noted Todd's tone turned guarded.

"Okay Roadhawg, Bedford's pet squirrel, Petey Boy Tanner, is going to be our new CO. I can't imagine the shit sandwiches he has scheduled for us." Jack got up and walked over to the fridge "I'm buying. Who wants another cold one?" Jack stood in front of the open door, and a strange chill came over him. Oh, shit. His chills were a precursor to bad news.

"Hey, buzzard breath, I'll take another one. And tell me what you've got up your sleeve for nailing Bedford," Todd hollered, breaking Jack's thoughts of looming trouble.

Jack took out two cans and handed one to Todd. "I'm going to the group legal officer tomorrow and file a request mast with the group CO. He'll have to listen."

"Damn it. Come on, Jack," Todd said. "You realize Bedford will sugar-coat today. Who's a bird colonel going to believe, a captain, or Major Hosier and Lieutenant Colonel Bedford?"

"Hopefully, all those worthless ribbons and awards from our last tour will give me a little bit of believability." Jack downed his cold Bud.

"Forget what the grunts will say. The group CO will stand behind his squadron CO. Besides, those two are asshole buddies from way back," Roadhawg said.

"I'm still going to do it."

"You're crazy. Pissin' in the wind. What if it doesn't work?" Todd held both palms up as though holding back danger.

"Jack, Toddy's right. You're going to lose, and then what?" Roadhawg watched as Jack took his .38 out and toyed with the shells in his hand. "Are you going to shoot him?"

"Hell, no. I've got something better in mind."

"What could be better?" Todd said.

"The money run." Jack aimed the weapon at the red overhead light and pulled the trigger. Todd and Roadhawg looked at each other.

"That was a game," Roadhawg said.

"Not anymore." Jack pointed the revolver at a beer can on the floor. The loud click drowned out all the noise, inside and out. The hooch was eerie silent.

"Jack, you're making me nervous. Put the damn gun away." Todd stood and faced Jack.

"And, what if I don't?"

Roadhawg, sitting next to Jack, sprang up and grabbed the pistol. "The both of you shut the hell up. I can't believe you two idiots."

"Okay, okay, I'm sorry. Let's head over to the club. I'm buying." Jack took the gun back.

The rest of the evening, the noise and drinks at the officers' club drowned out the animosity and anger.

The clock on the wall said three minutes to eight. Jack tried to relax at the group headquarters legal office in front of Major R. F. Jones. The building was on the other side of the runway. Insulation and central air conditioning would've made one think they were back in the world of the living.

Jack read the degrees hanging on the wall. And now a major no less, but no wings. An ass kisser if I ever saw one. Jesus, he looks like he's never passed the physical fitness test. Fat bastard.

R. F. Jones leaned back in his chair behind his full-sized mahogany desk. After he'd finished reading Jack's grievance, he rolled his eyes and locked in on Jack's. "Captain Higgins, let's get this straight. You want to have a request mast with the group CO about Lieutenant Colonel Bedford?"

"Yes, sir," Jack blurted out.

"These are serious charges." He glared at Jack.

"They're facts."

"I'll brief the group's commanding officer. Be back at one this afternoon. The colonel said he'll see you then." Major Jones stood, straightening his starched camouflaged jungle utilities uniform.

At twelve-forty, Jack walked into the group admin office.

"Hey, Jack, long time no see," Captain Robert Johnson, the group admin officer, said as he walked in.

"Time flies."

"Yeah, it's been almost. . .what? Three years since the last time we were in country?" He motioned for Jack to step into his office. Jack absorbed the fact that the lanky, red-headed officer was in his short-sleeved working uniform and not jungle utilities.

"Something like that. Closer to two. Hey, I hear you got picked up and are good for twenty," Jack said, following him into his small office.

"Yeah." Bob sighed. "I'm a lifer now. That's why I took this job here at group." He didn't look at Jack.

"Gotta be good for your career pattern," Jack said. "Bob, you look like a lifer."

"Jack, listen," Bob whispered, leaning across his desk. "The colonel called Bedford, and. . .you know. He's got Bedford's version."

"So it's already dead."

Bob nodded his head. Jack heard boots approaching. The colonel walked by, stopped, then turned and stepped into the office.

"Captain Higgins?" The colonel said. They shook hands.

"Yes, sir."

"Come on into my office, and, Bob, hold all my calls."

Bob ignored Jack saying, "Yes, sir, Colonel."

Jack sat in front of the colonel's desk. The trim, commanding officer of the base wore utilities and sported more salt than pepper in his cropped hair. He removed his glasses and began. "I've read the allegations. After the inquiry, you'll be informed of the findings." He thanked Jack for his concerns and assured Jack he was very serious about the whole affair.

Thirty minutes later, Jack changed into his flight suit in their hooch. Todd walked in. "Well, we're all checked in the squadron. How'd it go at the group?"

"He called Bedford. Got his bullshit lies. Thanked me for my concern. Informed me it was a first for him. One Marine alleging another Marine's cowardice." Jack exhaled, looking at the ceiling. "Thanks for getting all the paper crap done."

"Not a biggie, but was it that bad?"

"Worse. I was out in less than five minutes. At least I tried, damn it."

"Jack, about yesterday, I, ah-h-h. . ."

"Never happened. We're still cool." Jack hugged him. "And for my part. I'm sorry."

The door to the hooch let in the bright light as Roadhawg entered.

"You two homos knock it off. Last night, you're wanting to shoot each other, and now this huggy homo shit. Jeez. So how'd it go?" Roadhawg walked in carrying two cases of beer.

Jack told him the whole thing was going nowhere.

Jack's frustration built as the three discussed the dead end to the request mast. Jack shared his thoughts on robbing the military payroll on Okinawa. Their combat brother, Captain Dan Burton, was the assistant scheduling officer in the CH-53 squadron back there. On their first tour together, back in '68, was where they first heard about the payroll and the delivery, called the money run, every first and fifteenth of the month.

Jack's plan was in the formative stages. Roadhawg and Todd both questioned his thinking He shared what little he had with them.

"And that's your plan? Show up and somehow fly the payroll?" Todd held his unopened beer and pointed it at Jack.

"Yes, mother Toad," Roadhawg teased. "And, Jack, that's really your plan?" He raised his empty can.

"Here, Joe," Todd said handing Roadhawg another cold beer. "Seriously, what in the hell are you really thinking, Jack?"

The draw backs were huge. If they took the money, then they could never go home. Jack's motive was to give money to John Ludwig and Dennis Lee, the two disabled combat brothers, an equal share from the heist. Ludwig and Dennis were the two Bedford bragged about selective scheduling. Jack knew they couldn't make ends meet on their small disability checks. Plus, Jack told Todd and Roadhawg, he wanted to put a hit on Bedford.

Todd and Roadhawg brought up how hard the transition would be, going from Marine Corps hero helicopter pilots extraordinaire, to the prince of thieves.

The three bounced around the motives. Jack told them revenge was his motive. He said he wasn't in it for the money. "Are you two interested," Jack asked.

"Truth be told, Jack," Roadhawg said. "It's hard to say yes and become a thief. So. . .hell, yes, I'm interested, and the payback is just fine and dandy, but I'm keeping my share."

"So, Roadhawg, you're in?" Jack looked at him.

"Well. . .like I already said, hell, yeah." Roadhawg's voice went up an octave.

Todd opened his can. "I see Bedford's little intellectual enema got you pissed off now. And somehow you're going to just appear and fly off into the sunset? Incredibly stupid."

Roadhawg said, "No, you dumb shit. Here's incredibly stupid. The thought of being successfully unemployed in six months when they kick us out. So, Jack, tell us, what're you thinking?"

Jack could tell Roadhawg was trying to calm the tempest. "Nawh, getting kicked out and not having a job's not the real reason." Jack glared at Todd, "If nobody'll listen now, by God we'll take their money, then everyone will pay attention. The Walter Cronkite's of the world will be all over it, and I'll be the one to tell."

"Are you guys getting serious? I mean this is insane," Todd said, sitting down.

After a long silence Roadhawg said, "Hell, yes, I'm serious. How about you? Are you in, Toddy?"

Jack sensed Todd's withdrawal. "Roadhawg, the Toddster has a future. He's got Cathy, and truth be told, I'd give it all up if I ever found the right chick."

"Boys, I think we could really do it. Knowing Dan, he'll be on board." Roadhawg stared at Todd in the darkened room. The vibrating air conditioner was drowned out by the rotor blades from a landing helo. It blocked all conversation for a moment.

"I hate to be the naysayer this time." Todd seemed lost in thought. "I didn't mean to come down so hard, Jack. By the way, your plan sucks. I just worry that you all will get your tit in a humongous wringer. That's all. And, if you do, they'll be all over me."

"Toddy, say you don't know anything." Jack grinned, trying to ease the tension.

Roadhawg laughed. "Shit, Toad, act stupid. That'd be a natural for you."

"Go piss up a rope." Todd gave Roadhawg the finger.

Jack stood, stretched his back, and put his hands on his hips. "We can't be talking about it except here in the hooch."

"Amen to that." Roadhawg sat up.

"We're all taking our R and R together with Danny. I mean, we could work out most of the plans then," Jack said.

"Shit, yes. Now you're talking." The Roadhawg grinned.

"Alright Joe, but Toddy and I'll be swamped for a couple of weeks while we transition back into Hueys." Jack glanced at the two guys.

"Jack, are you sure this time? When we farted around about it last tour, you were the Boy Scout. But are you serious, because I'm in and I'm damned-dead serious."

"I'm one hundred percent serious. That cocky little bastard iced the cake yesterday."

"Just so I'm clear on this. You ain't in it for the money?" Roadhawg pointed his beer at Jack.

"Nawh, not really," Jack answered.

"Well, that's just fine and Jim dandy. Because if that's the case, how about giving me your share?"

"Kiss my ass and go to hell. I'll keep my share." Jack chuckled over Todd and Roadhawg's laughter.

"It's about time somebody nailed that bastard. And I'm going to be mighty proud it'll be us." Roadhawg unzipped his flight suit to his waist and sat back down in one of the bean bag chairs.

"Me, too," Jack began. "Gimme another beer. So, here's what I've got so far."

CHAPTER FOUR

Two weeks later, Jack walked down the line of metal walled parking spots for helicopters called revetments, a Huey parked in each one. He and his copilot, Captain Hal Zamora, were on their way to begin pre-flighting his bird. They'd flown together in country back in `67 and `68. Everyone called him Z. He always made people grin.

"Hey, Z, think we'll get some sun after the coastal fog burns off?"

"Yeah, man, but it'll keep us close to the ground. I hope the VC doesn't feel like target practice `til the overcast clears up."

The gray sky appeared thin to Jack, but the cool breeze startled him and gave him goose bumps. Doesn't seem so chilly. I gotta get over these shakes. He thought about his premonitions.

"Z, check this out." Jack felt he needed to bond with Todd to dispel his fears. Jack yelled at Todd pre-flighting his Huey. "Oh, Toddy, I got your good time here." Jack grabbed his crotch.

"Nawh, Jackson, this is the good time you dream about," Todd said as he mimicked Jack. He turned back to his work.

Jack watched Todd as he finished his preflight. Todd's blond hair stood out more than usual—a little bit longer than regulation—and for some reason he appeared shorter than his tall, lanky frame.

"Hey, Jackson," Todd said. "Today makes me wish I'd never left life guarding Cathy in California. I long for those golden days in Newport." He winked and patted the picture of Cathy in his pocket.

"Know what you mean. Hey, man," Jack said, walking toward him. "We're working a few miles to the west of you. Holler if you get your tit in a wringer."

"You know I will." Todd pounded his chest like Tarzan.

"Hey, seriously, just remember I got your six today."

"Yes, mother." Todd turned, waved, then blew a kiss to Jack, as he and his co-pilot climbed into his Huey.

Jack hustled to his bird. He and Z hurried their pre-flight. "I think the reason they got Captain Bailey as Todd's copilot is to squeal on us to Tanner." Jack did his half smile.

"That surprises you? Jack, you've got a keen sense for the obvious."

"Kilo mike alpha, Z."

"You can kiss my ass, too. You don't have to be so professional." Z grinned. "Hey, Jack, ah-h-h, about Tanner, there's something I need to tell you. He talked to me last night. Asshole thinks I'm one of his boys. Said he wants me to squeal on you if you do anything wrong today." Z glanced around as though somebody might be listening. "It gets worse. I heard Tanner and that imbecile Hosier talking. The two of them are dumber than a stump. I heard the back-stabbin' prick, Hosier, say that Bedford told him you and Todd are supposed to catch all the shit sandwiches. I mean, he told him to give you all the night medevacs and. . ."

"Thanks man, but we've already figured that." Jack put

his arm around Z. "You, me, and Toddy survived the Tet back in sixty-eight. This gig's a milk run compared to the Tet. But today, I'm a little worried about Toddy. So, let's get the show on the road. He's about ten minutes ahead of us."

Jack and Z briefed their crew chief and gunner. The crew chief was the second gunner on the helo. Jack smiled and shook his head as they hustled into their cockpit. Once in the air, they monitored the squadron's radio frequency. Jack was comfortable but nervous because this was his first flight as a HAC on a real mission, not some candy-ass, USO show run.

Today's the real stuff. I wonder if Z knows I'm sweatin' it? He glanced at Z behind his lowered sun visor. If he sensed something, he wasn't letting on.

About twenty minutes into the hop, Jack's radio came to life.

"Any aircraft, any aircraft, this is echo two four bravo six. We have an immediate urgent medevac and need air support." The voice was that of the CO from Bravo Company.

Comprise was the Huey Squadron's call sign. Four four was Todd's number or handle.

Jack, ten miles away, listened to the call, ready to abandon his mission and respond.

"Bravo six, Comprise four four. We're inbound to your position with re-supply. Go ahead," Todd answered.

Jack knew in his gut Todd had it covered, but still. . .

Jack and Z looked at each other through their clear face shields.

Hang in there, Todd. We've got your six, their expressions seemed to say.

CHAPTER FIVE

Jack listened as the UHF tactical radio lit up like a Christmas tree. He pushed the airspeed past the red line and the Huey vibrated more than normal. Shit. We should've launched together so I could cover Todd's ass.

"Comprise four four, we have immediate medevac's," the grunt CO repeated. "Be advised, we're under heavy fire and incoming. Do you have any fire support?"

"Roger that. We've got two full rocket pods," Todd said. "Can the medevacs wait? I see you're hot. We need to lay down some fire so we can get in."

"Roger that. I see you. We can use all the firepower you've got."

"Bravo six," Todd said. "We're going hot. Stand by. We're almost to your pos. I think I see you. Pop smoke. I'll get a bead on Charley and we'll fry their asses."

In Vietnam, the VC, or Victor Charley, was called Charley or Mr. Charles.

The hair on the back of Jack's neck tingled, and his chills returned.

"Roger four four. We have your bird in sight. We're popping green smoke now. Do you have us at your two o'clock?"

Hell, yes, you dumb bastard. Jack pushed his Huey harder.

"Roger," Todd answered. "We have your smoke and see the zone. Looks like Charley is busy. Confirm your incoming fire positions."

"Comprise four four," the grunt CO shouted. "The fire will be at your eleven and one o'clock position as you head straight in. Second platoon is pinned down by the river at your eleven, and third platoon is engaging Charley at your one. The LZ is surrounded by first and fourth platoon, but we're pinned down in a firefight," he yelled over the gunfire in the background.

The ground CO asked Todd to lay down as much fire support as he could. The ground officer said the VC had a superior force. His position was on the verge of being overrun. He told Todd, if his Huey could knock out the enemy, then Todd could try to resupply them and pick up the medevacs.

"Again, Comprise four four, the zone's too hot for you to land at this time," the ground CO said.

"Roger. We see muzzle flashes and have you in sight. We'll call in additional support. We're rolling in hot."

When Jack heard Todd over the radio, he gripped the controls tighter than crushing an empty beer can. Todd gave his call sign, location and asked for any aircraft that could assist because the zone was being overrun and his single helo wasn't enough. This was the equivalent of a police call saying an officer was down.

Jack could hear enemy rounds puncturing Todd's Huey over the radio. "Comprise four four, this is double deuce," Jack said. "We're about two miles out and hauling ass. We've got the entire zone in sight. If you'll wait a minute, we'll join up and cover your six."

From Jack's vantage point, he saw Comprise four four circle the zone with both .60 caliber machine guns firing away. They had located the source from the main enemy fire and rolled in with their rockets and the .60 cals. The rockets from the helo did the job. The incoming subsided.

"Okay, Bravo six. That seemed to slow them down. We're rolling in to get the medevacs," Todd said.

Thank you, Lord. Jack sighed.

Jack looked over at Z, and Z gave him a thumbs up.

"How many medevacs do you have?"

"We've got three. One immediate. Over," Bravo six said.

"You're in sight now, and. . .ah-h-h, mother fucker. . .we're taking a shit pot full of hits," Todd yelled. "Bravo, we're waving off. We've got Charley all over us from the one o'clock position. If we can get back around, we'll light up their ass with more rockets."

Jack watched Todd's Huey as smoke came from the exhaust, and more smoke when the rockets left the pods. The bird was dangerously low and slowing down, fighting to stay airborne and taking too many hits.

The radio picked up Todd's voice. "Damn it, get the copilot out of the cockpit. He's on the controls, and let me know how bad he's hit." A pause, then, "Shit, the cockpit's nothin' but flashing emergency and caution lights."

"Comprise four four, this is double deuce," Jack shouted. "We're at your six and will light `em up. You need to get your bird out of here or on the deck."

Jack's bird circled as he followed the smoking Huey in front of him. Jack's Huey shuddered as their rockets launched. The expended brass and rocket exhaust filled the cockpit with the unmistakable smell of cordite smoke. He could see Todd struggle to stay airborne; all the while laying down an accurate barrage of fire.

"God damn it, we're hit. There's blood everywhere," Todd shouted over the radio. He continued to attack the enemy position from his damaged Huey. The scene took on a slow-motion effect as Jack watched. Todd's bird slowed and started a fatal spiral, the nose dropped too low. It almost looked like the helo, by some miracle, had recovered as Todd tried to hover.

Jack kept his eye on the crippled Huey as he continued to circle the LZ.

"Damn it." Jack heard Todd yell over the radio. "Shit, shit, oh, shit. Hang on." Jack saw Todd had banked his Huey hard to keep over the zone. The aircraft started to spin. When Todd attempted to hover, the bird crashed in a spinning motion, rolling over to the right side. The main rotor impacted the ground, broke off, and violently threw the aircraft on its left side.

Jack's aircraft cleared the tree line. He and Z opened fire on the attacking North Vietnamese. He spotted Todd right in front of him, struggling to run from his destroyed aircraft. His left arm dangled limp, with the injured Captain Bailey flung over his right shoulder. He stumbled as he tried to get to the safety of Bravo six's position.

From behind Todd, automatic weapon muzzle flashes coincided with the bullets hitting the ground, closing in on them. Rounds penetrated Todd's leg as he fell to the ground, blood spots appeared on his flight suit.

"Take this, you mother fuckers," Jack shouted as he launched several rockets straight in on the enemy position.

Todd tried to stand, but several rounds struck him in the upper torso.

Jack watched in horror as Todd crumpled to the ground.

"Aw, fuck me. We're taking a shit pot of hits. Nail those bastards," Jack shouted. His two .60 cal gunners continued to pummel the enemy.

Rounds came through the cockpit. "We're still okay," Jack reported to the gunners. Out of his side vision he could see Z struggle to monitor and reset the popped circuit breakers. The Huey shuddered as he launched more rockets.

"Can you see if they're okay or moving?" Jack banked

the bird hard to keep the zone in sight. He could see several muzzle flashes still shooting at Todd and his crew. Jack pulled the nose up and transitioned to a circling hover about ten feet off the ground, between Todd's crew and the attacking VC.

"You slimy fuckers. Take this." Jack began launching rockets from the pods, point blank into the enemy's position, less than a hundred feet away.

"Z, are we still good?" Jack asked as numerous rounds hit their Huey.

"Jeez, Jack, they were waiting for us, but we're still good," Z yelled over the ICS.

Jack checked out the stinging sensation from his right leg and saw a hole torn in his flight suit. He was bleeding.

"Jack, your leg." Z motioned with his head.

"It's nothin'. Shit, maybe you'd better take the bird." After a moment, the zone cooled down. This time Jack couldn't control the shakes. The taste of bile filled the back of his throat.

Z hovered back toward Todd and Captain Bailey. Jack stared in shock. The two of them made no attempt to move.

"Comprise. . .you're cleared to land," Bravo six said.

Jack watched the troops run to Todd and his copilot. The Marines carried Todd and Bailey back to safety behind their lines.

Z sat the Huey down less than ten yards in front of Bravo six's bunker.

"I'll be right back." Jack bolted from the aircraft and ran to Todd.

The medic knelt beside Todd and his copilot.

"How are they?" Jack asked as he knelt down on one knee.

"I'm sorry, sir." The medic closed Todd's eyes. "Did you know them?"

No, damn it! Lord, this can't be.

The medic shook Jack. "I need to take a look at that leg and make sure you're not going into shock." He opened the torn leg of Jack's flight suit, but Jack couldn't look away from Todd.

"Hunker down." The medic pulled Jack down farther into the safety of the dugout bunker. "This zone is still hot, and we just might be between some gook's crosshairs."

After the Marines loaded the wounded and the KIA in Jack's Huey, he glanced back at Todd from the right seat in the cockpit. Todd's helmet was off, and sweat had stuck his blond hair to his head.

Jack's helo medevacked the wounded and the KIA Marines back to Marble Mountain.

Jack couldn't erase Todd's image from his mind from that morning's pre-flight.

Todd was gone. Come on God, why isn't it Toddy flying me home? The words of an old hymn stuck in Jack's mind. Swing low, sweet chariot, coming for to carry me home. This is all my fault.

Z put a hand on Jack's shoulder. "Are you okay?"

"Yeah, I was just thinking, we're a long ways from home." Jack shook his head, trying to clear his thoughts. Why Todd? Why couldn't it've been me?

Jack swallowed, trying to get rid of the lump in his throat. Images of Herb hadn't resurfaced after his death. But with Todd, it was different. It was today.

Moisture welled up from his eyes as he promised himself, he'd never rest until Bedford paid. God as my witness. He glanced over at Z to see if he was watching, then Jack wiped the tears from the corners of his eyes.

CHAPTER SIX

Released from the dispensary, Jack made his way back to the hooch and crashed on one of the black, beanbag chairs scattered around the floor. After a while, he retrieved a can of beer from the fridge and stared at the ebony emptiness of their hooch. He was more lonely than alone.

The guilt of the last few hours overwhelmed Jack. With Herb, he never saw him after his death, but Todd's image would be burned forever in his memory.

Jack jerked from the sound of loud knocking on the door.

"Captain Higgins, there's a WATS line call from Okinawa," the duty driver said, peeking through a crack in the door.

"Come on in. It's okay."

"Sir, it's a call for you from a Captain Burton. He heard about Captain Emmitt and said he'd call back in twenty minutes."

Jack sat there, absorbing all the noise from the constant laboring of helicopter blades landing and taking off in the background. "Give me a minute," Jack said.

Making sure the tears were gone, he walked out of the

33

hootch to a waiting jeep. They rode in silence to the squadron.

Outside the metal building housing the squadron's work spaces, a lieutenant approached him.

"Excuse me, sir, but I talked to Captain Z, and he said I needed to tell you this."

Jack nodded. The lieutenant's last name was Rodgers, his nickname was Roy. He told Jack he worked in the awards office and Lieutenant Colonel Tanner told him to throw away the write up for Jack's flight today.

Jack told him it was okay and he'd just as soon forget about it.

Roy said, "Well, sir, I put his endorsement on the paperwork and sent the package on to the group for approval. The ones I shit-can are his bullshit write-ups for himself. I swear, he's the biggest phony I've ever seen."

"Way to go, Roy." Jack chuckled. "A man after my own heart."

"But the guy at group is tight with the fifty-three squadron CO, Bedford, so. . ."

Jack put his arm around the first tour pilot's shoulder. "Thanks anyway, Roy. I owe you, man.".

Jack parted from Roy and headed for the squadron spaces. The sun had set casting an unexpected feeling of cool calmness.

The duty clerk stood, as he told Jack a call was on hold.

Jack took a seat at the open desk in the ready room and punched the blinking light. "Dan, is that you?"

"Yeah, I can't believe the news. Are you okay?"

"Shit, Danny, I don't know. It's all my fault. I screwed up and got me and Todd reassigned back here."

"Jack, listen. I know this is a really bad time, but I've got a ton of news. And we've only got a little time on this phone. You've been assigned to escort Todd home. You can pass on it, but it's your call. It's official. I'm looking at the orders." Dan paused a moment. "Man, are you sure you're okay? I understand you were wounded, again."

Jack told him the leg was nothing, just a couple of stitches, and they'd wrapped it. He tried to tell Dan about the whole incident, but stopped. Jack choked up as a lump in his throat took his voice and tears flowed. He wiped his eyes.

"Jack, this is hard on all of us, but you've got to get your act together. Todd'd be kicking your ass."

"But I owe him."

"Then for his sake, you're the one taking him home. Can you do that?"

"Sure I can. Taking him home's the least I can do. I don't know what to tell the family though, or Cathy."

"Hang in there. I've been coordinating everything from here. MAG-Sixteen will cut your orders in less than an hour. You'll depart tomorrow at eleven hundred local, arrive here in Okinawa at seventeen hundred. I'll meet you at Kadena. You'll remain overnight and depart for Honolulu. There you'll go commercial to Dallas and meet the family there."

"God, Dan, this is so hard. Why Todd? Why not me?"

"Jack. Listen to me," Dan shouted. "You didn't schedule the hop, and from what they're saying, you're up for something higher than the Navy Cross."

"I don't want it, Dan. You gotta know all I could do was watch those bastards shoot Todd. None of it makes sense. This morning we were cutting up, and. . ." Jack couldn't go on.

"Jack, it's going to be okay. Here, I've got more news and this is important." Dan told him MAG-16 would be standing down in less than a month and pulling out of Marble Mountain. The squadron would rotate back to Kaneohe in Hawaii, but the personnel would come back to Okinawa to finish out their overseas tour.

Jack shook his head in disbelief.

"Jack, did you hear me?"

"You gotta be kidding me."

"No, I'm not. I'm holding a copy of the orders. And, specifically, you and Joe will be back here."

"You mean we were this close to getting out of here?"

"Yeah."

"I can't believe it. Un-fucking-believable. Oh, God, it's all been for nothing."

"Captain Higgins, are you about finished with the phone? I need to speak to you on a couple of matters." Lieutenant Colonel Tanner interrupted, standing behind Jack.

Jack turned. "Don't crowd me."

"You're way out of line, Captain."

"Danny, I've got the schedule, and I'll see you tomorrow. I gotta git now. I'm going to unscrew this mother fuckers head and dip shit out for the whole world to show how full of shit this worthless son of a bitch is."

"Jack, Jack, listen to me. Cool it. Do you hear me?"

Jack hung up, stood, and glared at Tanner.

"Captain, if you're talking about me, you're about this close to getting your ass thrown in the brig. Do you understand me?" Tanner pressed his thumb and forefinger together.

Jack glared at him in silence. He could see Tanner glance around, no doubt to make sure the other officers standing in the ready room were listening. "Captain Higgins, a couple of things. We're all extremely upset about Captain Emmitt."

"Bullshit. You got just what you wanted. . .cherry picking our missions. Deny that," Jack whispered.

Tanner told Jack to go tell the group CO again. And that Tanner was sure the group CO would want to hear all about everything. Tanner mentioned his last request mast session findings came back that afternoon. "Your insinuations against Colonel Bedford and Major Hosier have been officially dismissed due to a lack of supportive evidence and past personal differences."

Jack took a deep breath. Let it go. There're too many witnesses. Don't do anything. Think.

Tanner looked over his shoulder at Z standing with a group of onlookers in the ready room. "I'm going to overlook your outburst on the phone. You need to go to the dispensary and get checked out.".

"Captain Zamora, I'm very concerned about Captain Higgins' mental state. I'd like you to escort him to the dispensary and report back to me. And Captain Mays," who was among the group standing in the ready room, "as the safety officer, I want Captain Higgins grounded for trauma and mental . . . hell, I don't know, but he ain't right. All of you witnessed his outburst. Enough said. Captain Zamora, you have your orders." Tanner turned and strutted out.

"Jack, you need to get out of here," Z whispered in Jack's ear.

CHAPTER SEVEN

The next morning, a bright blue sky hung over the South China Sea. Roadhawg and Z waited with Jack for Todd's flight home. The Air Force Base in Da Nang welcomed every soldier, whether arriving or departing, even those going back to the world in a coffin. Not a breath of breeze stirred the stagnant air. The humidity was higher than an upper ninety-degree temperature. Sweat covered the three Marines.

"I'll be back in little over a week," Jack said to nobody in particular.

"Man, I wish I could be going with you." Roadhawg hung his head talking to the tarmac.

Jack wiped the perspiratiot from his forehead as he turned to look at the sheet-metal oven that served as a terminal building. "Every time we've ever been here, it's been hotter than hell."

"Hey, let's get out of here," Z said.

They moved outside to find some shade.

Roadhawg wiped his brow. "Even out here it's hotter that hell."

"Speaking of hotter than hell, Tanner was livid last

night." Z squinted against the sun. Jack wiped moisture from his sun glasses.

"Chicken shit just turned and walked away," Jack said.

"Well, Jack, he was talking with the legal officer about bringing up charges. But the legal O told him to cool it. The word's out about them selectively scheduling ya'll."

Jack closed his eyes and tried to hold back the tears. "They'll never prove it."

"But I think they're running a little scared because Tanner dropped it. There's too much scuttlebutt going around about selective scheduling," Z said. Shaking his head, Z put his arm around Jack's shoulder. "By the way, the safety officer came over to my hooch and basically said everything got dropped. End of story."

"Hey, they're calling your row." Roadhawg hugged Jack. "Call me when you get back to Okinawa, and I'll make sure to pick you up."

Z patted Jack on the back. "So, don't worry about all that crap from last night."

"Thanks, but Tanner doesn't scare me." Jack turned and walked toward the waiting aircraft.

The turbulence on the way to Okinawa didn't seem to interfere with Jack's attention as his thoughts bounced around on the Air America 727.

So, Toddy, here we are pulling into Kadena. I would've never. . . He tried to compose himself as the engines shut down. It'd be good to see Dan.

"Excuse me, Captain it's your turn." A fellow Marine motioned for Jack to go.

He nodded. "Thanks."

The sun still shone high in the sky above the western Pacific. Jack put on his sunglasses and stepped down the portable boarding stairway. The sea breeze felt good, soothing.

Dan Burton, Captain, United States Marine Corps, walked out on the tarmac to meet Jack. Easy to spot, Dan stood about half a head over the crowd. His dark-brown tan was inherited from his Native American granddad and Hispanic grandmother, along with a whole lot of time exposed to the elements. Dan's attire screamed anything but official that Thursday afternoon in his cut-off sweatshirt and jeans.

"Now that's a typical Dan Burton. Just show up casual and then throw that rank around to get anywhere you want. Man, thanks for coming over."

The military-gray painted terminal was too small for the 727. So the aircraft sat on the blistering heat of the tarmac as the homeward bound Marines congregated. Dan broke through the confusion and hugged Jack.

"Come on, let's get out of here. I've got everything set-up for you." Dan said. They'd be heading home at zero-dark-thirty the next morning. In the meantime, they had a boat load of stuff to cover. "Excuse us," Dan yelled at the service men standing around. "Could you please move on?"

Jack tried to smile as they moved through the terminal and out to the parking lot. Dan seemed on the verge of choking up as he said, "Okay, Jack, I've gotta change the channel. Ah-h-h, all your gear and dress blues are packed and ready for you. I've got a place where we can go talk in private." Dan pointed. "The limo is parked over there."

"What the hell is this?"

A black '64 Pontiac, station wagon sat alone in the reserved parking spaces for colonels and above.

"By God, Jackson, it's got power windows and everything else. I dropped three deuces on it for a little more performance. She'll smoke the tires all the way through low, even with the air on full blast."

"I should've guessed it. You're still a biased Injun." Jack managed his half Steve McQueen grin as they got in the wagon.

Dan relaxed in the seat and looked at Jack. "It ain't just Injun. It's Apache. Always has been, always will be. Listen, we're off to a little base between here and Futema." Dan motioned with his head toward the main gate and then the Pacific. "It's an Army air base that's disguised as a yacht harbor. My man, I swear the other services have it sweet. Makes me realize how frugal the Corps is."

"Hell, our branch is tighter than bark on a tree when it comes to spending money on us." Jack rubbed his forehead. As scattered as he was, he'd brought up the money run subject. Tapping his finger on the dash board, he said, "Seeing as how we're all coming back here, I'm wanting to do it."

Dan drove, never looking at Jack, who continued to tell Dan about wanting to give some of the money to Herb, Dennis and Ludwig. Jack asked if Dan wanted to be in on the deal and checked his expression.

"You putz. Hell, yes, I'll be in. We'll need me, as a matter of fact. I write the flight schedules now."

"I know that. . .makes it all the easier. We'll all be back here soon. Those of us left, anyway."

"I think we can pull it off. I've been daydreaming about the money run for months. I'll tell you my thoughts about it in a minute." A faint smile formed on Dan's face. He reached for his ID as he drove up to the gate at Hamby, the Army's Recreation Marina base.

They approached the little marina on the west side of the island. The golden-orange sun reflected off the water. Once parked, Jack opened his door and inhaled the fresh sea breeze. "My God, are all these boats. . ."

"All of them. . .owned by service personnel stationed here. There're a few rentals but special services has those. The rest of them are owned by military personnel. You'll never see anything like this on any Marine Corps base. And the Army built this place just for their recreation."

Jack closed his eyes and relaxed. "How peaceful. Just

listen to those lanyards banging against the masts. And the sea gulls, and the boats rubbing against the docks. And almost no one around. Sure is different than being in country." Jack hesitated as he took in the full effect of the marina.

"Oh, hell yes, it's different. Just wait till you see the view from the bar and dining room. Come on. The first round is on me. Look," Dan motioned to Jack. "I told you, the place is empty."

The cool air inside the bar and dining room was a welcome relief. The humidity had the windows moist from condensation. The bar lined one wall. The dining area faced the westward sunset. They walked to a table near the windows. The bartender came out from the back.

Dan waved. "Hey, Bill, a round of cold ones for me and my good friend."

"Coming right up." The bartender brought two frosty Buds to them. "So how you doing, Dan?"

"We could be doing better. We're here to commiserate over the loss of a good friend. Jack's here 'til the morning. He's on funeral escort, taking Todd home."

Bill shook his head. "I'm so sorry. Tonight the drinks are on the club. Let me leave you guys alone."

"Many thanks," Dan said as Bill walked away.

"Man, here's to good times, good friends, and more of the same." Dan held up his drink in a toast to Todd. Then he got down to business. "And, Jack, we've got a lot to go over. Here, I've got everything written down."

Jack smiled. "Now that's a first. . .You writing anything down."

Dan had printed out Jack's flight itinerary all the way to Dallas. Todd's folks had moved there almost three years before. He handed Jack several sheets of paper. Jack tried to make sense out of it as the reality of it sank in. At last the words, times, and dates began to register.

"Jack, here's the deal. You can fly in your utilities from

here to Honolulu. Then you'll need to be in your dress blues as the escort. I just picked them up from the cleaners. They've been cleaned and pressed. And, ah, I took the liberty to add your air medals."

"Thanks, man. You seem to have taken care of everything. I'm so scattered." Jack looked out at the endless blue Pacific and noticed Dan doing the same.

Silence prevailed as the two Marines sat deep in their own thoughts. At last, Dan tapped his index finger on the table and said, "I thought losing Herb was bad, but . . .sorry, man, I'd do better if I don't talk about Todd just right now."

Jack worked on the knot in his throat as he noticed Dan wiping his eyes. Jack could still see Todd lying on the ground near his helo. He took a deep breath. "Let's change the channel."

After several moments of silence, Dan whispered, "Okay, Jack."

CHAPTER EIGHT

"Okay, here's what I've got so far." Dan checked around as though someone in the empty club was listening. He told Jack that in less than six weeks, MAG-16 would be pulled out of Vietnam. The scuttle butt was no later than the first part of June."

"I know. The Roadhawg told me last night. It just makes losing Todd even more senseless."

"Yeah."

"So tell me about the re-deployments."

Marine Air Group 16 would deploy for Kaneohe Bay in Hawaii. But the personnel would deploy to Okinawa. Jack and Roadhawg would be back in HMH-462 flying `53s with Dan.

"Well, I'll be good God-damned." Jack twirled the near empty bottle while his mind tried to grasp what Dan had just told him.

"By God, believe it and I pulled a couple of strings." Dan wiggled his eyebrows like Groucho Marx. He'd called Roadhawg that morning to tell him.

"So," Jack said, "we're still thinking about the money run?"

Dan nodded his head. "All right, Jack my boy, tell me the whole story."

Jack went into detail about his thoughts on the plan he'd shared with Todd and Roadhawg. "You, me, and Roadhawg will still be taking our R and R the first part of July." Jack paused. "When I'm back in Oklahoma, I'm going to talk to Dennis. I plan on him being our point of contact. We'll get a hold of Ludwig. I'm thinking of having the two of them sail east of here to rendezvous with us after we get the you-know-what." Jack tried to keep his same expression as he looked around to insure nobody was listening.

"Damn, that's slick. Everyone would naturally think we'd head west to Taipei."

"So we'd take the money on the bird and rendezvous with them, scuttle the bird, and sail back to Hawaii. Split from there to Switzerland. Put the money in a Swiss bank and disappear." Jack eased back in his chair.

"I think we can pull it off. Dennis Lee and John Ludwig are making plans as we speak to meet up with all of us in Hawaii for a supposed surprise reunion for you, Roadhawg and . . . Toddy. Anyway, the whole gang would have been in Hawaii. So we'll be able to get a lot finalized?" Dan smiled as he looked around again.

"Shit, this is taking shape." Jack also checked out the empty bar.

They agreed there was a whole lot all of the players needed to get coordinated and worked out.

"So here's what we've got so far. Luds and Dennis and their spouses are going to meet up with us in Hawaii."

"Do you mean like Dennis and Georgia, and Luds and Diane?" Jack interrupted.

Dan winked and tapped his index finger on the table, "We still have a boat-load of planning, and, by God, we're going to need your creativity. You were the only holdout when we were daydreaming about it back when we first heard about the money run."

"I'm getting jazzed just thinking about all of us being together again."

Dan looked at Jack's empty, turned around and held up two fingers for Bill. "By God, more swill for our tankards, innkeeper."

Bill brought two cold ones, then retreated into the kitchen.

"I'd be really surprised if Dennis doesn't go for it," Jack said. He relayed how Dennis' disability checks didn't even cover the basics. And Dennis was struggling, teaching school part time. "Remember?" Jack continued. "He was the original one who talked and talked about the money run way back in sixty-eight. And here's the icing on the cake. Luds is a sailor and has the boats."

"By God, I can't believe it's all falling together. Who would've thought? Even in our wildest imaginations."

"Well, here's the deal, Danny, and this is for real, no shit. We can't talk about it in any correspondence or on the land-line.

"When I stop here on my way back down south, we'll talk some more."

Jack stared down at his beer. After a bit of silence, he became serious. "But, here's the pisser. I dread meeting with the Emmitts. I know they'll probably have questions."

"Oh, yeah, I forgot. But we need to change the subject, because I've got a little update for you. Cathy has flown to Dallas to be with the Emmitts for the funeral. And ah-h-h. . ."

"Oh, Lord, I dread talking to her. Toddy had to have told her about me getting us kicked out of the fifty-three squadron. Danny, I mean it's all my fault." Jack began to choke up again.

"That's bullshit and you know it, Jack. Tanner and Bedford scheduled us in sixty-eight and then you, all the rest of this time. We all know it."

46

Jack held up his hand and began. "Yeah, but it was me that got us back in Hueys."

Dan interrupted, "And Bedford sent you all off. Pure and simple. Murder."

Jack looked straight at Dan. "When we pull the gig, I'm writing a letter and telling them why I took the money run. It's to finally get somebody's attention hoping they'll listen."

"By God, I'll tell them I'll give it all back if they'll finally hold those bastards accountable. I mean it, Jack."

Jack's thoughts went back to taking Todd home.

"What if Cathy and the Emmitts blame me and don't want anything to do with me?" Jack pursed his lips.

"Come on, man. From what I heard, Toddy was writing her every day. She has to know the truth. We all know. You did nothing wrong." Dan grabbed Jack's forearm. "Listen to me. Jack...you're not listening. You did nothing wrong. What you did in the zone, the grunts put you in for the Medal of Honor. But Tanner and his cronies did the scheduling, not you."

"Yeah, but I just wish it'd been me." Jack caught the tear from his eye right before it ran down his cheek. "Todd had everything going for him. He had Cathy, and I've got nobody." Jack couldn't finish because his lip began to quiver.

"I wish I could go back with you, man."

"Me, too."

"But listen. Just tell them the truth. If they ask a question. . .answer it. They know you and that you're honest."

"It's just going to be so hard to be there with Todd in a casket," Jack tried to gather himself. "Bedford, and Tanner are going to pay this time. I promise, Dan."

"Jack, I feel for you. Is there anything I can do? Anything to help you with the funeral?"

"Not really, Dan. Honestly, I don't know if I can do his

eulogy. I know they'll want me to say something. I know I'll break down and cry like a baby." Jack put his elbows on the table, then placed his head in his hands and massaged his temples.

He was massaging his temples when the flight attendant touched his shoulder.

"Excuse me, Captain. They've turned on the fasten seatbelts sign. You need to bring your seat up right. We're on final for Dallas."

Jack looked forward at nothing, furrowed his brow and wiped the moisture from his eyes. What if Cathy told the Emmitts who got Todd kicked out of the `53 squadron? He could see why they wouldn't want anything to do with him. They'd know Todd's death was his fault.

The flight attendant brought him back to the present. "Are you meeting the family here?"

Jack didn't answer.

CHAPTER NINE

The boarding area in Dallas was congested with people standing around, hugging, and blocking the exit for the arriving passengers. The noise at the gate, with the constant arrival and departure broadcast, and all the happy families, added to Jack's anxiety. He stood out in his dress blues. Besides, his uniform felt like a sauna. He began searching the crowd.

That must be them. I recognize them. Yeah, there's Cathy waving at me. Jack waved at her, and at Mr. and Mrs. Emmitt. Cathy, in tears, came running to him with both arms open. He carried his white hat as he moved through the crowd toward them. He tried to compose himself.

"Oh, Jack," is all she said as she threw her arms around him. The Emmitts were right behind her making their way through the congestion.

"Good to see you, Jack." Mr. Emmitt hugged him with a moist handkerchief in his hand.

"Sir, I wish we could be. . .well, you know," Jack managed to say.

Clutching a wad of tissues, Todd's mother tried to speak but tears took over.

Jack looked up at the terminal ceiling to keep from crying.

"As hot as that uniform looks, you must be terribly uncomfortable," Mr. Emmitt said. "Let's get out of here. It's almost lunch-time, and Betty's got food waiting for us." He motioned toward his wife. Cathy held on to Jack. And then she let go of him.

"Sir, that sounds nice and everything, but I've got to admit, I don't have much of an appetite."

"Jack, call me Will, and Betty goes by Betty," Mr. Emmitt smiled, then put his arm around Jack's shoulder as they headed for the baggage area.

Betty handed Cathy more tissues as they waited for the baggage.

"Hey, guys, my plane for Tulsa doesn't leave until five and I'd be glad to get to visit with you all 'til then, if you'd like." Jack watched their expressions. He saw no animosity.

"Jack," Cathy began, "I'm staying at the Emmitts, and they have an extra room if you want to stay here."

"That sounds nice, but I thought I'd go to Tulsa and see my folks for a couple of days." He caught himself before he said, "one last time."

They made small talk as they grabbed Jack's luggage.

Jack sat in the back seat of their station wagon. Lost in thought, he looked at the passing traffic. His mind drifted back to that fateful day. Lord, help me get through all of this.

"Jack, the kids are at the house, and they, ah, well, they'd like to know if you could tell us a little bit more about what happened." Mr. Emmitt's voice caught. He cleared his throat as his words broke into Jack's thoughts.

"Yes, sir, I could. I was there in the zone and saw it all," Jack said as they pulled into the driveway. Todd's sister and his twin brothers came outside, and introduced themselves.

"Jack," Betty turned to face him, wiping the corner of her eye with a tissue. "I know it must be tough for you, but if it'd be okay. . .the military told us virtually nothing. First, let's get inside and let you change clothes." Everyone walked toward the house.

"And, even though we were engaged . . .they haven't contacted me." Cathy started to weep. Jack reached over, put his arm around her shoulder, and gave her a hug.

Once inside, Jack got into jeans and a polo shirt before he joined Todd's family at the dining room table. The aroma of pot roast filled the house. The food was ready to be served in the kitchen, but nobody fixed a plate. Betty brought glasses and tea for everyone. Jack sat with his back to the wall. The shades were down on the windows in the dining room, just enough to keep the afternoon light comfortable in the room.

Mr. Emmitt said, "Jack, we were only told that Todd died in action south of Quang Tri, Vietnam. Can you tell us anything else?"

Jack was silent as he gathered his thoughts. He took a sip of tea. "I was there. Are you all sure you want to know?"

Jack looked at Mr. Emmitt, Betty, Todd's sister and his brothers. They all nodded. He looked at Cathy. She nodded, too.

Jack moved his index finger back and forth on the tablecloth. "We launched just after breakfast. Todd was about ten minutes ahead of me." He paused.

Mr. Emmitt said, "Was it early morning?"

"About eight. The zone was south of Quang Tri and west into the mountains. The troops on the ground called for air support and medevac's." Jack made eye contact with the family and tried to regain his emotions. "Todd went in and came under heavy fire. He waived off, and I heard him say his copilot was wounded."

"Do you know if Todd was injured at that time?" Mr. Emmitt said.

"No, sir, not for sure. After he waved off, he launched a

direct attack with his rockets. He kept circling the zone, firing. As we approached, we saw way too much smoke coming out of Todd's helo. . .the engine, and I could tell he was struggling to keep the bird in the air."

"Is that when he was shot down?" one of Todd's brothers said.

"No, he actually made a hell of a recovery and almost landed. But the bird started spinning. They rolled over, and the main rotor impacted the ground. That threw the aircraft hard on the other side." Jack shifted in his chair.

"Did he survive the crash?" the other brother said.

Jack looked at Cathy. She had her head down. Her entire body was shaking.

"Yes, he got out, immediately. Whew," Jack exhaled as he tried to gather himself. "Then he grabbed the wounded copilot, had him in a fireman's carry and was running to our lines. He was shot in the leg. He stumbled, got back up, but was still stumbling. That's when the sons of bitches shot him in the back."

Realizing what he'd just said, he cleared his throat. "Sorry, I, ah-h-h, I hate `em."

"That's all right," Mr. Emmitt said. "It's hard not to feel anything but contempt. I know they're people, too, but. . ."

Betty did not try to hide her grief.

Jack stared at the ceiling, trying to compose himself until he could continue. "He died right there with the wounded copilot still on his shoulder. They didn't have to shoot him. He was running away from them."

Then Jack told them about carrying Todd back in his Huey. "They said he'll be awarded his second Silver Star. That level of sacrifice speaks for itself. He died trying to save others." Jack choked up.

Waving his hand, Mr. Emmitt struggled to talk. "We know how he didn't care about the ribbons. But, Jack, it means the world to us to know what happened." His voice quivered, and he shook as he wept.

Jack stood and turned away. "I know. I know. . .this just hurts so much". Todd's brothers went to him and wrapped their arms around him. Then, Todd's sister, his mom and his dad huddled close.

Cathy remained seated. She said, "Todd wrote me and told me how you called Bedford out and how proud he was of you." Jack went to her, leaned down and hugged her as tears ran down his cheeks on to her blouse.

"Jack, I know it must've been terrible to watch. I can't imagine." Betty sobbed.

"We've got to stop this," Jack said. "Todd would never have allowed all this. Let me tell you some funny Todd stories." Jack looked at every one in the room. Feeling he had their approval, Jack told about several good times they had in the cave, and the conversation led to the family remembering the good times they'd had with Todd.

Half an hour later, Cathy volunteered to drive Jack to the airport. She said, "Todd told me about the selective scheduling, and. . ."

"Cathy, with God as my witness, they're going to pay. And there's something else."

CHAPTER TEN

At the gate in Tulsa, everyone was waiting for someone. Jack rubbed his aching temples as he searched the crowd, trying to relieve the throbbing. He saw his parents before they saw him. All right, there they are. I guess this will be the last time they come to pick me up. I can't tell them what I told Cathy. Shit, goodbyes suck.

"Hey, son." His dad hustled through the crowd and hugged him.

"Oh, Jack, I'm so glad you're home safe and sound." His mother cried as she moved his dad out of the way and held Jack tight.

"Son, you look good. Here, let me carry your bag. I thought you'd be wearing your uniform. Why don't you have your uniform on?"

Jack kissed his mother.

"Why ain't you wearin' your uniform?" his dad repeated.

"I don't have to or want to."

"That's okay." His dad blinked. "Well, we just knew that you'd be okay and make it home. I never had any doubts. I know you said this time wouldn't be as tough as the first, but how come you're home so early?"

"I'll tell you all about it." That's a big lie. They don't even know why I'm home.

"This isn't your R and R, is it?" his mother said.

"Well, yeah, kind of." Jack managed to hold it together as they moved from the boarding area. Another big fat lie. His thoughts danced around in his head. This'll be the last time I'll see you all for a long time.

The crowd was nothing like Dallas. His tried to clear his mind as they walked toward the baggage claim. Nothing changed, but everything was different. Then he heard his mother saying something.

"Jack, I prayed every night that you'd come home safe and sound." She laughed and cried at the same time as she squeezed his hand.

Yeah, I'm sure Todd's family thought the same bullshit. He wasn't paying attention but caught a part of what his dad was saying.

"Son, I remember how glad I was when I came home from the war."

"Yeah, I'm glad to be home again, Dad." An even bigger lie.

His Dad leaned over and whispered while looking around to make sure no one overheard him. "Son, did you have any close calls?"

"Dad, it was a walk in the park. I never really had any close calls." Another big lie. . . and I'm smilin' about it.

"I know you probably don't want to talk about it anytime soon. One of the guys at the plant had a boy over there, and his boy said that it was pure h-e-double l. His son only loaded bombs on them jets. I don't think he ever saw any action like you did."

Jack rubbed his six o'clock beard and looked at the floor as they walked to the baggage claim area. "Yeah, Dad, I imagine it was rough on some of them." He shifted the heavy carry-on to his free hand. "Where's Lee?"

"Your brother's still at work. He said to tell you that

he'll meet you back at the house. Your momma has some of your favorites cooked up tonight. Turkey and dressing, mashed potatoes, biscuits, and gravy . . ."

His dad was going on and on, but Jack lost his train of thought. Biscuits and gravy were Todd's favorite. Todd's grandma won't ever get to make them for him again. Shit, I'm about to lose it. I can't let them see me like this. Change the channel.

"Hey, Daddy, Lee's done a great job taking care of my GTO, and I've been thinking about letting him buy it from me because I'm gettin' a new convertible." He pressed his lips together to keep from saying something he'd regret.

The car had been a sore spot with his dad. Lee hadn't gotten his driver's license until the summer before Jack left to go to Vietnam.

Jack remembered well that day. They were driving in an old 1953 pickup that his dad borrowed from a deacon at the church. The truck was loaded with furniture they were moving for their parents, and Jack told Lee to drive.

"I can't," Lee whispered. "I don't have a license."

Bullshit. Jack thought, and right then he drove Lee to the DMV in west Tulsa and told him to get his butt out of the truck and take the written test.

Lee came out later, all grins, and announced that he'd passed.

"Get your ass back in there and tell 'em you're taking the driving test."

The old `53 Chevy truck was missing second gear and looked like something from The Grapes of Wrath, but it ran well enough to get Lee his license. Jack made the newest driver in all of Tulsa drive home, but when their father saw Lee parking the truck, he threw a fit. Letting his brother keep his GTO when he left was going to piss his dad off even more.

His dad watched the conveyer belt, avoiding Jack's eyes. "That boy don't need that car."

"I know how you feel Daddy, but it'll be between Lee and me," Jack said. "He's taken care of the GTO and shown a lot of maturity with the responsibility. I know you think that it's too nice of a car for an eighteen-year-old, but Lee did a hell of a job taking care of it last year. If he can afford it, that'll be between Lee and me."

"We'll talk about it. But, boy, it sure is good to have you back home. I just knew you'd be coming home." His dad grinned as put his arm around his returning hero.

I don't even know where home is right now. God, I've got to get out of here. They're going to drive me crazy. I wonder what the church people momma is always trying to impress will think when I turn out to be the king of thieves.

When they entered the house, it smelled like Thanksgiving. Jack headed to his old bedroom. It looked like a shrine. His baseball, wrestling, and track trophies still sat on the shelves. He picked up the picture of him after he won the state sectional half-mile. He put it back and went into the dining room to join his parents.

Jack asked if he could make a long distance call to Dennis in Duncan. Jack caught his dad checking the time. Jack knew his dad wanted to make sure the rates had dropped. He offered to pay, but a small squabble ensued.

He dialed. "Hey, Georgia, this is Jack." He told her about the Emmitts, and the funeral times. Then he made some small talk. Dennis was out running errands. She promised he'd call as soon as he got in, and told Jack they'd planned a big feast for his visit.

"Ah, Georgia, I've got some real important stuff to talk to you and Dennis about when I get there. It'd be best if the kids are in bed."

"Is everything all right?"

57

CHAPTER ELEVEN

"Jack, will you come to church with us on Sunday?" his mother said. She reached over and held his forearm. "I'd really like for you to wear your uniform. Could you do that for your mother?"

"Momma, I know you want to show me off, but I don't want to wear that uniform," he whispered, looking off into nothing.

"Son, your mother is proud of you and all of your accomplishments. . .getting promoted to captain and winning all of those medals. She knows they just don't give 'em away. And how proud I was wearin' my uniform when I came home."

"I might have to leave before Sunday," Jack blurted out. "I have to go visit some friends." He looked down at his plate. I've got to get out of here.

"But, son, that's only a couple of days from now," his mother said.

"Well, here's what I'm doing. Tomorrow I'm going to buy a new Corvette convertible."

His dad shook his head in disgust and glanced at his mom for support. She closed her eyes and put her hand over her mouth. Jack knew their disapproval was coming, and he upped the ante.

"The GTO doesn't go fast enough, and I need one that has air conditioning. Lee, do you want to go with me? I'll need your help on all the new hot-shit stuff."

Oops. Thank goodness it came out just "shit" and not "fuckin' shit." I've gotta get out of here.

"Hey," Lee said, "I've got the afternoon off from school. Tomorrow. We could go down to Bill White's Chevrolet. I can tell you all the stuff you want. You'll want the new high-performance four fifty-four. It's the hottest thing on the street." He was just getting started when his dad held up both hands and gave a "cut" signal.

"That's enough car talk. What do you say about church on Sunday, son? You know your mother doesn't ask much." He dropped his eyebrows, pinched his lips, and gave the "I'm talkin' to you, boy" look.

"I'm flat-out not wearing the uniform just to have you brag that I made it home. Besides, I'm more than a little pissed off at God right now."

"I won't allow that kind of talk in my house, boy," his dad yelled.

"I know, and that's why I have to be leaving."

"Both of you stop it." His mother started to cry.

"It isn't you. I just need to go, Momma."

He wanted to be thousands of miles from there, but the hootch was a lifetime away. It would never be like it was before, and he knew it.

The next afternoon in the showroom at Bill White's Chevrolet, Jack and Lee sat in a brand-new convertible. The smell of the new interior and tires had helped lure them into the dealership. Jack was convinced they had some kind of new car interior spray that they used in the showroom. The Corvette at was a four-speed convertible. But it didn't have air or the high-performance package, and Jack wouldn't buy it if it wasn't everything he wanted. He and Lee admired the bucket seats and watched the top fold away. Jack watched his brother with pleasure.

Jack rubbed his hands together as the anxious salesman noted Jack's list of must have items. "How soon can you have one with the air and everything else that I want?"

"The one you want is over in Oklahoma City, and I could have it here tomorrow."

"Hell, it's only one o'clock or so." Jack looked at his watch. "How about my brother and I drive over there and pick it up for you?"

Jack could tell the salesman didn't want to lose the sale, because he started to stammer. "Well, well, ah-h-h, let me make a call and see if they'll release it to you."

"If they don't, I'll make the deal with them," Jack broke out with his half smile.

The salesman hurried off and came back. Jack wrote a check for the car. On the way over to the other dealership, he worked out a payment schedule for Lee to buy his old '69 Pontiac GTO Judge convertible.

"Miss one payment and I'll have Daddy repossess it." Jack said, giving Lee a serious look. "Get more than two speeding tickets, and you give it up."

"Oh, man, that's cool. And, brother," Lee said, pointing to himself, "you got my word. Well, you know I'll hold 'er down. Heck, I've done good so far."

Later that afternoon, the two of them decided to spend the night in Oklahoma City. Jack didn't see the rush to get back to the parents.

"Hey, Jack, this is far out. . .a motel room and my big brother all to myself. Plus, you've got a new 'Vette, and now I own the Judge. Hey, I never knew how easy it was to get a motel room."

"I'd better never catch you usin' one with your girlfriend," Jack teased. "I think we'll get up and have a late breakfast and try to get home about noon. Then I gotta run down to Duncan to visit a friend."

"Works for me," Lee said.

His thoughts drifted to Dennis. Jack really wanted to go to Duncan and visit him, but at the same time, he felt hesitant. It wasn't that he didn't need to see Dennis. It was just that he didn't want to talk about Todd anymore. But it'd be good to talk about the run some more. See if I can relay anything to Dan. Plus get the inside on Dennis and Luds sailing to Okinawa.

"Hey, Jack," Lee was saying, trying to get his attention.

"Sorry, I guess I was drifting off. Let's call it a night. I've got a lot of thinking to do."

Jack fell asleep dreaming about his brand-new four-speed convertible with air and a high-performance package. It made him smile knowing how foolish it was to buy the Corvette, because he'd never be able to use it after they took the money.

CHAPTER TWELVE

After a late Saturday-morning breakfast, Jack and Lee drove east on the Turner Turnpike to Tulsa. Jack finally let loose with a smile. He'd decided. . .take the money, no regrets. Buying the car... just plain stupid. Better hurry up and enjoy the hell out of it. I won't be coming back here. Boy, Lee's going to be surprised when he discovers I put the title in both Jack and Lee Higgins names. That made Jack smile. Then he frowned. I've still got to talk to him about not joining the military.

When they pulled up to his parents' house, Jack was hesitant to go inside. Lee was in a hurry to pick up his girlfriend. Jack wasted time walking around the new `Vette. He knew his dad was aggravated because he'd bought the car.

His dad strode out the front door.

"Hey, Daddy, what do you think? Pretty snazzy, huh?"

"I thought we could go bowling. Your momma would like to do something together."

"I don't know." Jack didn't look at his dad.

"Son, why don't you want to spend any time with your mother and me?

"Dad, bowling is your thing. You all know I don't dig bowling. But if it'll make you all happy, let's go." Jack tried to smile.

"Good. I'll go get your momma. I still don't know why you need that thing," his dad said, no doubt making sure it was loud enough for Jack to hear as he headed back toward the house.

Just then, his mother walked out.

She shook her head.

"Hey, Momma, wanna go for a ride in my car?"

His dad had to ask again why Jack needed a new car. And remind Jack that it was a waste of money. Followed by, he'd like to know why Jack couldn't go to church with his mother and him.

Jack walked around the car seeming to ignore the questions, and then blurted out. "First of all, I bought the car because I could pay cash for it and I wanted it. Okay? And Momma and Daddy, I'm not going to church. So could we let it rest?"

Jack glared at his dad. Bowling sounded about as much fun as an ice water enema. "But if it'll make you all happy. Let's go bowling."

"Okay, son, that sounds good. Momma, come on."

"Alright, Dad, wanna ride in my new car? Hey, how about you drivin' us there?" Jack held up the keys.

Tension had reached the boiling point. His dad refused, saying the seats looked too uncomfortable, and spoke for Jack's mother when he said she didn't want to, either. Lee had been the silent observer. He hurried away saying he was going to go pick up his girlfriend, Abby. He reminded Jack she still hadn't met him.

"Suit yourselves. I'm gonna drive my new Corvette, if anybody would like to ride." He spoke loud enough for his dad to hear.

Lee grinned as they walked to their cars. He whispered to Jack that Abby didn't like bowling, either.

"Great. Don't ride with me," Jack mumbled to nobody as he slammed the Corvette's door.

When they got to the bowling alley, the Saturday League Night crowd was insane. Lord, can't those parents control all their little bastards? Herds of kids ran around him, screaming and yelling, and the place reeked with the smell of stale beer. Jack rubbed his temples as his head started to pound. He saw his dad at the check-in counter and walked over.

"They won't have an alley open for about twenty minutes," his dad hollered.

Jack pointed. "There's three seats over there."

"What?" His dad looked lost.

Jack yelled in his dad's ear, who nodded and told Jack's mother. They made their way to the seats in front of an alley. After they were seated, the tension in Jack's temples grew intense. His dad sat, arms folded, a huge frown on his face, and the best part—he never spoke a word. Jack could feel the tension rising. Lee and his girlfriend arrived, and Lee yelled over the racket to introduce her.

Jack smiled at Lee and Abby. "Who'd like a coke?"

"Me," Lee answered. His girlfriend nodded yes. Jack could tell Lee sensed the growing tension.

"Dad? Momma?" Jack yelled. They each shook their heads.

Lee, Abby, and Jack walked into the grill and bar in the bowling alley, leaving his parents behind. Jack ordered from the bar. He knew his parents would never enter any establishment that served alcohol. The air was as frosty as the draft beer Jack held in his hand. The beer would ease some of Jack's tension. But he knew if his parents saw a mug of it in his hand, the beer would cause a major confrontation with his dad.

The noise in the bar and grill was just a touch less than that in the bowling alley. The hamburgers on the grill smelled great to Jack. He noticed several guys shooting pool, and several women watching, and the juke box was playing Sonny and Cher's, "The Beat Goes On."

God, there were guys in country, and the beat goes on over here. None of it made sense to him.

Two gals walked toward Jack as he stood by the bar waiting for his order. One snarled, "With that hair cut you've got to be in the service."

"You guessed it." Jack glared, taking a swallow from his Coors.

"Home on leave?" The other girl rolled her eyes.

Jack just shook his head.

"He looks like a baby killer to me." The first one smirked.

"I'd let it go," Jack said, turning to face them.

"Ooh, big bad war monger. Well, we ain't no Okies from Muskogee," the other one said as she got in Jack's face.

"Whatever." Jack picked up his order and walked over to the table. He said, "Lee, Abby, sorry about all that." Jack started to take another drink when one of the women popped the back of his head, making the beer spill as the mug struck his teeth.

He spun around to face her "If you were a guy. . .I'd kick your ass." He noticed Bob Reynolds, a trouble maker from high school, heading his way. Jack ignored him. Bob handed his pool cue to the obnoxious woman.

"Well, looky here what we got. Is that you, Jack? The big bad-ass Marine?" Bob laughed.

Jack faced him. "Bob, I'd let it go."

"So, I hear you've become quite the hero." Bob smirked.

Jack didn't answer.

"He said he'd like to kick my ass," the woman said.

Bob stepped closer. "Is that right?"

"For the last time, Bob. Just let it go. Okay?"

His girlfriend moved from behind Bob, and said,

"Chicken shit won't admit it now?"

Jack looked at Lee, and shook his head, "Why don't you take Abby, and the Cokes out of here? I'll be out in just a minute."

Lee stared at Bob. Handing his Coke to Abby, he said, "Abs, take this out to Mom and Dad." Abby took his Coke, and left.

Then Bob smirked. "Well, I guess the two of you make it fair against me."

"I said let it go, Bob." Jack stretched his six-inches-less-than-six-foot frame off the bar stool. He felt good as his McQueen half smile broke out. He noticed the loud mouth gal holding Bob's pool cue as she stood beside Bob. Jack inhaled. Relaxed. Flexed his fist.

"I hate beating the shit out of a guy half my size." Bob laughed.

"I kicked your ass in high school, and I'll do it again if I have to," Jack said.

"That guy kicked your butt?" The girlfriend laughed.

"Take your best shot." Jack felt the adrenaline rush.

Bob drew back. Jack kicked him in the groin before Bob's swing was half-way home. Bob bent over. Jack never hesitated. He kicked him in the head, grabbed the pool cue from the chick, and began to beat Bob's back and head. The pool cue broke. With the shortened club-like handle he kept hitting Bob.

Lee grabbed Jack from behind. Jack broke free and started to hit Lee. Lee shouted in his face, "Jack. Jack, it's me. It's Lee."

Jack blinked, relaxed a bit, and said, "Okay, okay, let's get out of here." He dropped the broken pool cue, and looked at the crowd.

The startled woman rushed to attend to Bob. Then she stood and spit in Jack's face, and said, "Mother fuckin' baby-killing asshole."

Jack shook his head and drew back his fist. But, for all

his fallen combat brothers he caught himself. The gal flinched, stepped back, slipped in Bob's beer she'd dropped, and fell on her butt. Jack wiped his cheek. "Wanna try and spit in my face again?" He nodded his head. "Good choice. Stay on your ass."

"God damn it, you made me fall. Asshole. You almost hit me."

Nodding his head, Jack said, "My record is still intact. I've never hit a lady. . .bitch."

"I'll kick your ass," she said, trying to get up.

"By God, I might have to knock you on your ass again," Jack said. "So, come on." She squirmed back down. "If you really wanted to see a baby killer, Baby, I'll show you one. A little advice, you ignoramus. Don't go spittin' on anybody again."

"Jack, let's get out of here." Lee pulled on his arm. Once they were outside the bar and grill, Lee continued. "Jack, I saw the bartender making a call. It's probably the cops."

"I don't doubt it. I'd better get out of here." Jack wiped the corner of his mouth. "If the cops show up, tell them exactly what happened. If they want to get me, tell them they can find me in Vietnam." Jack began to laugh as they walked toward their parents.

"Jack, go on and get out of here."

"God almighty, Lee, I just wanted to get the folks off my back."

Jack's momma and daddy were walking toward Jack. Lee held the blank bowling paper in his hand.

"Hey, they just called our names. We've got an alley," Jack's dad said.

"Momma, Daddy, I've got to go. I'll see you all later." Jack sat down to take off his bowling shoes.

"Son, what about church tomorrow?" His daddy said above all the noise as Jack stood.

Why is he pissing me off? Damn, I feel like I can't breathe.

"Son, where are you going? I thought we came here to bowl."

Jack sat back down and grabbed his shoes.

"What's wrong with him, now? I swear, he acts like he's gone haywire or something." His daddy looked at Lee and his mom.

Abby was wide-eyed, glancing from Lee and then at Jack.

Jack shook his head, finished putting on his shoes, and walked over to his momma and kissed her.

"Bye, Momma. I love you." He hugged her. He knew she watched him leave.

Lee jumped up and followed Jack out to the parking lot. Jack unlocked the Corvette. "Hey, Lee, tell 'em that it isn't them, it's me." Jack hesitated as he opened the car door. He hugged Lee. "You have to promise me that If you have to join the service, you'll join the Air Force or Navy if you have to. I couldn't handle it if you have to go to Vietnam. Do I have your word? I'm dead serious."

"Sure. Okay, you got my word, brother," Lee answered. "But, I'm worried about you. Are you okay?"

"Shit, I don't know. Probably, but I'd better get out of here before the cops show up. I'll keep in touch."

Lee stood there as Jack got into the convertible, put the top down, and drove off.

Jack slipped a new tape in the eight-track stereo and looked at the next one. Ah, sweet Jesus, the Beatles' Greatest Hits. Buddy Holly's next.

A few hours later, somewhere between Joplin and St. Louis, the motel lights looked inviting, but he kept driving. The road had, for the time being, put his mind at rest. He missed his hootch, and he missed his "family."

That evening as he continued east, he inhaled the late spring air and smiled. The smell was nothing like Marble Mountain Marine Corps Air Station, Da Nang, South Vietnam. The air was fresh. He was glad that at least something felt good. He shook his head. He didn't know what day it was.

His thoughts were all over the place, like the pollen blowing in the breeze.

CHAPTER THIRTEEN

Jack wore sunglasses to keep him inconspicuous, which made no sense at all in a new ticket-me-first red Corvette with the top down after dusk. On the highway, he opened it up to see how fast it could go. He was sure a hundred miles per hour was breaking someone's rules. *Like I give a shit. The war made us break a bunch of rules.*

At last he noticed something in the rearview mirror. *Holy crap, the pinball machine must've just hit the jackpot. I wonder if the local law-enforcement agent can keep up.* Jack smiled as he floored the new 454 big block. As the speed increased, the noise and the feel of the wind felt soothing, giving his rambling mind a break. After winning the challenge, he pulled over and walked up to the approaching siren-blaring, lights-flashing cruiser.

"Officer, I just wanted to see how well this baby could run," he said, patting the patrol car's front fender. "But I think I won. Whadda ya think?" He flashed a devil-may-care grin and held up his palms.

"Okay, flyboy, let's see your license and registration." The highway patrolman poked his finger at Jack.

"How'd you know I was a pilot?"

"Are you?"

"Hell, yes. Just got back here from Vietnam, and, just so you know, I don't give a flyin' fuck. By the way, I ain't payin' the ticket, so just haul my goddamned ass off to jail. It's a whole lot better than where I've been the last few months." He leaned against the cruiser's front fender, getting comfortable.

"You just got back from Nam? Are you in the Air Force?" he said.

"Hell, no. I fly helicopters in the Marine Corps."

"Whoa, there. You probably had it pretty rough. I bet it feels good to be back home again." He looked at Jack and tossed his citation pad onto his front seat.

"To tell you the truth, I don't know what the hell I feel right about now. I went home, and it didn't feel like home anymore. I don't know where home is. It sure isn't anywhere around here." He looked at the ground and shook his head. Then he locked onto the officer's face.

"Tell ya what I'm going to do. I'm going to let you go this time, but I want you to promise me that you'll hold it down, okay?"

"Thanks, officer. I'll try," but he knew it was another big lie. He'd become a patented liar.

Jack jumped back into the convertible and took off. He didn't know exactly where he was being drawn, but it was like he was being pulled by a magnet. As he drove through Missouri heading nowhere, he thought about how the military had spent so much money getting guys who were just out of high school ready to go into combat, but not a single cent to get them back into the world. No "detoxification," just turn us all loose on society.

The only thing he knew for sure was he had to bury Todd in about two days. He'd head anywhere to get away from the Marine Corps.

As he drove, he wanted to think good thoughts, but he kept returning to the morbid ones. The lack of mufflers on the Corvette produced a deep rumble. That's something good. The smell of the new car was good, so there was another good thing. Driving with the top down felt good—another good thought. Freezing my butt off—bad thought. I need to get laid. Now there's a really good thought.

I miss Herb, and Todd, and the rest of them.

His mind was tired from thinking too much. All he had really wanted was to come home, and when he did, all he could think of was leaving. He didn't fit in anymore. His daddy couldn't browbeat him. His momma couldn't make him feel guilty about his behavior. He wanted to hug them, and he wanted them to make the bad feelings go away. On the radio, The Righteous Brothers were singing, "You've lost that lovin' feelin'."

Somebody save me.

CHAPTER FOURTEEN

The engine of the new Corvette glided along as the ribbon of interstate carved its way on through Missouri. The highway patrolman had seemed nice enough by only giving Jack a warning. Somewhere past Joplin, the truck stop looked comfortable and nonthreatening.

The tank needed filling, so he pulled in. From the parking lot, he noticed the truckers inside enjoying dinner. That smell—bacon. Man, that smelled good.

He walked into the all-night diner. The warmth and noise were soothing, but the process of ordering food was going to take some thought.

The mess hall was just a place to eat whatever they had. Here I got to pick out something . . . and order. I've gotta start functioning. He relaxed in the imitation-leather booth and smiled as he looked at the table. The Formica showed brown worn circles. The condensation droplets from the water glass formed small puddles on its surface. Yes, that was familiar. Then something caught his attention. Someone asked him something. He jumped back into the present.

"I'm sorry," he said as he read the nametag. "Rayette,

ah, what did you say?" He attempted to clear his throat.

"No problem. What'll ya have, honey?"

Jack began to panic. "I'm sorry. My mind was drifting. What do you have that's good at this hour?" He pretended to look at the menu.

"All the breakfast menu's available, along with the dinner menu. We still have some of the dinner special, meatloaf with mashed potatoes. The hamburgers are always good. What sounds good to you?" She stood, pen ready to write on her order pad.

"All of a sudden everything sounds good. I'm leanin' towards breakfast. Could I get two eggs over easy, with hash browns, bacon or sausage, and some biscuits and gravy? Do ya'll have biscuits?"

"Honey, do we ever. The gravy's made from country sausage. Would you like some?"

He relaxed. "God, that sounds outta-fuckin'-sight. I haven't had country gravy in a month of Sundays."

She tilted her head, puzzling Jack. She smiled and put away her pad. "You're just back, aren't ya?"

He thought he'd hidden it behind his sunglasses. "How can you tell?" he said, taking them off.

"I see more and more of you guys these days." She winked at him. "Really, it was your military haircut. Everyone else has long hair now. I kinda like it your way."

I can't believe she pegged me that easy. In combat, if they recognize you, they could kill you.

"Anyway, I'll have your order right up. What'll ya have to drink?"

"Ah, Pepsi, Coke. . .ah-h-h, either one is okay."

She brought him his breakfast and left. In less than five minutes she was back. "You made short work of that. Would you like some dessert, honey?"

Jack picked up the folded napkin, wiped his mouth, and nodded his head with a still-hungry smile. "Why not? Hey, do you have hot apple pie with ice cream on top? Do you have that?"

"Lemme see." She turned to survey the pie rack. "Looks like you're in luck. Any coffee, or another Pepsi?"

"Pepsi, please. Okay, here's the deal. I'd like the apple pie with the ice cream on top and all the fuckin' chocolate syrup in the world on top of that," he said. "Bet you haven't heard of that combination, have ya?"

"I haven't heard of that, but I can get it for you." She grinned, nodded her head, and walked away to fix up his special concoction.

I like this place. It's peaceful. He looked out the window into the night. I really like the looks of my new Corvette, and I'm beginnin' to like the wing on the back. Well, Jack, you oughta like it. You paid cash for the wing, along with the rest of the car. That made him laugh.

"What are you laughin' at?" The waitress said with a bewildered look. "Here ya go. So you're really goin' to eat this?" She laughed with him.

"Oh, yes," he said, the fork clenched in his fist.

After the pie and ice cream, she came back with the check. "Enjoy the dessert?'

"Is a forty-pound robin fat?" he answered.

"What?"

"I'm saying absolutely yes. Rayette, this was fan-fuckin'-tastic." A couple had just sat down in the booth next to him. The guy leaned over to make eye contact, frowned, and stared at Jack. In a heartbeat, Jack's grin went away as he realized for the first time he'd slipped back into the "in country" verbiage.

"Hey, buddy, we got women in here," the man said. "This ain't that hippie haven Frisco or that Chicago Democratic Convention. It's Missouri."

"Man, I'm sorry," Jack said as he slid out of the booth. He looked at Rayette and ducked his head. "I really apologize. I didn't realize that I'm ah-h-h, here. . .back." He got up and started to get his billfold.

"Hey, it's okay. I understand. Not like it's the first time I ever heard it. Sit back down and relax."

"Thank you for your hospitality, and keep the change, but I really need to be going," he blurted out, then hurried through the door to his car.

He didn't burn rubber as he left, but he fully accelerated through second and third gears. At well over a hundred miles an hour, he shifted with ease into fourth and let off the gas. He couldn't believe he'd just screwed up in there. Gawd, he didn't mean to make a scene. He'd beaten the shit out of some guy back in the bowling alley, almost knocked some bitch on her ass, and cussed in that diner. Yeah, I need to go. Disappear. I could take the money and run. Easy, real easy. I'll never have to come back. Jack, you're in.

As he headed east on I-44, his brain caught up with his speedometer, and the clock.

Holy shit. Jack locked up the brakes, barely making the exit. What've I done?

CHAPTER FIFTEEN

The Corvette was silent after Jack shut off the engine, and coasted to a stop in front of his parents' house. His watch read ten after ten, well after his folks' bedtime. He let himself in with the hidden key above the front door trim. He woke Lee, whispered for him to get dressed, and they slipped outside.

"Lee, I've screwed up big time. My flight to Dallas left about four hours ago. So, I need you to drive me to Duncan. Do you think you could do that?"

"Duncan? Like south of Oklahoma City, Duncan?"

"That's right, brother. I told Dennis I'd meet him there, and I'm way late."

Lee checked his jeans. "I've got my billfold. . .let's go."

"We'll take the `Vette. You'll be home way before daybreak, if we hurry."

"Ah, this won't count if I get a ticket, will it?" Lee cut up.

"That's my brother, always looking for an out," Jack teased back at Lee. They hustled to the waiting Corvette.

Jack stopped, got a slew of quarters, and called Dennis.

"Hello," he said when Dennis's wife, Georgia, answered

the phone.

"Hey, I'll give you five bucks if you can tell me who this is."

"Jack, you owe me five bucks. Where are you?"

"About a couple of hours away."

"Well, get your butt in gear and get here. Cathy called and told us about the funeral. We're going to go tomorrow. Are you okay, Jack?"

"I think so. Hell, I don't know."

"Here's Dennis. He's about to yank the phone away from me."

"Man, I can't believe it. How are you holding up?"

"I'm fine, but I won't be in Duncan for another hour and a half."

"Don't sweat it. It's eleven now, so haul ass and we'll see you a little after midnight."

The ride down was a mental blessing. He and Lee laughed and cut up about the time Jack got caught sneaking out past midnight in his underwear, and the time his mother found a half pack of used condoms in the wash. Their mother accused Jack and he told her she had the wrong son. Jack didn't talk about the war. They made it to Duncan a little after midnight.

Jack made Lee head back to Tulsa and then Jack began a gradual effort to unwind. Jack noticed that Dennis still relied too much on his cane. The Marine macho thing never bothered any of them. Once inside, the two heroes hugged. Jack felt the tears on his face. Georgia grabbed the two of them in a three-way hug.

"Jack, honey, the kids are at Mom and Dad's, so we're all good here."

Jack nodded.

Dennis searched Jack's face. "Let's sit down. I called Danny, and he told me most of what happened with Todd. But can you fill me in?"

"Man, I saw it all. But the worst part of that day was flying back to the base with him and the other two crew members."

"Danny said they shot Todd as he was carrying the crew chief to our guys."

"He was defenseless, and. . . " Jack couldn't continue. Silence filled the room.

"So he was already gone," Dennis said more than asked, all the while looking at the floor. Jack just nodded his head, although Dennis wasn't watching.

"Jack, can I get you anything? When did you eat last?" Georgia reached over and held his forearm.

"I'm fine. But I could use a Coke, Pepsi, or whatever."

Jack and Dennis talked in soft tones, finished and sat in silence. When Georgia came back with three Cokes, she joined them at the table.

"I'd like to hear about what happened to Herb, Ludwig, and Dennis." Georgia checked with Dennis. "He doesn't remember much, and you were there. If it's okay."

"I'll tell you what I know," Jack said. "Bedford finally admitted that he, Tanner, and Hosier had us flying the suicide missions."

"So, he finally admitted it? I hate that bastard. I'd like to kill him with my bare hands." Georgia got up and stood behind Jack, leaned over and hugged him.

"Yeah. I think he was trying to get Toddy or me to slug him before he kicked us out of the squadron." Jack watched Dennis, and asked, "But are you alright with that?"

Dennis motioned with his hands.

Jack took a sip of Coke and began. "Well, it was a flight of four. Herb was the lead. Dennis and Ludwig were dash two. Roadhawg and I were dash three, with Toddy and Danny as tail-end Charley. The zone was hot, and we all circled. Finally, Herb attempted to get in the zone. He waved it off and we laid down a bunch of fire."

"I remember all of that," Dennis said sitting and gazing

at nothing. "Then Herb went in, and we followed. The zone was quiet until we got the medevacs on board. And then I don't remember shit." He placed his head in his hands.

"Herb lifted and took a ton of fire. The Huey rolled, inverted and went in from about two hundred feet. You guys never stood a chance of departing the zone," Jack said to Dennis. "Your engine was unwinding as we landed."

"I read your citation," Georgia spoke up. "It said you left your Huey and went back for Dennis and Ludwig."

"That's what happened. Either one of them would've done the same. I was in a daze. I knew Herb was gone. I couldn't think of Luds or Dennis getting hurt. Yet when I got to them, they were unconscious. I just remember trying to run as fast as I could." Jack wiped his chin.

"Honey," Georgia said, wiping her tears as she squeezed Dennis' arm. "Is that when you got shot?"

"I honestly don't remember getting shot."

"So you don't know if it was your leg that was shot first?"

"Nope. I don't have a clue."

"Shit, I weighed about two hundred at the time, and you were less than one-fifty. I'm still amazed you hauled my ass out of that burning wreck."

"I was scared. I remember taking you first because the fire was closest to you."

After moments of silence, Dennis stirred. "Let's change the subject. I called the Emmitts and told them you were spending the night here and we'd be down at ten in the morning."

"Thanks, man. I've been so screwed up. I don't know if I'm comin' or goin'."

Small talk followed as they tried to put the war behind them. Jack told them about the FAC tour and flying Hueys.

"Well, I've decided on getting even with him, the Marine Corps, and all those hippy-loving assholes that want to spit on me and call us baby killers." Jack tapped his finger on the table.

"How are you going to do that?" Dennis said sitting up.

"You remember telling us about the payroll flight on Okinawa?"

"Sure. So?" Dennis furrowed his eyebrows.

Jack pointed his finger at Dennis like a gun. "Danny works in the S-3 in the `53 squadron and writes the schedule. I talked with him a couple of days ago. Marine Air Group 16 is standing down. We're being reassigned to Okinawa."

"You gotta be shitting me. The three of you back in four sixty-two flyin' fifty-three's?"

"That's a fact, and Danny said he's in on the deal. The Roadhawg is in, and so am I. I'm going to need Ludwig's and your help."

"Hell, yes, I'm in. What's the plan? How will we get the money off the island?" Dennis stood and leaned on the table without his cane.

"Simple," Jack said. "You and Ludwig will sail one of his boats west of Iwo Jima. We'll make them think we're going to go west to Taipei, but we'll fly east. Meet up with you all. Unload the money, scuttle the aircraft, and sail back to Hawaii."

Dennis nodded his head.

"Then we'll leave from there," Jack said. "Take the money to Zurich, deposit it in one of those Swiss banks. We'll split it equally. . .between the six of us. . .Luds, you, me, Roadhawg, Danny, and one crew chief who we'll pick pretty quick."

"I like that."

"I'd like us to give some to Herb's family and some to Cathy, and then each of us can do whatever we'd like." Jack leaned back and grinned.

"I'm a hundred percent with that. And, damn, what a sweet idea. I think it just might work. But, Jack, that's a long sail."

"I know but, here's the deal with me. I'm going to contact the media and give my share back if they'll let me tell what Bedford, Tanner, and Hosier did. I don't know if it'd do any good, but maybe someone will listen. If they don't. . . I'm putting a hit on Bedford's ass."

"My James Dean." Georgia ruffled Jack's short hair. "The rebel with a cause. You'd really put a hit on Bedford?"

"Not only yes, but hell, yes. I'm just so sick of all of it. Shit, I may keep the money and you know what they say. . .living the good life is the best revenge."

They began to work out some of the details, then Dennis called Ludwig on St. Thomas in the Virgin Islands.

"Hey, Ludwig, it's Dennis. I know it's late, but Jack's here," Dennis filled him in on the skeletal plans and smiled, giving Jack and Georgia a thumbs up.

After he hung up, he said, "Here's the deal. Luds said he's on board. Now here's the sweet deal. One of his thirty-six-foot charters is sailing one way to Honolulu. He said they'll be there in about a month. He doesn't have a charter sailing it back, yet. So we could meet you all there on your R and R, iron out the wrinkles, and sail for Iwo Jima."

"Sweet, and here's the best part of the whole shebang." Jack held up his index finger. "They'll be all over Roadhawg and me. They won't have shit on Danny. He'll say he knows nothing. Plus, they won't have diddly on you or Luds. Just say you were sailing his boat home and took your time."

"Oh, yeah, he told me when we had to talk about it let's refer to it as 'the picnic' from now on when we're on the phone." Dennis rubbed his hands together.

"You all are serious." Georgia looked from Dennis to Jack.

Dennis watched her for a moment. "I should've asked you."

"Hell, yes, we're in." Georgia hugged Dennis.

CHAPTER SIXTEEN

Later that morning, Jack checked his watch. "I've never changed Mickey since I left Tulsa over four years ago. Mickey says it's five forty-six, so I'm turning in."

"Yeah, we should leave by at least seven to make Todd's service at eleven. Give us two hours to get to the Emmitts', then to the chapel. We'll be lucky to get a nap in. Wanna have a kick-ass breakfast and make it an all-nighter?" Dennis stood, nodding his head.

Jack chuckled. "Hell, yes. We're only gonna be young once."

"I'll start the biscuits and the potatoes and onions. You two can start the sausage, and get the gravy going," Georgia spoke over her shoulder as she walked into the kitchen.

After breakfast, showers and dressing, they didn't stand a chance of a seven o'clock departure. But by seven-thirty they were well on their way to Dallas. The early-summer Oklahoma morning had a clear sunrise. However, black storm clouds soon appeared.

"Guys, I'm not feeling good about the service today," Jack said.

"How come? What's up?" Dennis never took his eyes

off the road.

"Dennis, I can't look at Todd again. I swear the last visual of him in the bird will haunt me forever. I know they want me to say something, but I can't go close to the coffin. They're having an open casket."

"I'll talk to the Emmitts and ask if it's okay for me to do the eulogy. Don't worry about it, brother. I've got you covered." Dennis turned on the windshield wipers as huge raindrops fell, followed by lightning and thunder.

Jack tried to thank him, but the knot in his throat choked him. Sitting beside Dennis in the front seat, he raised his hand. Georgia leaned forward from the back seat and patted his shoulder.

Dennis parked in front of the Emmitt's a little after nine. They walked to the front door and rang the doorbell. Cathy met them at the door. Each of them seemed to be holding back their tears. Jack could tell the Emmitt's were getting ready for the service.

"Cathy, could we talk? I've, ah-h-h, got a problem," Jack said.

She stepped outside with him. "What's the matter, Jack?"

"I don't think I can memorialize Toddy. . . I'll get too emotional. Shit, I can hardly talk to you about it." Jack inhaled to gather himself. "Dennis said he'd be honored to do it if the Emmitts are okay with it."

She made eye contact with Jack and said, "I'm sure it'll be fine."

"And there's something else." Jack stammered, searching for the right words. "You and I both know Todd would be throwing a shit fit if he knew he was in his dress blues."

"They're so proud of him. I see you've got yours on," Cathy said.

"I'm wearing them out of respect for them. Personally, right now, I don't ever want to wear them again."

"Jack, we won't say a thing about him in his uniform, but thanks. I know they'll be so pleased that you're in your dress blues."

"Hey, Jack, there you are. We've been looking for you." Will Emmitt opened the front door and stepped through. Nodding his head, he said, "I just spoke with Dennis. We'd love to have Dennis do the eulogy. And if you change your mind, just follow Dennis."

"Mr. Emmitt, thanks. Thanks for understanding. It's just so hard. . ."

Will wiped his eyes and put his arm around Jack's shoulder and said, "Let's go inside."

At the service, Dennis struggled to walk without his cane for the first time in public. He tried to speak, but his tears wouldn't stop. At last he said, "It's hard to define this war. Many have judged the participants and the war itself in very derogatory terms. I am proud to say Todd joined the Marine Corps to serve his country, to be the best. To that end, he gave everything and was the best." Dennis stopped and appeared to try and compose himself, but his voice broke as he continued, "I am blessed to have known him and to have flown with him."

Then Dennis broke down. Jack walked up to him, and put both arms around Dennis, then tried to stem his own tears. The silence lasted well over a minute as the two wept. In a quivering voice, Jack began. "I am not ashamed to cry here today and say I loved Todd without abandon. I will miss him. . . until we meet in heaven. I wish I could have given him my life."

Jack assisted Dennis back to his seat.

"You guys, that was more than words can say." Georgia sniffed and blotted her tears with a tissue.

At the gravesite, Dennis spoke. "God, this is hard. I feel so deeply for the Emmitts."

"I couldn't imagine losing one of ours," Georgia said.

After the preacher spoke, the crowd dwindled except for Jack, Cathy, Dennis and Georgia. "Hey, Jackson, we'd better be going. You've got a flight to catch," Dennis whispered.

"Guys, saying goodbye is going to be a bitch. If you all could try and understand, I'd like to have you drop me off outside the terminal."

"We more than understand," Dennis said.

"And the Marine Corps' rules and regulations can kiss my ass. I'm not flying in this uniform, ever again, just so we look good in public to a grateful nation? Screw 'em." He walked into the men's room. Dennis followed him. Jack started unbuttoning his dress-blue blouse and said, "I can't stand wearing these. I'm getting into my civvies."

Jack said his goodbyes to the Emmitts at the chapel, after he'd changed clothes, and left with Dennis, Georgia, and Cathy for the airport.

"Today's been one of the hardest days of my life," Jack said as Dennis drove.

Cathy squeezed his hand from the back seat. "Amen."

Dennis parked in the unloading zone, got out and came around the car. The rest of them got out and stood by Jack. Cathy and Georgia both hugged Jack. Dennis walked with Jack into the terminal.

"Jack, Ludwig and I'll get everything done on this end. When you get to Okinawa, we'll keep the calls short."

Jack turned, waved over his shoulder and walked away.

Later that evening, Jack stood in line trying to ignore the deplaning crowd's insanity at the Dallas Fort Worth airport gate. The gray overcast mirrored his mood. A big show is all it was with Toddy wearing all his ribbons and medals in his dress blues. And everyone sayin' how good he looked. Idiots, he's dead. He looked dead. How good is that? I don't ever want to look at dead people. . .ever again.

He rubbed his temples to get some relief and sighed.

What are they going to do to me if I don't wear that damn uniform? Make me shave off all my hair and fly helicopters in combat?

"Young man, the line's moving," a voice behind him announced. The elderly lady repeated herself, then tapped his arm. "Excuse me, young man. Are you in line for flight eighty-two to Los Angeles?"

Jack nodded. "Yes, ma'am."

"Then you need to move along. They're taking the tickets." She motioned ahead and continued. "Are you going to L. A. or going on?"

"Yes, ma'am, I'm going on to Vietnam."

"I thought you might be in the Army. Now, I must tell you," she said, moving right behind him, "I think the war is wrong. You boys should do something and come home. It's just not our fight, and it's wrong what you're doing over there."

"Look, we don't like the war, and there's not a whole lot we can do about it. But I sure appreciate your support." He was hoping that would be the end of it.

"Young man, I lost my grandson over there, and. . .and for what? Can you tell me?"

"I just came home and buried one of my best friends. Do you think I'm all for it? It's not like we've got a whole hell of a lot of say about this war," Jack blurted out as they walked down the aisle of the aircraft.

Damn, just my luck, he thought, because he and the lady had adjoining seats.

"Why can't you do something about it?" she said as the plane taxied to the runway.

She turned to gaze out the window.

He thought about the last time he'd seen Roadhawg on his way out of country—what he'd wanted to say to him but didn't.

"We're finally headed to the big payday," he mumbled,

though the old woman didn't seem to have heard him.

CHAPTER SEVENTEEN

Eight weeks later...

Jack had plenty of room on the plane as it started its descent to Kadena Air Base, Okinawa. *Strange how crowded the aircraft was back in '68 when I was leaving, and how empty the flight was now.* Jack got comfortable and looked out over the vast Pacific.

He and Roadhawg had survived the last few weeks in country and were now headed to beautiful Okinawa to finish their tour, along with one hundred and thirty or forty other Marines. The big 707 was about half full. He got out of his seat and walked up two rows to where Roadhawg was stretched out, catching up on his sleep from the celebration they'd shared the night before.

"Hey, wake up. We're about ten minutes out," Jack shouted.

"Hey, you just messed up my dream."

"Ain't no dream. We're out of the suck once and for all. Free at last, free at last."

"Come back and get me up when we pull up to the terminal." Roadhawg gave him the finger as he rolled over and ignored Jack.

"Nawh, get your lazy butt up. We're finally going to Okinawa, and Danny's waiting for us." Jack took the aisle seat beside him as the "Fasten seatbelts" light illuminated.

Shortly thereafter, the airplane touched down and taxied to the air terminal at Kadena.

"Thank you, Air America," Roadhawg said and then burped.

"Well, it says that on the outside, but we both know it's CIA on the inside," Jack answered as the jet engines quieted down. Everyone stood, anxious to leave. When the door opened, the line moved down the stairs. Several Marines ran, jumped, and a few even kissed the tarmac. But Jack was looking for Dan.

"There he is. What a galoot. Look at him in his cutoff sweatshirt and shades." Jack pointed as he and Roadhawg deplaned.

"By God, there they are. . .two of the Marine Corps' finest combat helicopter aviators. Make way. Give 'em some space, you slackards," Dan yelled as he slapped both Jack and Roadhawg on their backs.

"Hey, where's my cold beer you promised?" Roadhawg belched again.

Dan held up a black-plastic garbage sack full of crushed ice and cans of something. "Hey, butt breath, I've got 'em right here." Dan adjusted his shades. "Did you bring your church key? I can't do everything for you."

"I got you both covered." Jack pulled out his handy government issued can opener from around his dog tags.

Roadhawg grabbed a can, almost broke Jack's dog tags opening it, and started chugging. Jack and Dan broke out in grins.

"Come on," Dan said. "Let's find your gear and get over to our base. I've already got you rooms. The AC is turned on full blast, and I've got three cases in my fridge."

Roadhawg bowed and waved his arm toward the terminal. "Spoken like a true officer and gentleman. Lead the way, Danny boy. I'll follow you anywhere."

Jack held up his carry-on. "This is it. We shipped everything else."

"Well, follow me, and we're outta here," Dan lead the way to his Pontiac wagon.

Once off the base, Dan began telling them the rules.

"By God, not a word gets spoken in our rooms in the Q, or anywhere on base. Once we're off the base we're clear. Anytime we need to talk, we need to go to Hamby. That's the little base where we talked the last time you were here." He looked at Jack.

Jack pointed out the Army yacht harbor as they drove by. Each one of them pointed out the fact the Marine Corps had nothing close to Hamby.

Dan told them as far as he was concerned, when it came to talking about the gig they were about to embark on, they needed to be one hundred percent serious.

"Okay, I'm cool with that, but Dan, you seem to be taking this awfully serious." Roadhawg leaned forward from the back seat to talk to Jack and Dan.

"Guys, I know we like to goof off and cut up. But when it comes to this. . ." Dan said as he drove. "Time is short, and we've got a lot to get nailed down."

Jack looked over at his two buddies. He nodded in agreement.

"As soon as I get you guys in your rooms," Dan said, "we'll have a cold one and be off to Hamby. We'll go over the details there."

"Alright, then, I take it that Dennis and Ludwig are going to meet us on our R and R." Roadhawg sat back in his seat.

"That's correct. Dennis and Ludwig are finalizing the sailboat. Luds rented his boat to a couple who's sailing it one way to Hawaii. So he and Diane are supposed to pick it up in several weeks." Dan held up five fingers and then rocked his hand side to side.

It'd been almost three years since Dennis and Luds had been shot down and injured. Now, they were going to do one more mission together. Roadhawg leaned forward and turned his head as he kept looking back at Hamby.

Dan grinned. "But on this mission, we'll be getting some payback."

Roadhawg nodded. "Thing're going to be happening very quick."

Their R & R was a little over a month away and would last well over a week.

Diane and Georgia were to fly to meet Luds and Dennis there. That would buy some time to get provisions and be ready to meet up with everyone, Dan told them.

Looking out the window, Roadhawg said, "I don't know much about sailing, but the five of us aboard a boat is going to be cramped."

"With the crew chief, it'll be six, but we'll manage. Luds has all that planned and will go over it with us when we get to Hawaii." Dan gave them the cut off sign as he maneuvered the Pontiac up the steep hill to Futema Marine Corps Air Station. "We'll continue this conversation after we get off base."

"Gotcha." Roadhawg finished his cold Bud and pointed to the gate at the base. "So this'll be our new home until we get the truck outta Dodge?"

Dan reached for his wallet to show the guard his ID.

The MP held up his hand for Dan to stop the Pontiac. "Excuse me, sir. Could you and the occupants please step out of the car?"

"Is there a problem, Corporal?" Dan said, as he opened the car door.

CHAPTER EIGHTEEN

"No, sir, nothing's wrong. We've moved to condition level two, and all vehicles must be inspected by the bomb dogs." The corporal pointed to the German shepherds.

The dogs searched inside the vehicle, noses in the air. When the guard motioned for them to get back in the wagon, Jack, Dan, and Roadhawg headed to the bachelor officer quarters or the "BOQ," and often called the "Q."

Roadhawg said, looking back at the guards, "I know we haven't done anything, but shit like that gets to me."

"I'm not kidding about us being careful where and when we talk," Dan said.

"No shit, Sherlock." Jack held up both of his hands. He took in the scenery as they passed through the gate and rode down the hill. "All right, Danny boy, let's hear about the gig."

Dan steered the big old Bonneville through the base.

"Well, here's what we've got so far. Ludwig and Dennis will sail from Hawaii to the rendezvous pickup point six hundred miles east of Okinawa." Dan motioned over his shoulder. "By God, what's sketchy is the sleeping quarters on Ludwig's Santana. They'll have to make stops across the

Pacific, and take on enough water and provisions." Dan stopped in front of the BOQ.

"Let's get our crap into the rooms, change, and head out." Jack grabbed his duffel bag and small carryon.

Dan handed them their room keys.

Within a few minutes, they'd dropped off their stuff and were on their way. When Dan pulled into the parking lot at Hamby, Jack noticed the empty parking lot. "Well, girls, looks like the place is standing room only."

Once inside they could the smell the Friday-night special, clam chowder, that permeated the room. The wall-to-wall mirror behind the bar revealed three women sitting by the windows. Jack smiled at Roadhawg. He could see Roadhawg was struck by the aroma, unlike Jack. He was struck by the cute brunette talking with two other attractive women. "Just a minute," he said as he left Dan and Roadhawg behind, and approached them.

Jack smiled and nodded as they made eye contact. Lord, have mercy, I'm in love. "I hope I'm not interrupting." Jack never broke eye contact with the brunette.

"Yes, as a matter of fact, you are," she said as she glared back at Jack.

The blond smiled at Jack. "Let me guess. You'd like to buy us a drink."

"Ladies, could we put it to a vote?" Jack rubbed his hands together as he sat down in the fourth chair at the table.

"We came here to avoid obnoxious aviators at the Kadena O club," the petite brunette said with a smirk. "And now we have you."

"Lemme guess." Jack pointed to the three women. "Officers in the United States Air Force, and you're tired of obnoxious aviators of the Air Force variety. Am I right?"

The brunette nodded.

Before she could say something, Jack said, "Well, that's a good thing. How about letting me buy you ladies a round and introduce my two friends?" He waved Dan and Roadhawg over.

The brunette said, "Larry and now Curley and Moe. I hate to mess up your smooth lines, but we were having a private conversation."

"Come on, Ellen." The blonde smiled at the approaching twosome. "If they want to waste their money buying us drinks, what's it going to hurt?"

"Hey, Ellen, come on." Jack was getting in to it. "As Ricky would have said to Claude Rains, 'Louis, I think this is the beginning of a beautiful friendship'."

Ellen raised a brow. "Ah ha, a Casablanca fan, but remember, it was at the end."

Roadhawg and Dan pulled up chairs and Dan motioned to Bill. He was ahead of Dan. With a wink and a grin, Bill was already on his way.

"A round of whatever the ladies are having, Bill. And some finger food. And my combat veterans will take some swill." Dan waved his arm in a circular motion.

Bill took the orders and hurried back to the bar.

"This is Joe and Dan." Jack smiled, gesturing. "So, this is Ellen, and, I don't know your names." He pointed to the other two. "But, guys, be respectful, They're Air Force officers."

The cute blonde smiled. "Sue, and, yes, I'm a captain."

"Nancy," the slender strawberry blonde said as she looked at Dan. "And you are?"

"The luckiest man on the face of the earth." Dan smiled as he stood, took her hand and shook it.

"Lucky, do you go by Dan?" She smiled at him and withdrew her hand.

"Dan. Dan Burton. By God, pleased to make your acquaintance. Should I call you sir or ma'am? My, my, has anyone ever told you that you look like Faye Dunaway?"

"Yes, as a matter of fact, my fiancé." She held up her engagement ring.

"Well, he ain't here, and I am," Dan said. "You reckon that'd be all right, Nancy?"

"For tonight, I guess."

Bill brought over the drinks and food.

The conversation continued, but Jack couldn't think past the cute brunette. Shit, she'd pass for Sally Fields. Lord, help me, I'm fallin'.

"So, Jack, what brings you to Okinawa? On your way home?" Ellen scooted back and glared at him. "What do you do? You in the Army?"

Whew, made it by a hair. She thought she'd shot us down with the Stooges line. Jack looked into her beautiful brown eyes and stammered. "No, ma'am, I'm not on my way home. I'm not in the Army. And why do you hate pilots?"

"They think they're God's gift to women. They see us as another notch on their guns. The base is full of their oversized egos."

"Probably a good thing I'm not an Air Force pilot."

"Don't tell me. . .you're a pilot."

Jack grinned, never taking his eyes off her. "Okay, Ellen, I won't tell you I'm a pilot tonight. So what do you all do for the Air Force at Kadena?"

"I work in the ATC." Ellen sighed.

"Wow, so you're all air traffic controllers?" Jack did his half grin.

"No, I work in the tower," Nancy said unable to take her eyes off Dan. The connection was obvious to Jack, even though she said she was engaged.

"And I work at ground control," Sue said to an attentive Roadhawg. "We make sure the aircraft taxi where they're supposed to."

He nodded also not taking his eyes off her.

Jack took a sip of his drink. "And, Ellen, you're an air traffic controller?"

"Among other things. I wear many different hats. I

guess you could say I'm the assistant provost marshal."

"Wow. So if I get a speeding ticket on base, you could take care of it for me?"

"Sure thing. Bring it to me, and I'll see that they lock you up." She didn't smile.

"Whoa. Hold on. I'm a uniformed armed forces member, Darlin'. I'm on your side." Jack half grinned.

"Hey, Bill, the ladies' glasses are almost empty." Dan waved for Bill.

Jack could see it wasn't hard to get Bill's attention in the empty club.

"Listen, I hate to break up your little party, but we've got duty very early tomorrow morning," Ellen said, looking as if for confirmation from Nancy and Sue.

"She's our boss. Plus, she's our ride. What can I say?" Sue smiled at Roadhawg as she stood.

"Let's go AWOL. I will if you will," He pleaded as Sue shook her head.

Nancy held up her hand for Dan to see. "Daniel, maybe another time. But remember, I'm engaged."

Dan took her engaged hand. "I really enjoyed this. What are you all doing tomorrow night?"

"We're on a twenty-four watch. Nice try," Ellen answered for the group.

"So this is it?" Jack said.

"By the way, Jack, what do you do?" Ellen rose from her chair.

"It'd be better if I didn't tell you. Come on, let me buy another round."

"The boss says no, and we've got to go." Nancy waved as they walked away.

Jack stepped ahead and opened the door for them. "Hey, Ellen, ah, I'm not at a loss for words, but could I, ah, maybe take you out for dinner after your twenty-four-hour duty?"

CHAPTER NINETEEN

"Jack, listen. . .no, never mind. I doubt you'd listen anyway. All of you guys think you can wine, dine, and sweep us off our feet. You've got your lines down pat, and I don't feel like being a next."

"Well, excuse me all to hell. You make it sound like a crime for a guy trying to be nice. What some other son of a bitch did to make you such an iceberg has nothing to do with right now. Maybe someday you'll melt and let somebody get to know you."

Ellen kept glaring at Jack.

"And all you can do is stare daggers at me?" Jack rolled his eyes.

Ellen turned and walked out. Nancy and Sue shook their heads and followed.

Silence filled the empty room. Jack held up his palms and looked from Dan to Roadhawg.

"Jack, you sure got the way with women." Roadhawg laughed.

"By God, Roadhawg, he's got the smooth of Ex-Lax, don't he?" Dan said.

"Screw it. We came here to talk, anyway. Although it

would've been a nice diversion." Jack stared out the window at Ellen's vanishing tail lights. "I ain't sorry for what I said. I'm sorry if I screwed up anything for you all. So what's on the agenda?"

"I'm cool. Besides, Nancy, was engaged out the ass." Dan rolled his eyes. "Anyway, you all get checked into the squadron tomorrow. You'll get your aircraft commander rides Monday. I wrote the schedule."

Roadhawg smirked. "Damn, Danny boy, it pays to know the scheduling officer."

"Here's why. Wednesday, I've got you two scheduled with the Kadena approach control. You'll fly over there and go meet them."

"What the hell for?" Jack said.

"We need to know where they can and can't hold us on their radar scope. When we head out with the pay load, it'd be nice to know when we go off their screens."

"We can do that. But why so soon?" Roadhawg looked from Dan to Jack. "It's still June. We've got till the middle of September."

"Good question. I'll tell you why." Dan looked around. Nobody was within earshot. He told them when they take off and head to the rendezvous, they'd need to know how soon the tower would lose them on radar. And, more important, if and where they could paint them on their scopes.

The chair Roadhawg sat in scraped across the floor as he scooted closer. "That was real smooth," he said as he looked around at the empty room. "So what's your plan, Dan?"

"I've got a three-hour hop scheduled. You'll go over to explain when we're flying back from Taipei, if we have an emergency and have to go low level. . .just where they show us on their radar. Then for the last hour, we'll fly patterns off to the east of the island and see how low we can go before they lose us."

"I see." Jack rubbed his chin. "The first couple of hours are misdirection, and then we'll sashay off to the east because that's what we really want to know if they can follow us on radar."

Dan closed his eyes. "Exactly. The ops section was having a fit when I suggested I'd be out for three-plus hours, and I ain't got a copilot to go along with this little ditty."

"Sounds good to me. Three more, please." Jack held up three fingers to Bill.

"That's not all of it." Dan fidgeted with his empty bottle. "The skipper here is harmless but he's a status climber. He's found out about your Navy Cross. Long story short, Stars and Stripes will be here Tuesday for the award. He's the one who pushed getting you two back in the squadron so that he could present the award."

"They can all kiss a fat Okie's ass in overtime. It's my fault Toddy got killed, and they ain't pinning a hero medal on me for that."

"Jack, listen. I know how you feel, but I had to do it to get you two in our fifty-three squadron. Understand me, man? I need you all here, and we need to be together to fly the run when it goes down."

"Hey, here comes the beer." Jack nodded as Bill approached. Jack asked if it was okay to call him Bill.

"Yes, sir, and what do you two go by?" Bill set the longnecks down.

"Shit head and shit bird." Dan laughed, pointing. "But they answer to Jack and Roadhawg."

"Jack, and Roadhawg. Any friend of Dan's is good by me." Bill nodded and left.

Dan said, "Jack, listen. We all know how you feel. It'll just be a little ceremony, Okay?"

"Not really, but I guess I don't have a choice."

CHAPTER TWENTY

The noonday sun was out, and the airfield was hot and silent the next Tuesday. A small breeze was the only thing that made Jack feel a little more comfortable. Every squadron was in attendance at parade rest. Jack sat on the presentation platform beside the guests of honor—all of the heavies getting their face time before the media cameras. Jack looked past the Marines at the purple Pacific in the distance and smiled.

Little ceremony, my ass. Look at the press—Stars and Stripes, CBS, NBC and A-fuckin'-BC. Shit, Momma and Daddy will sure as hell see this. And here I sit in these hotter than hell dress blues.

The wing general from Iwakuni, Japan, introduced the Secretary of Defense, Melvin R. Laird. Then Secretary Laird read the citation and finished with a message from President Nixon.

"And, Captain Higgins," Secretary Laird said, smiling for the cameras, "on behalf of the president and a grateful nation, I am pleased to award you the nation's second-highest award."

After pinning it on, the secretary looked at Jack and

continued. "Captain Higgins, I know how proud your family must be. Your comments, please." He motioned for Jack to step to the microphone.

Jack frowned and squinted against the sun. "I'd rather have Captain Emmitt back than have anything to do with this presentation. Thank you."

He turned and walked away from the podium and glared at Dan, who was standing in the formation. Little ceremony, my ass. The whole base is here in formation givin' me a medal that cost me one of my best friends' life. Just wait a couple of months, and see how you assholes feel about me, then.

Dan smiled, winked, and puckered like he was kissing him.

CHAPTER TWENTY-ONE

Jack and Roadhawg took off from Futema and were on their way to Kadena in a CH 53 the next morning. It was a very short five-minute hop.

"Don't know about you, Jackson, but it sure feels good to be flyin' shitters again."

"Amen, and, Lance, it's good to be flying with you again," Jack said over the ICS.

The crew chief, Lance Van Dolson, had flown with them down south in the CH-53 squadron, HMH- 463. He always had a great grin. About a head above Jack and one of the brightest crew chiefs, VD was his nickname, one of the better crew members. He began talking over the ICS as he pulled the jump seat down and sat in the cockpit.

"Good morning, Cap'n Jack, and you, too, Roadhawg. What a slice of heaven, having you all back flying fifty-three's and outta the suck. Yes, sir, life don't get no better than this." He pushed up the sleeves of his flight suit.

"I couldn't agree more." Jack signaled for Roadhawg to take the bird.

"I got it. I'll call Kadena." Roadhawg clicked the trigger switch on the control stick, saying, "Kadena tower, this is

Yankee Hotel one four, on your one-seven-zero radial at a thousand feet and about five miles out for landing."

"Rog, Yankee Hotel one four. We have you in sight. Call your gear on final. We'll have you land on spot four. The blue van will assist you with parking and transport you to your meeting."

"Hey, Roadhawg, I've got the flight supplement out, and on the airport diagram it shows spot four is on the east side of the mat, past the tower. I think I see it right over there." Jack pointed to his right.

"I see it." Roadhawg clicked the trigger switch again. "Kadena Tower, Yankee Hotel one four's on final with three down and locked for spot four. We have your blue van in sight."

"Roger, one four. You're cleared to land. Contact ground at your discretion."

They touched down and taxied to a spot to shut down. Then VD deplaned to put in the chocks, and assisted in shutting down the bird. He spoke to Jack and Roadhawg from outside the big helo while the rotor wound down.

"Hey, guys, if it's all the same to you, I'm going to run to the snack bar and get something fabulous for breakfast, seeing as how we're going to miss lunch."

"We'll see you back here, VD. I'll have the driver take you wherever you want."

They walked to the waiting van that drove them to the front of a nondescript, gray, three-story cinder block building that looked like the others beside it. Jack and Roadhawg climbed out. They left VD with the van. They waited at the security check-in until a sergeant arrived to escort them. Their meeting room was on the third floor. Everyone was busy in their cubicles. Jack liked the temperature and the lack of lights. The only lights were from the many radar screens. Jack loved the feeling. The room was downright chilly dark—just like the hootch.

Several people were looking at individual radar screens

as Jack and Roadhawg went through a strange airtight door into a bright illuminated room.

"Roadhawg, the door's supposed to keep the light out. Only the Air Force would do something like this," Jack joked as they walked into the conference room.

A major was waiting for them. "Hey, I recognize you. You're the Marine guy that was on TV yesterday. Captain, I'm Richard Jordan. Pleased to make your acquaintance."

"It's really not a big deal," Jack replied wanting to change the subject.

"What a pleasure to meet you. Okay. So here's what I've got scheduled for you." He took out a map and discussed what they would be doing for the next three hours.

"Is your low-level coverage the same to the north, south, east and west," Jack asked.

"You know, Captain, we're not certain. That's why we're doing this joint exercise today. With our arrival and departure corridors, we've never had any reason to check out the effective radar coverage at low altitudes."

"So, mostly your coverage is east and west arrivals and departures?" Roadhawg said.

"Yes. And if we had any threat, it would have to come from high altitude. He rubbed his chin, and looked a little embarrassed.

Major Jordan reviewed the flight itinerary for the second time. "If I could have one of you come with me into the dark room, I'll show you how we'll paint you on the screens."

"Captain Hegidio will do that. I think I'll grab a Coke." Jack grinned.

"Why, thank you, Captain Higgins," Roadhawg mimicked back.

"Hey, let me get Captain Stevens to take you to the cafeteria." The major jumped up and hurried out of the room. When he came back he said. "She'll be right with you."

"Thanks, ass wipe," Roadhawg whispered. "I get the scopes, and you get to scope out the chicks." Roadhawg gave him the finger.

Jack winked at Roadhawg. He began to study a wall map when he heard the door open behind him. He turned around as Captain Stevens walked in.

You gotta be shitting me.

CHAPTER TWENTY-TWO

Jack shook his head. "Out of all the gin joints in all the towns in all the world, you've got to walk into mine."

"You. . .you're that Marine captain that was on TV." Ellen looked wide-eyed.

"Yes, ma'am. That'd be me."

"Oh, my God. Major Jordan said the Marine captain who was on the TV was here." She tilted her head to study Jack.

God, why does she have to be so attractive?

"I didn't watch any of it," Jack mumbled.

"Look, you must think I'm an airhead. I. . .I just put two and two together. It. . .it is you from Friday night." She put her hand over her eyes. "I want to apologize for my attitude."

"Let me guess. Now that I've made the six o'clock news and I'm not an Army warrant officer, would you like to reconsider having that drink?" Jack narrowed his eyes.

"Listen," she said, moving closer. "You were right, Friday night. You were trying to be nice, and I was being anything but nice. Here's the deal. I just got out of a relationship that was terrible, and I took it out on you. You were the first guy to come along who was being decent. I want to apologize. My attitude was unacceptable." Her cheeks began to blush.

"Apology accepted." He was more than curt.

"Okay, this is going to be tough for me." She inhaled, hesitated and looked into his eyes. "Could I buy you a drink later this afternoon at the Hamby marine bar?"

"Thanks, but I've got plans."

"Now you want to make it a crime for a girl to say she's sorry? At least I tried. What's got you so pissed off?"

Jack was silent as her killer brown eyes worked their way with him. It was the faint Bogart grin that seemed to catch her attention.

"You're smiling, Captain. Come on, get off your high horse." She grinned.

"Play it again, Sam." Jack let loose the Higgins grin. He knew the correct line was, "You played it for her, you can play it for me." But he went for the recognized line.

"Does that mean yes?"

"If you can tell me the name of the song." Jack began to melt.

"As Time Goes By." She pointed her finger at him and winked.

"Hell, yes, I'd like to have a drink with you, but I'd like to buy dinner if that's all right. But tell me it's not because of the TV thing."

"I swear to God. Want to know something else?"

Jack wondered where that question was going. "Sure."

"I was going back to the marina tonight in hopes of seeing you there to apologize. And, well, now here you are." She turned her head and looked away from Jack.

"Well?" Jack felt his face flush as he half grinned.

"You're embarrassing me. Your grin says that you're enjoying every minute of this."

"You want to know something else, Captain Ellen?"

She didn't answer.

"You had me hook, line, and sinker the instant you walked into this room." Jack winked.

"And you put me through all this bull crap? Are you usually this pig-headed?"

"I didn't want to get shot down again. I really, really wanted to see you, and then in you walk all dressed up, and me in a flight suit knowing how much you hate pilots, and on top of that you were thinking I was some Army guy. Okay, so maybe I didn't handle it right." He tilted his head from side to side.

"It's Jack, right?"

"Yes, Jack Higgins."

"Jack, you're a mess."

"I heard the major say Captain Stevens. So you're Ellen Stevens?"

She nodded.

Shit, I could be in big trouble.

"Okay, I get off at three. Let's say around four at Hamby's?" Ellen said. "Should I bring Sue and Nancy? And you bring your two friends."

Jack shook his head and tried not to grin too much. "How's about just you and me? I like the rest of them, but. . ." He broke into a full grin.

CHAPTER TWENTY-THREE

Jack drove Dan's Pontiac around the last bend before he entered the Hamby parking lot. The sun was still about five hours from setting, and bright enough to blind his vision of the vehicles parked there. Damn it. He didn't want to be there first, he noted as he turned off the ignition.

He rubbed his eyes. The window was down, and the sea breeze was pure Pacific fresh. In the distance the lanyards were banging on the hollow aluminum masts. Jack inhaled and massaged his temples.

He didn't hear the footsteps. "You don't have a headache, do you?"

Jack jumped. The voice was too close. "Shit. I'm sorry. You, ah-h-h, startled me."

"I'm sorry. I didn't mean to." Ellen touched his shoulder as he got out of the car.

"No, I didn't see your car. Thought you weren't here, yet. Where is your car?"

"Sue needed to borrow it. She's supposed to be back in a bit."

"I like your outfit." Jack took in the shorts, deck shoes, and long sleeves.

She gave him a basket and told him she had a surprise for him.

He looked inside and asked if it was a picnic basket. She asked him if he was prone to getting seasick.

"Me? I'm a Marine. I don't get seasick."

"That's good to know. I've rented us a twenty-one-foot sailboat. I'm glad to see your tennies." She pointed to his shoes. "I'm taking you on a three-hour cruise. Come on, Gilligan."

"Wow. I've been on aircraft carriers and deep-sea fishing boats when I was in Southern California, but never sailing. This oughta be far out." Jack checked out the boats as they walked toward the wooden dock, wondering which one was theirs.

"I've got some wine and I grabbed some dinner."

Jack smiled. He took the picnic basket from her.

"I didn't know if you liked red or white, so I got a nice chardonnay and a merlot." She took his hand and squeezed it.

"I'll like whatever you have."

Ellen stopped. She checked the slip of paper in her hand as she swung her arm out in front of a sleek, white sailboat with blue trim. "Okay, here we go." She stepped aboard. Jack followed.

"What can I do to help?" Jack mumbled as he looked around.

"Untie those lines on the other side while I start the engine."

Jack sat the picnic basket down, undid the fore and aft lines, coiled the ropes, and laid them on the boat. He heard the engine cough and start, ending in a smooth idle.

"If all else fails, the iron spinnaker works," she announced as she checked the gauges. "If you'll untie the last two lines, I can get us out."

Jack stowed the lines, admiring her skill at backing out of the slip.

He stood beside her as she turned the boat out of the marina. "You're pretty good."

She glanced at him. "I got bored and took lessons, and now I'm hooked. It's a great release."

"It seems sedate and relaxing." Jack looked at the marina behind them.

"Come here and steer. I'll hoist the main sail, and we'll be under way."

Jack watched as she winched up the main. When she finished, she stepped down and tied off the boom. "Okay, ready to be under way?" She cut off the engine.

The boat took on a list as she steered into the wind.

"This is called a tack," she said. "We'll zigzag, changing tacks as we go out."

The wake they were leaving was faint and left little eddies. Jack relaxed. The silence engulfed him.

"Here, I'll let you hold the tiller." She motioned to him. "I'll get us a snack."

She went below to the cabin, while he toyed with the rudder, checking out how the sailboat would change direction. When she returned with the picnic basket, she sat beside him.

"Hey, isn't the Marine Corps technically a department of the Navy?" She elbowed him.

"Yeah. The men's department." Jack grinned, never looking at her.

"That's a good one. I like your sense of humor."

"Little by little, I'm getting there."

She nudged his shoulder. "Cute, real cute."

"So, Cap'n, where are we off to?"

"I'm still learning, but I'm getting there." She grinned. "We'll tack out for a couple of hours and then sail with the wind behind us. Coming back's a whole lot quicker."

Wonder if she's ever thought of a trans-Pacific sail?

"Okay, Matey, we're going to change tack. So, we'll use the winch to pull the boom with the main sail to the other side while we use the rudder to put the nose about sixty degrees from the left to the right."

"Do I turn the rudder?"

"Uh, huh, and then I'll wrap this line around the winch, and you put the handle in and winch the boom around. While you're winching it, I'll release the other side. The trick is to not let my side slip loose, or the boom will head your way. If that happens, it'll snap over very quickly, and that's dangerous."

"I'll be watching."

"On sailing vessels the term is hard-a-lee, and then you do it."

"Say when." Jack got ready with the handle in the winch.

"Hard-a-lee," she yelled.

Jack turned the rudder and started winching the mainsail.

"Jack, watch out," she screamed.

Jack looked up as her line came off her winch and the boom slammed into him, knocking him overboard.

The first sensation was a freezing cold numbness. He surfaced and tried to catch his breath. In the swells he could see the life line being thrown past him. The forward motion of the boat brought the life preserver right in front of him. Groggy, he grabbed the ring and held on. He started treading water to stir up some inner heat.

"Hold on," Ellen shouted as she dropped the main sail. The forward motion came to a stop. She pulled the line as fast as she could to the stern of the boat.

"Are you okay?" She grabbed the back of his shirt.

"I was a little lightheaded, but the water woke me up. Let me see if I can get myself back on board." Jack hoisted himself into the boat as she tugged on his shirt and then the waist of his shorts.

Rolling around on to the deck of the boat, he started laughing.

"What's so funny?" she cried as she helped him sit up.

"First date, and I'm flopping around on the deck like a tuna."

"You scared me to death. That was my first man overboard, and I. . ." She grabbed a towel and wrapped it around him.

"If I could get this kind of attention, I'd go overboard all the time." He raised his eyebrows.

"Well, we're heading back. Our picnic will be just as good tied up at the dock. Jack, I'm so sorry. That's never happened before. Something let go in the winch, and it just spun."

"You mean it's broke?"

"I think so." She reached back and spun the cylinder.

"Can we get back okay?"

"Yeah, we'll just be extra careful. I can't believe it just went bad. I bet it was brought back in this condition, and they never told anyone."

"Hey, I'm fine. And a private party at the marina sounds good to me."

"Are you cold?"

"Yes, now that you ask. Maybe you could hold me. I'll wrap a blanket around us, solely

for . . . ah-h-h safety reasons. You know, getting my body temp back up."

"There goes your sense of humor, again." She chuckled. "You're terrible, but come on over here. You realize I'm only doing this because you look so cold."

A couple of minutes later, their lips met. It wasn't an ordinary first kiss.

Uh, oh, that made something besides my temperature rise. Lord, help me.

"Okay, Jack, for safety reasons, I'd better stop. You seem overly warmed up."

"No. I'm freezing to death."

She glanced down. "I don't think so." She unwrapped the blanket.

114

"Just when you had me where you wanted me."

"You're terrible." She pecked his cheek, "Now get over here and help me get this thing headed toward the marina."

Jack changed into some dry gym clothes he had in the duffle he'd brought along. They made it back in no time at all. He dropped the main-sail as she fired up the engine and maneuvered the boat like an expert into the slip.

Once there, Ellen and Jack tied off the boat and opened the picnic basket.

After white wine, cheese, crackers, and sliced beef, Ellen said, "Well, Jack, you've probably never been on a first date this messed up."

"I had a good. . .no, make that a fantastic time." He squeezed her hand.

"Really?" She reached over and caressed his cheek.

"Cross my heart." Jack mimicked crossing his heart and leaned forward to kiss her, then stopped as they gazed into each other's eyes.

"I really enjoyed being with you. I was worried how this would go."

"Did I do well enough for us to go out again?"

"You baboon, what do you think?"

CHAPTER TWENTY-FOUR

Jack opened the door to his room at the BOQ, and there stood Ellen, well before the six o'clock brief. Clad in a flight suit and boots, she cut a cute figure.

"Welcome to my version of living quarters." Jack motioned her to come in. "Joe should be here anytime. Wow, you make that flight suit look awfully good, Captain Stevens." Jack looked her up and down and grinned.

She turned and struck a modeling pose. "I know you better than that. But do you think it looks okay?"

"Yes, it makes your butt look very cute."

"You're terrible. Really does it look. . . all right?"

"Hang on. I've always fantasized about kissing a female in a flight suit." He wrapped his arms around her, but her lips met his before his met hers.

"Hey, knock it off," Roadhawg yelled as he opened the door.

Jack held her a moment more.

"I hate to break up this tender moment, but we've got a brief. I take pride in being professional and punctual, and in demonstrating Marine Corps leadership."

"She doesn't believe you for one second," Jack shot

back.

"Well, it sounded good. Let's hit the trail." Roadhawg held the door open as he bowed and motioned them out with a sweeping arm.

They rode to the flight line in the Impala. After signing for the bird, preflight, start-up, and take off, Jack asked Ellen what she thought. She wore a helmet and could listen to the intercom and the radios.

"This helicopter is huge. And it doesn't vibrate at all. How high are we?"

"See this gauge?" Jack pointed to the altimeter. "It says we're at a thousand feet."

Sitting on the jump seat between Roadhawg and Jack, Ellen could see everything forward as well as they could. Jack pointed ahead to the huge runways at Kadena.

"There's where you work. It's only about three minutes or so by air." Jack pointed with his gloved hand.

"Wow, it really is close, and you can see everything from up here," she said.

Jack called Kadena for landing instructions.

"Hey, today's payday. Are we flying the money run?" She looked at Jack.

"That'd be a yes." He nodded as Roadwhag completed the landing checklist.

"No kidding, all that money in here with just us?"

"That'd also be a yes." Jack set the helicopter down as smooth as silk.

"I've never thought about it, but how much is it?"

"Honey, they don't tell us things like that."

The payroll van approached, and the guards and crew began loading the locked strong boxes onto the aircraft. Ellen turned around and appeared over engrossed with the whole procedure. Once the money was loaded, along with two armed Air Force guards, Jack called for takeoff to Camp Sukeran.

The money run was heading south from Kadena. As

soon as they lifted, the huge Army base at Camp Sukeran took up almost the full windscreen at one thousand feet. The base looked busy, with trucks and military equipment hustling and bustling around.

"Wow, look at that. I was thinking Camp Sukeran has about thirty thousand soldiers stationed there. So let's say two hundred average per payday. And that's on the low side. Good Lord, is my math right. . .six million dollars?" Ellen put her hand over her mouth.

Jack slowed down as the helo landing pad by the headquarters grew larger before them. He set their approach path into the wind, which was indicated by the flag pole in front of the three-story building.

"I ain't no math major, Captain Stevens," Roadhawg said.

"Sounds about right." Jack didn't look at her. He pretended to be busy with putting the '53 exactly on the big X on the landing pad. The touchdown was smooth as the last landing, and when he eased the power off the engine with the collective, the noise faded.

"Look at all those locked boxes they're unloading." She watched the Air Force guards loading the reinforced strongboxes. They finished and their crew chief, Sergeant Van Dolson, gave Jack a thumbs up for clear to take off.

Jack keyed the mic, got Roadhawg's attention and gave him a thumbs up. Roadhawg acknowledged that Jack had completed the takeoff check. The noise increased as the engines responded, and then they were airborne again.

Jack tapped her shoulder to get her attention. "Hey, Captain Stevens, when we get rid of all of this filthy lucre, would you want to fly it around for a while?"

"Oh, yeah, but I can't get my mind off all that money back here. I thought the sailing thing was a big deal, but, Jack, this takes the cake. I mean, nobody would believe it if I told them."

"Okay, Sweetie, but you can't be telling everyone.

Officially we aren't supposed to be taking passengers. They might think you would want to steal it or something."

"I can't believe you officers would even be talking that way." V. D. chuckled. "We lowly enlisted swine would never think of such a thing."

"Hey, let's keep the enlisted chatter from the peanut gallery to a minimum." Jack laughed as V. D. strapped the last box securely to the floor.

The Marine Corps Air Base at Futema, less than a couple of miles away, appeared in front of them. Jack called the tower and again landed by the building with the flag pole. The same hurried routine followed with two guards coming out to escort and help carry the payroll safely inside.

"Jack, we're all good to lift," V. D. called out from the back of the aircraft.

After he radioed the tower, they lifted and began the other deliveries. True to the schedule, after about an hour and a half, they returned to Kadena and dropped off the two Air Force payroll guards.

"Okay, Ellen, are you ready to see how it feels at the controls?" Jack looked at her.

"I don't know, I. . ."

Getting out of the copilot's seat, Roadhawg told her, "You'll be fine. Jack's in control."

V. D. and Roadhawg helped get her seatbelts comfortable. Jack lifted, and they headed north to the Marine Corps' Northern Training Area.

"Wow, Jack, the green looks so lush from up here. I never imagined how fabulous the island could be. The water, the sky, the clouds, they're all so. . . beautiful."

"Are you ready to fly us around a while?" Jack pointed at her as he let go of the controls.

"Hey, don't do that." Ellen said.

"We're okay. The trim system will automatically hold the last altitude and attitude it recorded. See, no hands." Jack raised his hands higher. "Now I'm going to be on the controls with you, so you can't mess up. Take hold. If you want to turn left, move the stick to the left. If you want to go up, you pull up the collective. That's this thing on your left. How about turning us to the right, and then you can do whatever you want."

Jack disengaged the trim, and she moved the control stick to the right. The aircraft made a slow and gentle turn to the right. Jack could feel her slightest input as the bird followed her movement. They leveled out on a new heading, crossing the island west to east. From that height, the late morning sun wasn't in her eyes.

"Oh, wow, this is far out. Can I go over there?" Ellen nodded to her left.

"Sure. Move the stick that way. All you can see here is the Marines' NTA."

She moved the cyclic stick and the aircraft followed making a gentle, but cautious turn. The turns became more natural and smoother as the aircraft soared high above the island and ocean. The only sound was the constant high pitched whine from the big two General Electric four thousand-plus horse power engines. When Jack looked over at Ellen, she was talking to herself with a big grin.

"Would you like me to show off a bit?"

"As long as you don't scare me."

"I won't do anything to hurt any of us. This is the free world's fastest and most maneuverable helicopter. I'll show you how we get into a hot zone."

"You're going to get even for me knocking you overboard, aren't you?"

"Not me." Jack lowered the collective with ease, which took off all the power, taking the cyclic stick hard to the right and pointing the nose down. "See that little clearing down there in the jungle?"

The helicopter began to spiral, nose down, then banked hard right, the ground spinning and growing closer. The noise from the engines became quiet, yet somehow the maneuver felt under control.

"This maneuver is called a corkscrew."

"My stomach is coming out my throat, Jack. You're scaring me." she said.

Jack glanced over at her and nodded. "Okay, I'll show you a little-old-lady approach to the zone. Be smooth as silk."

"Boo," V. D. moaned over the ICS.

"And hiss. Just when we were beginning to have some fun," Roadhawg said.

Jack leveled the wings and raised the nose as he prepared the aircraft for a more-normal landing. The rate of descent decreased, and Jack saw Ellen put her hand to her chest in relief. Jack reached over and pulled the landing-gear handle down. With a loud thunk, the gear indicator showed the three landing wheels were down and locked. Sitting on the jump-seat between Jack and Ellen, Roadhawg made a circling motion around the cockpit and then gave a thumbs up, signaling that the landing checklist was complete. Jack acknowledged with a helmet nod to Roadhawg and put the big bird down on the ground.

"I barely felt that," Ellen said.

"This'll be a max-speed take-off. Count to five and then look at the air speed indicator. It registers in knots per hour." Jack pointed to a gauge in front of her.

"We'll be well over a hundred knots indicated," Roadhawg bragged.

"All ready in the back." V. D. let Jack know he was buckled in and braced.

Then Jack pulled full power, lifted, and put the nose almost sixty degrees down as they accelerated out of the zone, with the engines delivering every ounce of power.

Ellen laughed. "That scared the hell out of me, but it was fun."

"Would you like to go low level over the water?" Jack

said.

"Groovy."

He headed to the shoreline and flew at about one hundred and fifty knots. The helicopter paralleled the shore, and Jack said over the ICS that at that low altitude, he was concentrating on things outside the helo. And he depended on Roadhawg, in the jump seat, to monitor the gauges.

"The radar altimeter is showing fifteen feet, Jack. Everything is in the green." Roadhawg rested his right hand on Jack's left shoulder.

"Oh, my God, what a rush," Ellen said. "This is unbelievable. I love it. I don't want to go back."

Jack glanced to his left at Ellen. *I think I'm falling for you.*

The helo seemed to blend in with the breaking waves, but the speed was surreal, sharp, and intoxicating. Everything peripheral increased to a blur.

CHAPTER TWENTY-FIVE

The flight ended, and before they left the helicopter, Ellen hugged and kissed Jack.

"That was incredible," she whispered in his ear.

Still holding her, Jack said, "How about getting Nancy and Sue, and you all join us at the local watering hole at Hamby for dinner? Say six or so?"

"We'll be there early." She took his hand as they walked from the helicopter.

"Last ones buy the first round?"

"I love it when you all lose." She hugged him again.

On the way to her car they met Roadhawg coming out of the line shack. Once Ellen left he said,

"She seemed very interested in the count and amount. You don't think, as a cop, she was considering Dialing for Dollars, do you?" Roadhawg said.

"It's reason for concern, but we'll talk about the diner later." Jack cut it off just as one of the majors in the squadron walked toward the line shack with his flight gear.

When the guys met the ladies, the breeze off the deep blue horizon chilled more than the atmosphere. Bill had opened the windows, and nature's air conditioner blew in a fresh, gentle breeze.

The three guys discussed the inquisitive Ellen and the payroll.

"Jack, you know her better than we do. What do you think?" Dan looked at the women approaching the parking lot.

"If she brings it up, then we need to be a little bit concerned." Jack frowned.

"I think she was impressed with the flight in general. The payroll was secondary to the fun she had flying," Roadhawg added.

"We'll see how it goes. Here they are." Dan pointed with his bottle.

"Are you girls up for a friendly bit of inter-service competition?" Jack wagged his head.

"Sure. We'd be glad to show the Marines up anytime," Ellen stuck her tongue out.

Jack motioned to the row of six or so machines. "You feeling lucky?"

Ellen glanced in that direction. "Guess we'll find out. I've never seen a penny slot before."

Roadhawg walked up with a small bucket of pennies. "Here's how it'll work." He held up a roll. "Everybody gets fifty cents' worth. When you've finished it, the one with the most winnings buys the next round."

Bill arrived with the first round and served the drinks.

"So you want to lose?" Sue raised a questioning brow.

Nancy looked at Dan. "That's just wrong."

Dan smiled. "By God, that way we won't feel bad when we beat you like a drum."

"I'm starting, and you're looking at the winner." Ellen grabbed the roll out of Roadhawg's hand and peeled back the paper.

"Jack," Sue said, "Ellen is over the rainbow about flying today." She smiled at Roadhawg. "I'd like to go flying sometime. What's a girl have to do?"

"Ah, yes," Roadhawg smiled, imitating W. C. Fields. "Wanna go for a ride, little girl?"

Sue shook her head. "You're terrible."

"Look at this." Ellen hit three oranges and won ten pennies.

"Way to go, El." Jack hugged her waist.

"By God, I'll take the both of you flying anytime you want." Dan said.

Ellen stopped and looked up. "I'm going if they're going."

"Ellen, Ellen." Jack shook his head. "What about me? I'll take you. . .anytime."

"What about you? I'll go flying if they're going."

Jack rolled his eyes, "Guess that tells me where I stand."

"I'd do anything to get to go," Sue said.

"Anything, little girl?" Roadhawg pretended to have a W. C. Fields cigar as he moved his eyes from side to side. "Ever wanted to join the mile-high club?"

Jack looked away as he tried to not to laugh.

"Mile-high club?" Sue and Nancy said in unison.

"Young Joseph is trying to be cute. Just ignore him," Jack said.

"What?" Ellen had just finished her roll of pennies and was digging the winnings out of the tray to put them into a plastic cup.

"Honey, I'll explain it later," Jack whispered in her ear.

The three women snickered because they knew.

Sue slugged Roadhawg's arm. She'd already started on her roll, pulling the lever. The slot machine rang when she hit two cherries, and pennies clanked.

The bell above the door jingled. Bedford and Tanner entered the bar. Bedford pointed at the party, smirked, and sauntered toward them.

"Jeez, we came down here to avoid those bastards," Roadhawg grumbled.

"It's a private party," Jack growled as Bedford approached them.

"A private party? Oh, my." Bedford reached into the container Ellen was holding and grabbed some of the pennies. "Well, my party would play with more than these cheapskates and their pennies."

"Last time. It's a private party, and you're out of line." Jack stepped toward Bedford. "Now get out of my sight."

"My, my, ladies," Bedford said, "are these boys," he flipped his wrist, "trying to impress you with their misplaced heroics? Goodness me, but have you heard how many of their buddies lost their lives over their misguided heroics?"

Jack drew back to hit Bedford, but Dan grabbed his fist.

"By God, Tanner, take your pet squirrel and get the hell out of our sight," Dan stood, facing Bedford. "Or I'm going to kick your ass." Dan shook his finger in Bedford's face.

"Oh, lordy, must've hit a raw nerve," Bedford retorted. "Ladies, we'll adjourn to the bar. If you'd like to play with real men, you know where we'll be."

"It just hasn't dawned on you two geniuses that there's an investigation over your selective scheduling." Dan moved to block Bedford's retreat and poked his finger in Bedford's chest. Bedford took a step backward.

Dan continued, "And downgrading Jack's Medal of Honor to a Navy Cross started another investigation from the grunts. Rumor is two squadron COs downgraded it, and the ground side is pushing their own investigation. Now, 3M, you know why you two are at group instead of in a squadron."

Roadhawg, still seated, winked at Bedford.

Bedford paced as he glanced at the three aviators. "Ladies," he said, smiling, "I'll have these poor excuses for officers up for insubordination first thing tomorrow. Then we'll see how full of themselves they are."

"Bedford, the only thing real about you is that you hide behind your rank. If I'm lyin', then meet me out back, you chicken shit." Roadhawg stood and stepped closer.

"Oh, you'd like that. But I won't succumb to your cowardly antics." As Bedford turned and swaggered toward the bar he said, "Ladies, you should move on from these vulgar little boys."

"You two are the ones who put them on the flight schedules in Vietnam. You ought to be shot," Ellen yelled above the din.

With exaggerated steps, Bedford waved his hand, not turning around.

Jack watched Tanner and Bedford as they spoke in hushed tones and then walked outside. Through the window he could see them looking at the storage sheds. Tanner pointed. Bedford folded his arms and nodded. What in the hell were they doing out there?

"I'm sorry, El. I just hate him." Jack watched as Bedford and Tanner walked along the row of pull-down door storage spaces that boat owners used to store gear.

"I don't know what they're doing down here. But you can bet they're up to no good." Jack tapped his finger on the bar as Dan nodded in agreement.

"By God, they sure can ruin a good time. Let's forget 'em. I'm buying. We'll play the slots later. Come on, Jack, you can help me carry the drinks back." Dan headed toward the bar.

Still staring at Bedford and Tanner, Jack said, "Just look at them. I think they came down here just to piss me off. But, I'm worried they're up to something."

Bill walked from the behind the bar. "Friends of yours?"

"Back-stabbing lifers and pricks."

Bill nodded. "They've been in a couple of times asking all kinds of questions. They've done everything but rent a boat."

"Who cares? How about another round?" Dan pointed

toward Bill.

Bill turned to get clean glasses.

"I get around them, and just lose it," Jack said. "I'd like to kill both of them."

"Take a number. But listen, Jack. Think about it. Those two keep showing up too often. I don't think they're on to us, yet. But we can't be too careful. . .especially this close," Dan lowered his voice as he picked up the drinks.

"Damn, Bedford's up to something, and I don't know if we're cool with him finding us here with Ellen," Jack said as he walked beside Dan.

"We can't get too lax," Dan added.

CHAPTER TWENTY-SIX

Jack drove Ellen back to her quarters at Kadena. They arrived as the sun was setting, and when she invited him inside, he felt romance in the air, or he was hoping, anyway.

"On second thought, El, going inside's probably not the best idea."

"Jack, thanks for. . .for taking things slow, but. . ."

He kissed her and held her at arm's length. "I said that we'd take our time. And I think it's working." He kissed her again and caressed her ear.

"Am I supposed to ignore that?"

"No. I just slipped up."

"Honest?"

No, it wasn't. And not being upfront is just as good as a lie. Think about something else.

"You're thinking something. What is it?"

"Things." He toyed with her hair.

"Tell me about one."

"I was thinking that I'd like to spend the night with you." You're such a sleaze bag, Jack. You know you're worried about her talking about the money run. Don't say a word. Maybe she's forgotten.

"I don't want you to go, but you'd better," she whispered, "before we get into trouble."

"I'd love to get into that kind of trouble, but I want us to wait . . . until it's right."

"Okay." She pecked his cheek. "See you tomorrow night."

Jack watched her walk into her living quarters.

Jack, Jack, what would you've done if she'd asked you to stay? That's a stupid question. He smiled as he fired up the Impala.

"Baby, the last couple of weeks I know we said we'd always be honest, but. . .what I mean is, ah-h-h, I'm getting all messed up." She shook her head and looked away.

She was driving her Comet, headed somewhere unfamiliar to Jack, along the road paralleling the coast.

"Come on, El. Remember how we said last night we'd never keep things from each other? Come on, 'fess up. What's on your mind?" Jack stared out the window at the local businesses along the road closing at dusk.

Technically, I haven't lied. I just haven't told her we're planning on taking the money run.

"This has nothing to do with our date tonight, but Nancy's telling Dan she's not engaged. It's been kind of a thing that she does to keep guys away."

"Really? She's not engaged?" Jack sat up.

"She really likes Dan. He's been very, ah-h-h you know. Hands off."

"Kind of like me, huh?" Jack waited a few moments, then said, "Something else is on your mind. Fess up."

"We've been going out for almost a month now, and you said you wanted me to do the initiating and, so well, you leave Tuesday for R and R."

"What are you trying to say?"

"Are you up for a surprise, maybe an adventure? I'm going out on a limb, Jack."

"I'm up for a little adventure. What are you up to, Captain Stevens?"

Ellen told him she was in the mood to go for it. She stopped talking as she pulled around a couple on a small motorcycle. Jack told her he loved the fact that she had something planned. She reached over, took his hand and told him they were going up to the north end of the island. Kadena's special services had recreation cabins there for rent. Neither of them had been to the site.

Then Ellen told him she had rented two cabins for the weekend, plus all the food, wine, etcetera was packed in the trunk of the Comet.

She stopped for a traffic light. Jack grinned and held up his index finger.

"What?" Ellen looked puzzled. "One what?"

"That's how many rooms I vote for."

"I've never done this before," she stammered. "Made the plans and now I'm getting really embarrassed."

"You haven't answered."

"One room sounds perfect." A slight curl formed on her lips.

Jack turned toward her as the Comet moved across the intersection. "El, I'm blown-away happy. I don't think I've ever been this jazzed."

"Jack, I don't want you to think badly of me."

"More than anything in the whole crazy world, I want to make love with you. There, I said it. I've had girlfriends before, but I've never ever felt this way. I can't do anything without you being in my thoughts."

Jack scooted closer to her and told her he'd never told any girlfriend that. She asked why. In his mind he knew why—because they were getting ready to steal millions of dollars and what would she think of him if she knew. God, Jack, you're screwed up.

"Come on, tell me what you're thinking," she pressed on.

131

"Just that this must be love." Jack, you can't tell her about the run. Jeez, I hate this. Why now?

"You seem like you're somewhere else."

"It's not us or you, honey. It's. . .I promise I'll to tell you later." He put his arm around her and kissed her cheek while she drove.

"Jack, are we going too fast? I know how I feel about you, but where am I with you?"

"You're right here with me on this bluff listening to the surf, watching the moon light up the ocean like a giant spotlight." Jack had both arms wrapped around Ellen who was sitting on the ground leaning against his chest.

"The moon's unbelievable. But, Jack, I mean, what about us? You're getting out of the Marine Corps soon, and I'm not far behind you."

"Ellen, I've never told a girlfriend I loved her and meant it, and I don't have any meaningful employment in the near future. But I know this. . .I love you."

Ellen leaned over and kissed his arm. She straightened back up and pulled the flannel blanket around them. "That's the first time you've ever said that. Tell the truth. When did you decide you liked me, and when did you know you loved me?"

"When I walked into Hamby's that first night, and I walked right straight to you. No cutting up with Sue or Nancy, Honey, I was drawn to you."

"And then what?" She squeezed his arm.

"Two things stand out. The typical guy thing. Your white short shorts that night. I thought, 'Lord, what a cute butt.'"

"That night wasn't one of my better nights."

"I remember." He laughed.

"I was still upset about the split with Ron. When we got to the car, Sue really raked me over the coals. She told me you were just trying to be nice, and I came across like a real witch." She shifted, snuggling closer against him. "I thought about it, and she was right. So I got this plan to go back and apologize, and there you were in my office, bigger than life. And it dawned on me you were the Marine pilot, so I panicked."

Jack told her he was almost speechless when she walked in. He half smiled as he thought about how he wasn't going to let her shoot him down again. They talked about how he was being a perfect jerk when he acted so piss cool collected with the Bogey line, 'she's got to walk into mine,' and then the 'apology accepted' bit. Like he could care less. She elbowed his ribs.

"So, I didn't think it through. I was. . .shocked to see you."

"Are you telling the truth, or is it because we're both naked, wrapped up in this blanket?" She kissed his forearm.

"The 'necked' part has a lot to do with it, but when did you decide that you liked me?"

"I was pretty sure when we went sailing, and then when you got knocked overboard, and joked and laughed about it. That was special to me."

"But when did you know you liked me enough to come up here?"

"The other night at my place, after the confrontation with Colonel Bedford, and I asked you what you were thinking. Remember?"

"Yeah, I said something like I wanted to make love with you."

"Yes, you were honest and considerate of my feelings and didn't press the issue. It got me thinking about what was really important to me. And it's you."

"El, see the moon? In just a little while, the sun will start coming up behind us. And on the other side of the island, the water will glow bright orange. That huge strobe light of a moon shining off the water in front of us will turn translucent to pale blue."

"So how many other girls have you watched this with?"

"Zero."

"And just how do you know all about this romantic sunrise, moonset?"

Jack took a deep breath. "All those night medevacs."

"Jack." She turned and drew him closer. "I'm so sorry. I didn't mean to bring any of that up."

"Honey, it's okay. I've never talked about any of that crap except with the guys. You know, that hero stuff is a bunch of garbage. Truthfully, all of us know we didn't premeditate anything. We were either trying to save our buddies or our own asses."

She pulled away to look into his eyes. "Yes, but in the middle of all that chaos, you all stood up and did the right thing, Jack. That's the difference. Lots of guys wouldn't."

And how's she going to feel about the stand-up guys when they stand up and take the money and run? He paused a moment. "We were just at the wrong place at the wrong time, that's all."

"No, Jack, it isn't. You don't brag about it or try to show off about it. At best you try to act like it never happened. Like no big deal. And that really matters to me." She wrapped her arms and legs around him. Her kiss aroused him.

"El, I'm getting into big trouble here."

"Not with me, you're not. Why do you think you're in big trouble?"

"The moon is turning translucent, and with you wrapped around me, and, well, I'm getting this tremendous hard on."

"Jack, Jack." She turned to look at the sky and then snuggled closer to him. "I really wanted to see this moon you've been talking about." She took his face in both hands, kissed him again, and then stopped. "Jack, I love you with all my heart," she kissed his eyed, and his cheeks, and the tip of his nose. "But, we'll have to catch the moon another night. I've got something else in mind, right now."

CHAPTER TWENTY-SEVEN

On Sunday evening, Ellen dropped Jack at the BOQ in Futema. Ellen had her twenty-four duty first thing Monday.

"Okay, Baby, get cleaned up. I'm picking up Sue and Nancy. It's dinner at Hamby. Don't be late because I'm starving."

"I could use a little nap," Jack yawned as she drove off. He made his way to his room. He heard Dan's stereo next door and banged on the wall.

Dan walked into Jack's room. "Jackson, get your butt up."

"Danny, I'm tired. Man, it's almost four-thirty. How about we take a rain check?"

"Get your running gear on. We need to talk." Dan shook his head and pointed to his ear—the sign for no talking. "Last one in the parking lot buys the next round."

With reluctance, Jack got into his PT gear and ambled out to the parking lot. Dan didn't say a word. He pointed to the start of the running track that wrapped around the base through head-tall bamboo. It gave them a lot of privacy. Dan looked around at the half-mile marker on the three-mile course. "So what's going on with you and Ellen?"

"This weekend was the best weekend of my entire life."

"You ain't falling in love or anything, are you?" Dan stopped and looked around.

Jack walked back to Dan. "I know I like her a whole lot."

"Jack, I love you like a brother. No, sir, closer than that. And I know you want the real deal. Ever since we've known you, we've teased you about being a walking romance looking for a place to happen? And how many times have we heard you say, 'I'd chuck the whole deal for the right one.'" Dan shook his finger at Jack.

Jack squinted into the sun as he looked at Dan. "You're worried that we're too close to doing the deal to let something blow it."

"You've got to think about the rest of us. Telling her anything about it could screw it all up, big time," Dan stared at the ground, shuffling from one foot to the other.

"Danny, Danny, I'd never do that."

"Honesty check. Have you thought about telling her?" Dan looked him in the eye.

"Yes, I've thought about it, but that's all. I've never said a word. Not one word."

"I know you too well. You'd trade the whole gig if the right one came along."

Jack hesitated. "I won't lie. I might."

"Well, then, we've got problems with meeting Luds and Dennis. Ludwig's worried that she's too much of an unknown this close to D-day. They don't want the girls to know anything about them at this point."

Jack raised his brows. "I don't think it's that big of a risk."

"Damn it, Jack. Listen to yourself."

"No, you listen," Jack shot back.

"By God, get a grip." Dan grabbed his bicep. "When we take it, everybody will know we did it, and they'll question the girls. Can you imagine when the girls tell them we met

Ludwig and Dennis in Hawaii, and they had a huge sailboat?" Dan frowned.

Jack looked into the distance. "That'd blow it all to hell."

Dan put his arm around Jack's shoulder. "Promise you won't say anything. If it's the real deal, you can write her before we do it. Explain it. And then ask her to meet you."

"Kind of like Steve McQueen in The Thomas Crowne Affair?"

"Wasn't thinking that, but why not? You know, 'meet me or see you later.' By God, if Thomas Crowne could do it, so can you."

"I don't know, Danny. I'd hate to lose her."

"What about losing the whole shebang, if you're wrong?"

"Okay, okay, but what about you and Nancy?"

"Like her more than I can say, but we're upfront. We've admitted it ain't love just yet. But we agree it's definitely lust."

"I guess if I wrote it out, that'd be one way. So, if she freaks out, she and I are done."

Dan stopped. Jack went forward a couple of paces more and turned around.

"You sure you could walk away. . .leave her?"

Jack walked back to Dan and nodded. "If she ain't in, it'll break my heart. But, I'm with you all."

Dan kicked the ground with the toe of his shoe. Jack promised he wouldn't tell her anything about it.

"Alright. Oh, yeah, Nancy's going to Hawaii. Most likely she and Ellen can fly Space A together, and we'll all fly back." Dan grinned at Jack. Then he told him that plans had been made to surprise him. Ellen, Nancy, and maybe Sue would be going too.

"You dog," Jack punched him on the arm. "So you planned on her going to Hawaii all along and said nothing about it?" "That's about the size of it. But let's have fun. .

.fun, fun 'til the money run flies away," Dan sang like a Beach Boy.

"Come on. I'll race you to the finish line."

The women were already at Hamby when Jack arrived with Dan and Roadhawg.

"Hey, Dan's buying. He lost the foot race." Jack cut loose the Higgins half grin.

"By God, if I don't let him win once in a while, he'll whine like a girl and cry."

"Hey, Bill, a round of swill," Roadhawg yelled as they walked into the empty diner. "And put it on Danny-boy's tab."

Bill dropped off the drinks on his way to another table.

"Come on, Ellen. Tell us all the nitty gritty," Sue teased.

"She wouldn't tell us anything," Nancy added.

"Okay, it was marvelous. There. Happy?"

"And I don't kiss and tell." Jack laughed.

Sue grinned. "Sounds like love is in the air."

"Somebody please contact Walter Cronkite on the six o'clock news," Jack said smiling at Ellen.

She moved her head near his ear and said. "You look kind of worried. Is everything okay?"

"Everything's great because we're meeting in Hawaii on Thursday." Jack kissed her neck.

"I'll have the leave papers signed tomorrow morning," Ellen said, "and Nancy and I have seats reserved Wednesday night on a C-141 arriving at Hickam at oh-nine-forty. Sue will follow in two days."

The guys had rented cabins at Bellows Air Force Recreation Station on the windward side of Oahu. It was the Air Force's R & R Center.

"Groovy." Jack clenched his fist and shook it in celebration. "Honey, this is going to be far out." He put his arm around her.

"You can't fool me," Ellen said. "Something's bothering

you."

Jack pulled her close. "Nothing, honey. Life couldn't be better." He looked over her shoulder at Dan, who was watching them.

Dan stared at Jack. "By God, sounds like it's going to be one big happy blow-out at Bellows."

CHAPTER TWENTY-EIGHT

Jack stood at the car rental with Dan and Roadhawg as three women in floral Hawaiian blouses worked to process their paperwork. The tropical evening breeze was scented with pineapple, and the swaying palms gave a false sense of tranquility. Waiting off to the side, John Ludwig and Dennis traded anxious glances.

Luds raked a shaky hand through his coal-black hair and whispered something to Dennis. Jack couldn't help staring at Luds' injured left arm. He realized rehab hadn't helped his friend much when Luds struggled to carry Jack's small suitcase back at the terminal. And he noticed Dennis relying, with a worried expression, on using his cane.

Their meeting at the airport had been strained. Not the band-of-brothers reunion Jack had expected. Jack whispered his concerns to Roadhawg.

"You boys look a hell of a lot better than after Jack pulled you out of that burning, shot-to-hell Huey," Roadhawg said, trying to lighten the mood.

"How's the arm?" Jack asked Luds.

"My arm isn't the problem, Jack. We've got a ton of stuff to go over when we get to the cabins, and we don't have a lot of time."

"We'll meet you all on the other side of the island." Dennis winced in pain as he struggled to keep up with Luds' pace.

Jack, Dan, and Roadhawg were the only riders on the shuttle. Dan shook his head. "By God, they ain't in the best of moods."

"Come on. They planned on it just being us. And now all the women are going to show up, and they didn't have a clue." Roadhawg shook his head.

"I get the feeling they're pissed at me." Jack stood to get off the shuttle when they arrived at the rental parking lot.

Dan stared down at the rental keys. "Nawh, I just think it'll be better once we get all the details worked out."

Jack eyed his Mustang convertible. "See you when we get to Bellows."

"Twenty bucks says I get there first," Roadhawg said.

"I'm in." Jack waved his keys.

Dan grinned. "By God, you're on."

The drive over to the Air Force Recreation Station could have been mistaken for an amateur road rally. On the two-lane road at the base, Jack was the first to attempt an illegal pass in the grass. In turn, Dan and Roadhawg blocked the narrow road, cutting off Jack. He fell behind, honking the horn, and Roadhawg gave him the finger. Jack cut to the inside grass again, taking a sharp turn, which put him in the lead. Glancing in his rearview mirror, he saw Dan's sunglasses fly off as Dan swerved to miss him.

When they pulled up, nobody came out. The tan-and-brown, flat-roofed cinder-block duplexes hadn't changed since their R & R back in '68.

Jack glanced at the cabins. "Where is everybody?"

"At least the breeze is warm," Dan said.

Luds' wife, Diane, came rushing out. She fixed a strand of her long, dark hair the breeze had caught, and smiled at Jack. "If you aren't a sight for sore eyes."

Georgia, drying her hands on a towel, came right behind Diane. Georgia wore her warm smile as she hugged Roadhawg and Dan.

The wives, girlfriends and non-squadron people never called the guys by their aviator nicknames. Like they'd call Roadhawg, Joe. And they'd call Luds by his first name, John, the two in the group who had long standing Marine nicknames.

Diane held on to Jack, then turned to Dan and Roadhawg. "Hey, dinner's almost ready. We've got the guys working on the grill."

"Perfect timing," Luds said, coming around the corner. "Just like the old days. We get it ready, and then you all show up. Come on back." He led the way around the cabin.

"Meat's about done. Let's chow down." Dennis didn't look up from the steaks he was turning.

After dinner they sat around the picnic table and in detail covered the rendezvous, the unloading of the money, and the most dangerous part—scuttling the '53.

Luds looked at his paperwork. "Sinking the bird gets really hairy. I'm sure we'll get it worked out. But let's get this out of the way." He handed a copy to everyone. "Here's the list of supplies and provisions for the sail to and from. Tomorrow we'll go to several of the bases and buy everything. . .to avoid any questions."

"Do we take the food and stuff directly to your boat?" Jack said.

"Yeah, we'll split into three parties. Next is the phone contact when we make Iwo Jima. This is very critical. If we're behind schedule, we're screwed and we'll have to hang around another two weeks." Diane and Georgia were the points of contact while Luds and Dennis were at sea.

"John will call me," Diane said, putting her arm around him, "and do a routine check-in. If everything's fine, then I'll call Dan in Okinawa from a payphone to ensure no

records of contact are made and let you know it's still a go."
She smiled. "Then I'll call John back and tell him."

"If you don't get the call from Luds and Dennis, we need to know as soon as possible." Dan glanced at Luds.

"No, kidding." Luds rolled his eyes. "We need to be there at least two days before we sail and get into position. Timing is critical at that point."

Diane rubbed her husband's arm. "Honey, calm down."

"Okay, I'll wait to hear back from her that you all are ready. If it's a bust, we'll sail for home." Luds looked at Roadhawg, then Jack, and at last—at Dan. Luds nodded to Georgia.

"I guess I'm next," she said. "I've got three passports, one for each of you." She handed them to Dan, Roadhawg, and Jack.

"That easy?" Jack looked at his picture on the fake passport.

Georgia told how she got and infant's date of death from a cemetery, wrote the county clerk, and asked for the birth certificate. The date had to correspond close to the guy's birth years. At that time, she sent a request to Social Security for a Social Security card, along with a birth certificate. They sent her a Social Security card in the deceased infant's name. When she got the card, she filled out the forms for a passport, along with the two pictures and the money. In a couple of weeks, they sent back a new passport—with a fake name.

Jack grinned. "So with this I'm William Burk."

"And whoever else's names are on the passports." Luds nodded at Dennis.

Dennis picked up one of the survival radios, admiring the hardware. "Thanks for the three PRC-90 radios."

"How does that work?" Diane said.

Luds broke into a smile. He explained to Diane how the radios had a pre-set channel. So when Jack, Roadhawg, and Dan radioed them, Dennis and Luds could key the mic to their radio, and tell them where the boat was located.

The radio instruments in the helicopter would point on the compass the exact direction to the radio signal and tell how many miles away they were.

"Won't other aircraft be able to hear?" Georgia said.

"They're line-of-sight radios, and we'll be four hundred miles out of Okinawa. That most likely puts us out of everyone's range," Roadhawg said.

"Chatter to a minimum," Jack continued. "We'll be Green, and the boat will be Blue." He explained when they made contact with the boat, they'd have to keep their mic depressed until the helo got the heading and mileage. Once the helo crew had the direction and distance, they'd say "Green copies."

"If for some reason it's a bust, and we want you to come on in to Okinawa, the call will be 'Execute white.' That means for you to call us when you get to White Beach on the east side of the island. And 'Execute black' tells you to turn around and sail back to Hawaii."

"I think we're all clear on that." Dennis let out a sigh of relief.

Luds folded his papers. "That just about covers it all."

"No. I'd like to address the new people in the mix," Dennis said. "We're leaving at least four days early because three women are coming here. What were you all thinking?" Dennis shook his head.

"Honey, we're all still friends. Cool it." Georgia walked over to Dennis.

"Guys, I'm a little upset. I want to know that we've not gone to all this trouble just to get our ass caught and thrown in jail. Damn it, we're too close. . .waited too long, and done a hell of a lot of planning to simply screw it up at the last minute because somebody talked too much or fell in love."

"Dennis," Jack said, getting to his feet, "you've got a right to be pissed, but calm down. I would never expose any of you or put you in harm's way. And it brings me up a bit short for you to infer differently. You need to think about what you're saying."

"You need to think about what you're doing. Will you deny that you haven't gotten serious with this Air Force captain?" Dennis crossed his arms over his chest and stared at Jack. "Your timing couldn't be worse. And now we've got to beat feet and leave here early so questions won't be asked." He winced and grabbed his thigh.

"I admit I've fallen for her, but I'm in. And I'm not going to compromise this now or in the future." Jack glared at Dennis.

"Jack, come on." Luds drummed his fingers on the table. "We've positioned the boat twenty-five-hundred miles over here, and we've depended on you guys to do your part and not screw it up at the midnight hour."

"Guys, nothing has been compromised." Diane reached over and silenced his drumming. "I'm happy for you, Jack. . .really I am. And deep down I know this big lug is, too." She stared daggers at her husband.

"Yeah, I'm happy that the whole world is happy, but damn it, you guys. What in the hell were you thinking? Come on, man? Do you think when we take the run, they won't be questioning everyone you know?" Dennis said.

Luds said, "And the women you're bringing here won't say anything about us when they start asking questions after you all take the run? Let alone, that we have a boat here? So many other things can go wrong, and we're leaving them a trail to follow. And I'm not sorry, Jack." He stood up and stormed back to his cabin.

CHAPTER TWENTY-NINE

Knocking on the cabin door woke Jack late that night. He looked at his watch—3:10—as he opened the door.

"Luds, Dennis, what's up?" Jack yawned and motioned them in.

Dennis hugged Jack. "We're leaving early this morning."

"This morning?" Jack looked at the two of them as he sat down.

Luds shrugged his shoulders. He explained how they'd gone down to the boat that evening, and somebody had been around asking too many questions. After everyone had left the barbeque, Dennis and Luds went back just to check things out, and to top it off, somebody had been aboard. The two of them packed everything, cleaned their cabin, and came to say goodbye.

"The real pisser is the lock on the cabin was jimmied. They didn't get in, but with everything else it's a good reason to leave. We've picked up the chrome lettering, paint, and decals to change the name on the boat once we're at sea." Dennis rubbed his eye. "So we're ready to sail."

Luds pulled out a chair from the table in the kitchen. In

the dim light from above the stove, Jack could see him fidgeting with his chin while he nodded his head. "Jack, Dennis and I are here to apologize and make sure there aren't any hard feelings." He avoided looking at Jack.

"I've been up till a couple of hours ago," Jack said, "and you all were right on. We should've never told the women a thing about meeting you guys. They could've come after you all were long gone."

"We overreacted. You girls didn't do anything that wrong." Dennis pulled out a chair.

"No, it was wrong. It's probably best that they don't see you all. We could've planned this better. Man, I hate it that you're pulling the chocks early."

"Jackson, it's all good. Cool it, man." Luds reached over and put his arm around Jack. "Besides, if we are out of here four or five days early, that's all groovy. Early's just what the doctor ordered."

"Yeah, we'd rather make Iwo Jima early. We'll find a deserted place and hang out until it's time to go meet you guys. So, honest, Jack, we're just fine. And I'm sorry for the way I acted this afternoon. You know me. I just worry."

Jack, with a knot in his throat, told Dennis and Luds that he was thinking if he, or Roadhawg or Dan suspect the women ask too much about who was Dennis Lee or John Ludwig. An alternative plan could be to sail north to Japan, get to Tokyo and leave from there.

Dennis fiddled with a tea towel. "That's a good idea. If they're looking for a boat sailing west, then north to Japan is a solid plan B."

"We'll see how it goes when we hook up at sea." Dennis seemed deep in thought. "I'll be relieved once everybody's on the boat." He looked at Jack and shook his head.

Jack cleared his throat. "I'm looking forward to all of us getting together. It's been too long."

Dennis stood and ruffled Jack's Marine Corps haircut. "We'll have a hell of a party when you get the bird sunk and we get under way. I promise it'll be a dandy. Jack, man, I was way out of line with my attitude. Are we cool?"

"Yeah, guys, we're fine." He winked, "Do you need a ride over to the boat?"

Luds said Diane and Georgia were driving them to the marina. And then the two women were on a 7:30 morning departure for L.A. Jack could see they were waiting in the car.

Jack walked outside to the car with Luds and Dennis. He leaned over and put his arms on the open, back door window. "Georgia, Diane, I'm sorry that. . .", he stammered, "you know. I'll make it up to everyone."

"Geez, Jack, give it a rest." Dennis hugged him.

"Would you shut up already?" Georgia put her hand on his arm and said, "Go have a good time, and we'll all be millionaires the next time we see each other."

Diane leaned over to hold Jack's hand and smiled. "You'll be disguised when we meet in Switzerland. We'll have a ball."

"Hell, these three stooges will probably be dressed as drag queens," Dennis laughed as he and Luds got into the car.

"Take care. It's a long way to sail." Jack moved to the front window, and squatted to looked at the guys. "Be careful."

"Yes, Mother." Luds said.

Jack watched them as they began to back their car out. "What the hell?" An MP car with lights on pulled up, blocking them.

A short MP guy bolted out of the vehicle. "Step away from the car," he said to Jack.

Jack held up his hands in front of his face blocking the bright flashing lights, and took two steps back. He kept his eye on a heavy-set MP with a shotgun.

"I'd like to see some ID," the short MP demanded of Luds and Dennis.

"Sergeant, what seems to be the problem?" Dennis said, getting out of the car.

Luds handed his retired ID to the shorter MP as Dennis got his out for the other guy.

"Here's mine." Jack handed his to the other MP. "Now, you recognize I'm a commissioned officer. I'd like to know why my guests are being questioned at three-fifteen in the morning." Jack knew the MPs were screwing with them for some reason, and the enlisted MP hadn't acknowledged the rank of any of them.

"We'll get to that." The MP glanced at Luds' ID.

"You're out of line, Sergeant. From now on, you'd best remember you're speaking to officers. Do you understand me. . . Sergeant?" Jack noticed Dan heading out of his cabin.

"Yes, sir," the short MP snapped.

Handing his ID to the man, Dan interrupted. "By God, you see from this ID I'm also a commissioned officer, and your attitude had better change right now. Your attitude is unacceptable. Do you understand me?"

A couple of guys emerged from their cabins to check out the commotion.

"Excuse me, sir." The big MP the put down the shotgun. "Sergeant Blevins has had a long night, and we've had a request to check IDs on the guest in this cabin. They appeared to be leaving, and our dispatch said to not let them leave until we checked that they are the registered guests."

"You've done that." Jack stepped up. "And I've identified them as my guests. Anything else? Because I'm following up on all of this. Understood?"

"Yes, sir." The short MP rolled his eyes as he backed up to his open driver's door.

"By God, hold on here. I don't like your tone of voice. Change it now," Dan ordered. "And who had you check IDs at oh-three-twenty-four? That's highly unusual."

"Sir, we're following orders. Now, we'll be out of your way," the short MP replied.

Dan and Jack watched them drive off. The gawkers went back into their cabins but left their outside lights on.

"Guys, make sure you aren't followed." Dan looked at Luds and Dennis.

"No shit, Sherlock. I'm glad we're outta here."

Jack followed the tail lights as Dennis and Luds drove off into the darkness. Dan motioned Jack back toward his cabin.

"Jackson, they'd told me they were leaving early," Dan said, pulling out a chair, "but the MP thing's weird."

"Someone had them checking on us," Jack said, "and I've got a pretty good idea who."

Roadhawg walked into Dan's cabin and they brought him up to date on the MP's. Jack went over the idea he'd presented to Luds and Dennis about plan B and leaving out of Tokyo.

The conversation bounced around about which crew chief to ask to join them. Dan felt uncomfortable because he didn't know them as well as Roadhawg and Jack, who said he was close to Pogany and he could ask without giving Pog too much information.

Dan brought up the MP's again. They all felt like it wasn't a coincidence. Jack volunteered to check it out with the head of security later that day.

In the pit of Jack's gut, he was worried.

CHAPTER THIRTY

Jack paced in the waiting area of the gray wooden terminal at Hickam Air Force Base. He watched the American Airlines 707 touch down on the runway both Honolulu International and the Air Force shared. The ten o'clock morning sun was behind him, and the rain over the mountain cast a double rainbow. He noticed the same looking MP vehicle from earlier that morning pull up in front of the building. Jack shivered. You're getting paranoid. Stop it.

In the distance, he spotted the big gray Air Force C-141 about three miles on final. That has to be hers. He smiled and looked at the fresh lei he'd bought for Ellen, taking his mind off the MPs who walked into the terminal.

"Jackson, can you believe we're here?" Dan said. "Let's go meet the bird and let the good times roll. You still cool? I mean about Luds and Dennis, and this morning?"

"I'm fine, and they're good. I just feel bad that we screwed up."

"By God, it's all going to work out, okay?" Dan looked Jack straight in the eye. "Hang in there. I'm the worry wart, not you. It's only a couple of months now."

"I'll feel better when we're all safe and sound in Switzerland. Then it'll be okay." Jack glanced in the opposite direction. "Dan, don't look now, but those MPs look like the guys from last night."

Dan checked out the men. "Give it a rest. It's nothing."

"Maybe you're right. That one's gut is too big." Jack looked away and toyed with the lei as they walked out to greet the 141.

The personnel door on the big cargo aircraft opened, and the first one out was Ellen, followed by Nancy.

"Typical Jack." Ellen grinned, approaching him. "Hawaiian shirt, shorts, flip flops, and on the flight line no less." She hugged him.

"I'm living on Hawaiian time." He stepped back and put the lei around her neck.

She took his hand. "I can't believe we're here."

"Come on. Let's grab your stuff and get outta here. Oh, did you see the double rainbow I ordered up just for you?" He pointed to the mountains in the east as they walked toward the terminal.

"Yes, I see it. I just can't believe it. Us. Here." Ellen turned to Jack. "How's Roadhawg taking Sue's leave getting cancelled?"

"Disappointed as hell," Jack said. "But what can he do?"

Jack was disappointed for him, too. But one less person meant one less complication, and for that he was grateful.

The two couples fetched the luggage from the baggage claim and agreed to meet for lunch back at the cabins.

"We need to find Roadhawg and make sure he's included," Nancy added.

Jack and Ellen headed for their cabin, parking in front.

Ellen took in the view, looking in all directions. "This place is fantastic," she said. "The beach runs on forever. And the turquoise water is like a picture postcard."

A glint near the pine trees caught Jack's attention. A

man in a coat and tie, wielding a camera, ducked out of view.

What the hell's going on?

"Jack?" Ellen tugged on his shirt sleeve. "Earth to Jack." She flashed him a smile. "So why did your friends have to leave?"

"One of Dennis's kids got sick, and Luds and Diane had business they needed to get back to," Jack lied. He glanced back over his shoulder, trying to put the strange man out of his mind. "Feel like a luau tonight?"

"That might be fun. Can we dress casual?"

"I don't see why not." Jack held his arms out, looking down at his ensemble. He moved his head enough to see the strange man with the camera was still half hidden behind a pine tree.

We've got a problem.

"Honey, why don't you get changed? I've got to run over to security and renew our parking pass."

Jack drove to the security/sick call building. At the desk he was told to wait for Captain Hoffmann, the OIC. An Air Force captain walked in and greeted Jack.

"I've got a complaint," Jack began after they were seated in Hoffman's office. "This morning around three or so, your MPs came to question us about unauthorized guests staying with me." Jack handed him his ID card.

The captain glanced over the card, avoiding eye contact, and handed it back. He told Jack he had received instructions late last night to check out the occupants in cabin 312-B. A Marine Corps lieutenant colonel from Okinawa thought unauthorized visitors might be staying there.

Jack asked if the lieutenant colonel in question had a name. Captain Hoffman said he didn't feel at liberty to divulge that.

"Captain Hoffman, I'm Marine Corps Captain Jack Higgins. I go by Jack." Jack held out his hand. Now as one

Captain to another. . . . I'd like to know who's so interested in me and my guests.

Captain Hoffman looked at Jack's extended hand, and shook it. "Captain Higgins, I'm the OIC here at Bellows, in addition to the head of the security detachment of Air Police. And if I say I'm not at liberty to divulge information, I think that should be clear."

"Well, Captain," Jack leaned back in his chair, and folded his arms across his chest. "It concerns me. And just for the record, Captain, I've got two tours in country. And I see by your single National Defense ribbon. . .you've never been in country. And now you want to play big shot, and uppity, being here as the O, I, C of this candy ass command."

"I've heard enough of your shit. Get out of my office."

Jack stood with a half Higgins grin, and said, "In the Marine Corps we're taught to kill, and I've done that. Now you can sit your ass back down, think about it, or try to throw me out of your office. You've got a choice. But one way or another I'll get the name."

They stood facing each other. Hoffman asked Jack to sit down. He apologized. In the next few minutes, he explained how he was awaken early that morning with an urgent set of orders to check out Jack's guest. When he located the paper work he gave Jack the name.

Jack thanked him and said, "That explains it. And is that your guy standing out there checking us out?" Jack motioned toward his cabin.

The captain shifted in his chair. "No, he's from the naval criminal investigation division. I think this lieutenant colonel from Okinawa is stirring the pot. The man in the suit checked in with me just this morning, and I saw the same name on his paperwork." The captain smirked. "You'd think they'd have better things to do."

Jack rose from his seat. "Thanks, Hoffman. I'd appreciate it if your report indicated nothing unusual."

"Can I call you Jack?"

"Absolutely."

"I go by Mike. And, Jack, I've already reported that everything checked out. Plus, my sergeant told me my airman was out of line and is supposed to stop by and apologize later."

"Mike, if you get time to stop by, I've got some cold ones in the 'fridge."

When they finished, Jack left to talk with Roadhawg and Dan. They both were a bit concerned, but not surprised. They were more concerned when Jack told them about the CID guy taking pictures.

They walked outside. "I kid you not." Jack rolled his eyes. "Don't turn around, but there's the guy in a suit and tie by the big pine tree taking pictures of us."

"By God, I'm going over there and stuff that camera where the sun don't shine" Dan took off on a run.

Jack followed. Spotting them, the man dashed for his black four-door sedan. He was long gone before they could catch him.

"That CID moron sure didn't want to talk to us." Jack tried to catch his breath. "Makes me glad John and Dennis left. Could you imagine those pictures going back to Bedford?"

Dan shook his head. "Jackson," he said, "we need to get Pogy on board and then cool it. Things are getting real squirrelly."

That night they dragged Roadhawg with them to Fort De Russy, the big time R and R center in Hawaii. The luau hit the top of the chart. In the next few days the two couples spent quite a bit of time sight-seeing. Roadhawg caught a space A hop back to Okinawa, leaving earlier than planned.

The night before their flight, Jack and Ellen were alone on the Bellows beach.

"I can't believe we've got to leave tomorrow," Ellen said

with her back to Jack. They were seated on the snow-white beach watching the spotlight of an almost full-moon.

"Life is made up of special moments. Some happen accidentally, some are planned, but they're all special." Jack kissed the back of her neck. "This moment tops 'em all, Ellen. I love you with all my heart." Jack held her a little closer. What am I going to do?

CHAPTER THIRTY-ONE

The two couples checked in at Hickam, and were relieved to find very few passengers for the Space A hop. The aircraft had bunks for transporting the injured, so they each had their own place to crash on the flight back to Okinawa.

Jack watched Ellen as she slept. The last five days they'd bonded more than Jack could have imagined. He'd seen the suited CID guy still lurking in the background and flipped him off when he took Roadhawg over to Hickam. On the way, Roadhawg said, Sue had called and made him an offer he couldn't refuse if he came back four days early.

Dan caught Jack's attention across the aisle and moved his eyes to indicate they meet at the rear of the big aircraft. Jack followed him to the galley.

Dan removed his ear plugs. "They could at least turn on the heaters."

"Wonder how noisy it'd be without this soundproofing?" Jack pulled at the gray material covering the walls.

"By God, the vibration and whatnot puts me to sleep, but Nancy can't get enough blankets."

"So, Danny, what's on your mind?"

Dan glanced around, "In hindsight, do you think we should've had the women over?"

"What we shouldn't have done was let the women know Dennis and Luds were even there." Jack rubbed his five o'clock stubble. "A little late now."

"It'd be a lot easier if the women were part of the deal, but they're not."

"When the authorities start questioning our recent movements, which they will, then we've got problems. It won't be that far of a leap to ask where Luds and Dennis are."

"Maybe we need to head to Japan, leave out of Tokyo, abandon the boat, and head to Switzerland with the money."

"I'd feel a lot easier if the women were part of the deal," Jack said.

"By God, I said that first."

"Danny, when we get back, I'll speak to Pog to see if he wants in. I'll get a feel for where he is, and then we'll make a decision. But we're down to a handful of weeks." He motioned toward their seats. "We'd better head back."

"Hey, if Pog's a no go, my vote'll be with V. D."

"I'm good with either one. They're both good guys."

"Hey, Pog, you got a second?" Jack made sure nobody was close to the `53 as Pog worked under the fuel sponson, changing the brake rotor.

"I'm getting paid by the hour. So what's on your mind, sweetheart?"

"There's something some of us have been kicking around. It'd involve a lot of money, but you could never go home. I mean enough money to never have to work again."

"I don't want to hurt your feelings, but I could've done the dope deal coming out of down south. Those guys brought a bale of one-hit shit back. I won't do no dope."

"Good. Neither will we."

"Then what are you talking about?" Pog put the new brake rotor on the ground and turned his full attention to Jack.

"For the time being, we've got to be extra cool. How about meeting Dan, Roadhawg, and me over here at the hangar at, say, eight tonight? We'll be in Dan's black Pontiac and have enough beer for about an hour." Jack grinned.

They picked Pog up and drove to the north end of the active-duty runway at Futema, where the golden sunset reflected over the endless Pacific, highlighting the helos as they took off. By a quarter past eight, the case of beer was about half gone.

They'd picked the spot for privacy, though the conversation was broken from time to time as a helo passed over them doing practice landings.

"Guys," Pog said, "I like it a lot. So we'll fly off with their friggin' payroll?"

"There are two more in on the deal. That means a six-way split," Jack said.

Pog shifted in his seat. "The rendezvous part is good. The extra fuel on board will get us further than they'll ever look. Going east instead of west is even better, but sinking the bird is going to be a bitch, to say the least."

"Yeah, we're worried about that." Dan rubbed his chin. "We've never practiced sinking a bird."

"I like the rotor-brake idea. But if the seas are rough and the blades hit the water with any speed, the bird could flip," Pog stared at the three pilots.

"Remember the bird in the Philippines that ran out of fuel and auto-rotated into the water? It didn't flip and floated for, what, three days?" Roadhawg held up both hands.

Dan shook his head. "If that happens, we'll need something to blow a hole in 'er and make it sink."

"Hey, I can get some grenades if she's still floating. Secure them, attach a long string, and. . ." Pog yanked his arm like he was pulling the pin. "Ka-boom."

"That'd do the job. We don't want any fire, smoke, or telltale signs giving away our location. But that'll be after we get all the money on board the boat." Roadhawg patted Pog's shoulder.

"That's fine, but how much do you figure it'll be?"

"Well, there's no guarantee, but we figure fifteen to twenty million." Jack toasted with his beer.

"Guys," Pog said. "That's more money than I've ever thought about."

"Well, the money is no doubt very big, but mostly we want to screw over them more than they've screwed us. It'd be the ultimate payback on the way out the door." Jack finished his beer.

"About the security," Roadhawg added. "We'll never talk about it on the base unless we're in one of the tanks." He pointed to the wagon and handed his empty to Dan. "Here, Miss Burton, I sure don't wanna accidentally drop an empty on the floor and have you piss and moan about trashin' the limo queen. You'd think this wagon was special."

"Kiss my ass. This baby is special." Dan tapped the steering wheel. "By God, in some ways it's better. It hauls your worthless ass around. Jeez, it's been two days since we got back from Hawaii, and ain't nobody going to say anything about the mag wheels I just put on this baby?"

Jack said, "We've been waiting to see how long it'd be before you started whining about nothing being mentioned. Yes, we've noticed them, along with everyone else on the base."

"I knew it. You dirt bags were screwing with me all along. You like 'em and you're jealous."

"Yes, princess," Roadhawg teased, "and they don't look too bad on a sled."

"So you admit they make it look cool." Dan paused. "I'm going to hate to abandon her after we take the run. Know what I mean?" He looked at the wagon with a contented smile.

"Guys," Pog said. "I know I need the money to bail out my mom after my dad's death, but why are you guys doing it?"Pog sent his mother most of his paycheck. She'd discovered his dad's business was deep in debt, and he'd been operating at a loss for years.

Roadhawg was the first to respond. He said he was pissed off at the military, the war, and the biggest reason was because the other guys were in and he wasn't going to be left out.

Dan being candid, said he'd toyed with the idea. But now that Dennis and Luds were in it, he felt justified in helping to take the money because of how the military had screwed all of them.

Jack added his reasons, once again. Listening to himself, his reason for revenge on Bedford sounded the weakest.

In the silence that followed, Jack thought, life would change a whole lot for all of them—afterwards. He knew they stood to lose a whole lot more. They'd lose each other, their families, and he stood a huge chance of losing Ellen. He kept remembering that the best revenge was living a good life.

Jack motioned with his head toward the departing aircraft. "There goes that ol' bastard Bedford, his pet squirrel, Petey Tanner, and Spit Hosier takin' off in the group's piece-of-shit

S-Two. Typical. A full moon and the field grades are out in force."

"That's why they call it a field grade moon," Dan said.

Jack beaded in on the S-2. "I don't feel good about those three flying over us."

CHAPTER THIRTY-TWO

Bedford and his cronies veered off course and buzzed the one-of-a-kind Pontiac.

"They let the whole base know when they go fly, like they're something special. Like they're the only ones who could fly an S-Two. What a bunch of morons." Roadhawg watched the twin-engine fixed-wing aircraft circle for another touch-and-go-landing.

On the next approach, the S-2 lifted off and made a sharp bank to the right to fly over the Pontiac at a low altitude again.

"Jeez," Jack said almost ducking. "They're borderline dangerous."

As darkness fell, Jack had an uneasy feeling as he watched Bedford join the traffic pattern for another landing.

"Danny boy," Jack said, "I think those ol' bastard's recognized this sweet ride of yours, and low-leveled us on purpose. Here they come again."

"Dan, get ready to turn on your lights," Roadhawg said. "Come on, guys. Let's get in front of this attention-getting magnet and moon 'em if they flat-hat us again."

Jack, Pog, and Roadhawg ran to line up by the runway while Dan sat ready to put the high beams on them. The aircraft was midway through the turn to final when Jack noticed the silhouette of the aircraft in the twilight. The landing gear was up, not in the down and locked position.

Roadhawg elbowed Jack. "That's strange, very strange."

"Look at him." Jack pointed. "That blithering idiot's got his gear up. That showoff bastard must be setting up for another low pass."

Roadhawg cupped his hands by his mouth and yelled. "Danny, get ready." The three of them dropped their pants. Dan waited with the bright lights.

"No, he's settin' up for a landing or touch and go," Pog said.

"Bullshit," Roadhawg yelled. "They've got their gear up."

"Hell, he's going long," Pog yelled as he stood up. "He's flaring to land."

"You morons," Roadhawg said pulling up his pants. "Drop your gear, you ignorant sons of bitches."

"Run for it," Jack shouted as he grabbed his pants.

Dan yelled, running between them toward the drainage ditch. "By God, they just drug the tail section. Shit, there go the props hittin' the runway. Get down. They're headin' this way."

The four of them dove into the drainage ditch as the wreck passed over them.

The S-2 showered them with a trail of sparks that paled Fourth of July fireworks. The fatally wounded aircraft skidded down the runway over the ditch and collided with Dan's wagon, part of the fuselage coming to rest on the top of the hood. Dan, Jack, Roadhawg, and Pog ran from the scene toward the safety of the runway.

"Holy shit, that thing is going to blow up," Pog yelled.

Just as they reached the far side of the runway, the crash-crew vehicles came barreling down the runway, lights flashing, over a half-mile away. Tanner, followed by Bedford, and then Hosier tumbled out of the personnel door.

"I guess we should've tried to save them," Pog said.

Roadhawg stood with his hands on his hips. "Like hell. If I'd thought about it, I'd have gone over and throwed a match on it. Jeez, why couldn't it've blown up?"

"Looks like the pinball machine hit the jackpot," Jack said as the crash crews approached the four of them on the runway.

The fire truck driver stopped beside them. "Are there any other survivors in the aircraft?"

"Dumb bastards totaled my car." Dan shook his head, not taking his eyes off the ruined wagon.

"Are you okay?" the driver asked.

"We weren't in the aircraft," Roadhawg said, pointing to Bedford and his boys, "but those three dumb bastards were. You might want to go check them out."

The fire truck driver surveyed the ditch. "Don't know if we can cross there," he said. Then he talked on his radio, saying, "You stay back to pull me out if I get stuck."

"Ten-four," the second truck driver acknowledged.

Jack and the others watched the fire truck make an attempt.

"They're stuck," Pog said, laughing. "It's not going anywhere."

"No," Jack said, "I think they got it."

"Amazing," Pog said, as the vehicle crawled to the other side.

"By God, why doesn't that abortion of a wreck light off? Should have been a huge-ass fireball by now. Then we'd have a crispy Freddy boy and his pet squirrels."

From behind them a military pickup approached the crash scene with flashing lights. The group safety officer, Major Bliss, took command of the accident scene, jumping out of the truck before it could come to a stop.

Bliss barked orders, and the crash crew began spraying fire-retardant foam over everything. Jack watched as the major walked over to take statements from Bedford and Tanner. Hosier was on a stretcher.

After a few minutes of flaying arms and finger-pointing, the major left Bedford and Tanner, and made his way toward Jack and the guys who were standing at the tailgate of what was left of the wagon.

Major Bliss looked perplexed. "I need to ask you all why you were here in this remote area at this time of the day."

"Well, sir, we were watching aircraft ops and the sunset, and this seemed like a good place," Jack answered.

Their cover story was that Sergeant Pogany had some problems with his girlfriend. She'd disappeared—the Red Cross, Navy Relief, her family—nobody could seem to give him an answer about where she'd gone.

The three pilots were simply helping out a fellow Marine with some personal problems.

"Yeah," Jack said. "We're just helping out our friend."

Dan kept staring at the crushed front end of the wagon.

"It still is, ah-h-h, unusual." Major Bliss looked from Jack to the others. "You've got to admit this isn't a spot many Marines on this base would normally visit."

"By God, I've had enough." Dan ran his fingers over the roof of the wagon. "Doesn't matter what the hell we were doing out here. Ain't no law against it. We saw the stupid sons of bitches crashing, heading this way, and made a run for it." He pointed toward the large drainage trench.

"We dove in the ditch," Dan continued, "and the wreck passes over us and destroys my car. And all you want to do is ask us the same stupid-assed question over and over. What about those three head-in-ass, forgot-to-lower-the-gear-handle, morons? Why ain't you giving them the third degree?"

"Major, unless you've got a good, and I mean it best be

166

good, reason to keep us, we're finished," Jack glared at Bliss and then he pointed his finger at Bliss. "You're way out of line, and we ain't lettin' it end here. I don't care if you are a major, sir, you're outta line."

"Okay, okay," Major Bliss said. "Both of the lieutenant colonels said there's bad blood between you all and them. They insinuated you were out here to distract them, and that's why, as they said, they overlooked lowering the landing-gear handle."

"Come on, Major Bliss," Roadhawg said. "You fly. What could we be doing that distracted them a mile away when they were on final? And way past sunset."

"Think about it," Jack said. "They just admitted there's bad blood between us. Shit, they buzzed us on purpose three times and were getting ready to do it again."

"And like you said," Pog added, "the tower didn't observe us doing anything."

Dan looked from his car to Major Bliss. "By God, let's go over there and ask them just what we were doing to distract them."

God knows how much I hate that moron, Jack thought as they walked toward Bedford. "Nice landing, Lieu-ten-ant Colonel Bedford."

Bedford glared at Jack, mumbling.

"Why don't you just admit you screwed up trying to buzz us?" Jack said.

"Ha, ha. Guess who's terminal rank now. Not a fart's chance in a whirlwind of getting promoted now," Roadhawg snickered.

Bedford shook his finger at them, but a helicopter taking off drowned his response.

After it passed, Roadhawg said, "If getting assigned a group job didn't wake you up, let me tell you. It's over for you. They'll probably have you out before us. And you thought you were so cute getting us out. Ha, ha, ha. You just self-destructed, Mon-San-to."

Bedford charged them. Jack advanced. Bedford slugged Jack on the jaw. Jack fell back and went to one knee. Bedford tried to kick him. Jack avoided the kick. Bedford swung again and missed, as Jack ducked. Then Jack nailed Bedford square in the face, knocked him down, and jumped on Bedford landing blow after blow to his head. When Bedford tried to cover his face with his hands, Jack pummeled his ribs.

The major and a couple of the firefighters jumped in to separate them.

"That's for Todd and Herb, you slimy maggot," Jack said as Dan and Roadhawg held him back.

Rescuers helped Bedford up. He broke free and rushed Jack.

"Come on, you moron," Jack yelled. When Bedford reached him, Jack kicked him in the groin.

"You son of a bitch," Bedford moaned as he curled into a fetal position. Dazed, he tried to stand, then staggered as Tanner propped him up. "I'll have you court-martialed," Bedford yelled.

Major Bliss stood toe to toe with Bedford. "No, you won't. You attacked him, and he defended himself." He pointed to the entangled S-2 and the remains of the Pontiac wagon. "And I'm not so sure it wasn't the first time you tried this evening."

CHAPTER THIRTY-THREE

The wrecker towed Dan's beloved wagon and gave the four survivors a ride back to the squadron. Jack called Ellen, and, after hearing what happened, she insisted on coming to Futema and taking him back to her quarters for the night.

Once there, she poured two glasses of wine. Toying with Jack's hair like she was looking for injuries, she said, "At least you got to hit him, but isn't there something the military can do to Bedford?"

"The best part was lifting him off the ground with the kick to his nuts. He's making noise about charges."

"They can't do anything. He hit you first. Isn't that enough for them to start looking at all the stuff he's pulled?"

"Nope. He killed Herb on our first tour, Toddy this time, and now in his fit of rage, he tried to kill all of us."

"But he crashed a plane. That's got to be serious."

"It might finish his career, but nothing serious will happen. I blame the whole system." Jack finished his wine.

"I'm pissed at the military for kicking you out and not him."

169

"Who knows? Maybe they will this time, but I doubt it."
Jack poured more wine from the bottle sitting on the coffee table in front of them. Then he held the bottle to her glass.

"No, I'm fine," she responded to his gesture. "It's not right."

"I know." Wait a few weeks until we take the money run. Then we'll right some of the wrongs. Jack broke into a faint smile.

"Honey," she said, "have you ever considered an interservice transfer? I talked to the Air Force recruiting folks back in D.C. I didn't mention any names, but I think they'd love to have you."

"Last year I looked into going over to the Navy, but you're getting out. How would that work if I stayed in?" Jack said as he put his hand on her arm.

"I was thinking about staying in, and the people in D.C. said they'd station us together. That'd be great, wouldn't it?"

Except I'll be on the ten most wanted in a couple of months. He shook his head to gather his thoughts.

"Why are you shaking your head?"

"I was thinking about getting out. Not having a job. Ellen, being together sounds good, but I just don't trust them to do what they say."

"What if I could get it in writing?" she shifted to face him.

"Honey, it's this simple. I don't have a whole lot of faith in the military powers-to-be right now." He frowned. "The fact remains; I won't have a job."

"You silly galoot. Not have a job? That doesn't sound like you. Where's that invincible John Charles Higgins I love?" She slugged his arm.

"You're right. It's just that there's a whole lot going to happen in the next six to ten weeks, and then I'm out."

"Jack, here's what I know. . .I love you, job or no job. I don't care what you'll do. I just want to be with you. But

170

you might look good in Air Force blue."

Jack didn't answer

"I can tell you're thinking something."

Don't answer her, Jack. Keep your big mouth shut. He looked into her eyes. "El, here's what I know. I love you, and if you'll hang in there and still love me after I get out, would you marry me?"

"Thank you for not making me ask you," Ellen said as she winked at him.

CHAPTER THIRTY-FOUR

Three weeks later, Jack dozed in his room. The blinds shed enough light for him to recognize the late afternoon sun. All of a sudden his mind went to full alert. The shadow through the Venetian blinds silhouetted a figure moving back and forth. He dropped to his knees. A knock on his door startled him. As the knock continued, Jack crawled to the door and opened it. "Pog?" Jack jumped back, and looked past his friend as he checked to make sure nobody had seen him.

Pog slid in. "Man, we gotta talk." He lowered his voice. "I know I'm not supposed to be in officers' country, but this shit is. . ." He shook his head. "Tomorrow's payday, and I saw the flight schedule. Tanner and Hosier are flying the payroll."

"Okay, but let's keep it to a whisper. We're still in their BOQ." Jack yawned and ran a hand through his hair, still in a daze.

"So I get to thinking, that's very coincidental. On the sly, I go check with Captain Burton. He froze. Said Major Weir told him he'd write the schedule this time."

"Yeah?"

172

"Then he checked with the major, you know, about Tanner and Hosier flying the payroll, and he said Bedford called over and requested to have them fly it. Some bull shit excuse about they needed flight time."

Jack raised an eyebrow.

"Captain Burton said to go shake down the crew chief. It's that back stabbin' prick, Johnson."

Jack frowned, trying to comprehend what Pog was saying.

Frantic, Pog whispered, "They're taking the money run tomorrow, Jack."

"Hosier and Tanner?" Jack forgot and raised his voice. "Are you shitting me?"

Pog moved closer to Jack. He said Captain Burton gave him the keys to a new Pontiac and to tell Jack and Captain Hegidio. "That's why I'm down here."

Damn it to hell. Jack turned and pounded the concrete block wall with his fist. I can't believe Bedford, Hosier, and Tanner are taking the money run. He shook his head in disbelief.

Pog explained he'd smelled a rat so he fished around. Then he took a chance and said, "Come on, Johnson. Tell me, or I'm blowin' the whistle on you guys if you don't cut me in."

Johnson said he had to clear it with the powers to be. Pog was to meet him at the squadron in forty-seven minutes. "Evidently he's running it by Bedford or Tanner," Pog added.

Jack took a deep breath. "Un-be-live-able. Okay, okay, let's think here for a second. Do you know any of the particulars?"

"Nothin' yet."

"It's four-fifteen now. I'll get Dan and Roadhawg, and we'll pick you up down the hill from the hangar at the usual place at five forty-five."

"Man, this really sucks," Pog said.

Before he hustled out, Jack whispered, "I've got an idea or two that just might work out for us in spades."

CHAPTER THIRTY-FIVE

They sat in Dan's wagon in the parking lot, going over the what-ifs and drinking beer. Dan started up the new Pontiac and drove down the hill a little before the rendezvous time.

Pog waited at the stoplight. Roadhawg opened the back door, and Pog jumped in. Dan drove off, heading in no particular direction.

"You wouldn't believe those cheap screws," Pog said, wiping the sweat from his forehead. "Here's the deal. Bedford, Hosier and Tanner are in on taking the money run, plus Johnson."

"I can't believe this shit." The Roadhawg shook his head. "Those simpletons are beating us to it."

Pog held up his hand. "Guess what? Those assholes are getting twenty-one apiece. Johnson's only getting sixteen percent."

"That doesn't equal a hundred percent," Jack interrupted.

"There's a mystery walk-on guy, and he gets the other twenty-one percent."

"That's typical of Bedford, Hosier, and Tanner. Screw everyone." Jack said.

"My five percent is coming out of Johnson's," Pog said. "He told me Bedford said something like, 'He doesn't deserve a million bucks. If he gets anything, it's coming out of yours.' And if I don't like it or go tell anyone, Johnson indicated I'd disappear. Gone. So, I could take it or leave it."

Dan turned to Pog. "By God, typical Bedford,"

Jack frowned and rubbed his chin in thought.

Roadhawg reminded Pog he only had forty-five minutes before he was to meet them.

Pog checked his watch. "I'm supposed to be grabbing some chow. Then we're supposed to get the bird ready for tomorrow's flight."

Dan headed the wagon to the hangar parking lot next door to their squadron. Nobody would see Pog get out, and he could hoof it on over to meet Johnson."

After Pog left, Jack said. "There's gotta be a way to put a spin on this. We could always, ah, turn them in for the reward and forget the whole deal."

Roadhawg frowned. "Jeez, Jack, we've got Luds and Dennis sailing here as we speak. Everything's set."

"Before we throw in the towel," Jack said to Roadhawg, "let's hear their plan. Maybe there's something in it for us."

"Their plan is a lot like ours. . . to get off the island," Pog said. "They're pulling in to our base to refuel, and then the fourth guy is walking on the bird from out of nowhere. If the Air Force guys don't leave, he pulls a gun and disarms them. If they get off the bird, no sweat."

"And if they stay on board and don't surrender the shotguns?" Roadhawg frowned.

"This bad ass has a silenced handgun, and they're history. Bedford and those guys don't care if they waste them or not."

"Screw it," Roadhawg said. "I say, let's blow the whistle on 'em."

"So, what if we do?" Dan paused. "I mean, you can't

prove a thing until after they've refueled. We can't wait until they whack the guards. That ain't right."

Jack looked out the window, deep in thought. "What a mess. What's the rest of the geniuses' plan? Wait a minute. Twenty-one percent times four is eighty-four and the cheap bastards are making Johnson take Pog's five percent out of Johnson's sixteen?"

"And, I'll bet," Roadhawg said, "the fourth guy's a pilot. They'll probably land at Bolo Point, dump the money, then fly to Iwo Shima."

"That little island a couple miles off shore," Dan stated more than asked.

"So," Jack held up his index finger, "they drop the money, fly to the remote island, and make it look like the bad guy headed west with the money?"

"Yeah." Pog frowned and looked out the window.

"Lord, I can't fathom that those ass wipes are beatin' us to it." Roadhawg got out of the back seat of the wagon, slammed the door, and stood by the driver's door, staring off into the evening sky.

Dan rolled down the electric window. "Hey, I know we're screwed to the wall, but go kill Freddy boy or Petey. Give the wagon a break. You'll hurt the door if you keep slammin' it like that."

Roadhawg shook his head and started to laugh. Silence lasted but a moment. Then Jack, with his Steve McQueen smirk, raised his Bud in a toast. "Don't worry, girls. I've got a plan. This is going to be sweet."

CHAPTER THIRTY-SIX

Thirty minutes later, Jack and Roadhawg stood in front of the counter at the motor pool on the backside of the base at Futema. The humid air in the metal shack office was stifling. The motor pool was where all sorts of trucks, jeeps, and other vehicles were kept on the base.

Roadhawg shifted his eyes side-to-side, wiped the perspiration from his brow, and a quiet voice asked Jack, "You think this will really work? Won't they be able to check the mileage? We'll have a boat load of miles driving up there and all around."

"Man, I've told you. It'll be easy. All I've got to do is reach up under the dash, unscrew the speedometer cable when we get to the lockers, and screw it back in when we get back."

"What if you can't get it undone or back together?"

Rolling his eyes, Jack mumbled, "You're going to make a great little ol' lady."

"Hey, Jack, I think you made the enlisted guy nervous."

"Officers do that to grunts." Jack pointed as he noticed their motor pool truck pulling up out front. With his back turned, Roadhawg didn't see the corporal getting out of the truck.

"But. . ."

Jack nudged Roadhawg as the clerk approached with the paperwork and the truck keys, handing them over to Jack.

The corporal escorted them out to inspect the canvas covered pickup and to brief Jack and Roadhawg on how everything operated. The motor pool was much like a rental car agency. Jack got in the truck as Roadhawg walked to Jack's wagon.

Lord, I hope this works. Jack shook his head. He hollered at the Roadhawg, "Wanna race back to the BOQ?" Jack started the cranky diesel engine and laughed as he saw the corporal turn around.

A few minutes later he parked the truck in the BOQ parking lot and walked to the waiting wagon.

"Come on, Joseph. Everything is going as planned." Jack said as Roadhawg slid onto the passenger seat.

"Yeah, yeah, this is the easy part, but there's so much that can go wrong."

Pointing a finger at him, Jack beamed. He repeated that they were stealing the money from Freddy, Spit and Petey boy. They weren't stealing it from any military personnel. They weren't stealing anything from the military, itself.

Roadhawg couldn't seem to get over the fact that they had no back-up plans.

Jack stared at him. How many times would he have to tell Roadhawg he thought their plan would work?

"It's just that we planned this whole damn thing down to a gnat's ass." Roadhawg moaned "Now, damn it, we're wingin' it."

"Trust me. It'll work," Jack said. "Now, let's go have dinner."

Roadhawg stopped the car in front of the club and cut the engine. He mumbled, "Yeah, our last dinner before we're thrown in the brig."

Ellen, sitting at the bar by the door, waved them over.

"Hey, stranger, where've you been? Out carousing?" Ellen was tapping her watch while she flashed a cute grin.

Jack scooted close to her.

"I was getting worried because you all were late."

"It took us longer than we planned on to get the truck. But now we've got a vehicle to move our crap tomorrow morning."

Dan raised his head and looked toward Nancy.

"Must be nice being a short-timer," Nancy said.

"It's a double-edged sword when you don't have a job and they're kicking you out." Dan looked at Roadhawg and Jack.

They both broke out in grins. Yet, it was another reason to hate Bedford for using his cronies to deny the guys rom staying in in the Marine Corps. Ellen along with Jack, Roadhawg and Dan were scheduled for separation out of the service before the end of October.

Ellen chimed in. "Hey, what about me? I'm out in less than three months."

Jack reminded her that she had a high paying job waiting with the FAA as a controller as soon as she left the Air Force. Then the banter picked up.

Roadhawg teased, "If I had that much time to do, Ellen, I'd dribble a basketball through a mine field."

Dan said, "Hell, I'm so short, I could free-fall off the edge of a razor blade."

Jack pointed at him, "If your hair was as short as I am, they'd call you a lifer."

Jack inhaled his food and checked the time on his Mickey Mouse. He was making sure he kept his nerves under control. He told himself not to worry, over and over. This time tomorrow, everything would be all good. Jack squeezed Ellen's hand for assurance.

As they were leaving, Jack said as he opened the car door for Ellen," Honey, I should head back to my place.

Roadhawg and I've got to get an early start to load up in the morning. And you've got to be on duty at six. How about we stop by for a bite of breakfast after that?"

"Just be careful," she said.

Jack pulled back and looked at her. "We're only loading our stereo junk and stuff."

She closed her eyes for a moment, then looked into his. "Yeah, sure," she said. "Promise you'll be careful." She repeated herself—like she knew something.

"You know I will, and we'll spend the day after doing whatever you want. Okay?"

Roadhawg waited, rubbing his hands. "Jack, tomorrow's insane. And you know it."

"Quit worrying. We'll get all out plans worked out tonight," Jack started the wagon.

Jack, Roadhawg and Dan used the excuse of getting the military canvas covered pickup to move their personnel effects they'd acquired while on Okinawa. The military paid to ship the officer's furniture and personnel effects. They had their usual assortment of pilot/officer high dollar stereo equipment, and odd and ends. The military had given them small storage units at Kadena to store their personnel effects. This was Jack's cover plan.

They stayed up late that night going over and over the contingencies for the next morning. By 6:00 they began their odyssey. At 6:30, they checked in with the guard at the storage facility, and as they knew he would, he told them the facility wouldn't open until 0900.

"Mission accomplished. He'll remember us for sure." Roadhawg sighed.

"Let's get out of sight and let me undo the speedometer cable." Jack played with the keys, waiting for the glow plugs in the diesel to warm up before he hit the starter.

They drove to a deserted parking lot where Jack scooted

181

under the dash. Giving enough time to worry Roadhawg about getting the cable loose, he said, "Damn it. See if you can find a set of pliers. This thing won't come loose."

Roadhawg opened the glove box and threw out the operator's manual, loose paperwork and one bent screwdriver. "No. Nothing in the glove box," he shouted, "and I sure as shit ain't got a set of pliers. I knew it. I just knew things would go to hell in a hand basket."

Jack squirmed out from under the dash and grinned. "I had it loose all the time. I was teasing you. There. As simple as that."

Roadhawg slugged him. "Shithead. That ain't funny."

Jack laughed. "Let's go." The diesel coughed to life.

The plan up to that point was going better than expected. The storage gate guard would be their alibi. They could establish the time they were there. The meal at the mess hall was iffy. They were getting the meals to go, but their story was that they were eating there, waiting until 0900. With hundreds of service men, they would be unnoticed. Jack was banking on that hour-and-a-half window to dovetail with the rest of the plan. The mess hall receipt had the time on it.

Only one H-53 would be flying into Kadena that morning from 0700 to 0715, and they both were searching the gray overcast horizon for the inbound bird. Once Bedford picked up the money, he'd fly back to Futema to refuel. Bedford needed the "thief" to board the aircraft during that refueling. Jack's plan was for Pog to deplane before they got to the fuel pits to refuel, claiming he was feeling ill.

The thing that worried the four guys was if the guards couldn't be talked off the helo, the mystery guy would shoot the guards, if necessary.

As they drove out the gate in the morning light, Roadhawg spotted a `53 inbound to Kadena, "There they are." Roadhawg checked his watch. "And it's seven twenty-three, exactly."

"Right on schedule." Jack sighed as he watched the doomed helo land.

"Yes, sir. Right on time. We gotta haul ass and get over there. Come on, man. Shake a leg."

"What if we don't get there on time?" Roadhawg said looking straight ahead.

Jack just shrugged his shoulder, drove out the gate, turned right, and floored the cranky diesel.

Once Jack hit forty miles an hour, the whole front end began to shake enough to bounce both of them in their seats.

The Roadhawg grabbed the dash. "What the hell? We don't need this."

CHAPTER THIRTY-SEVEN

After a couple of miles, the access road appeared. "Hey, see, here we are." Jack turned and drove off the road on purpose, bouncing both of them even though the ground was level.

"Jeez, Jack, slow this deathtrap down."

Jack laughed as they bounced down the two ruts of a dirt trail.

"Okay, where's the abandoned runway?" Jack said.

"Hell, how do I know?" Roadhawg yelled as he held on to the door's open window frame.

"Last night you said you knew where it was."

"Bullshit. I said I've flown over it a few times. I've never driven up here."

Roadhawg flipped him the bird.

"I'm teasing you. On the map it looks like we should take this road up and over that rise. There should be a small valley with a landing strip."

They cleared the hill and pressed on toward the rendezvous spot, leaving a cloud of dust behind them. Jack drove onto the pavement of an abandoned landing strip.

"Ha. Look down there to the right, at the end of the

blacktop. See that road?" Jack shifted into high gear. "I see a piss-poor job of trying to hide their truck. I wonder where they got it?"

"Are you lying to me? I don't see jack shit."

Jack could see Roadhawg squint as he tried to follow where Jack pointed.

"Man, right down there between those trees."

"Oh, yeah. Now I see it. Looks just like ours. Know what's funny?"

"I give up. What?" Jack glanced out the window.

"Stenciled on the doors is 'For Official Use Only.' Think they'll add No Unauthorized Use of Military Vehicles,on it when we get busted?"

"We're not getting busted. Now, help me find a place to hide this rattle trap."

They needed a spot where they could park their truck, yet keep their eyes on the old runway. Jack grunted as he steered off the end of the hard-top pavement again onto the dusty two-rut trail. Seeing a dry stream crossing, Jack grinned. He slowed down and pretended to get stuck.

"Oh, shit, I should've hit it a little quicker." Jack began to rock the rig back and forth.

"Damn it, Jack. Quit screwing around. Time's running close."

Jack smiled as he drove over the top of the small rise. "Had you going, didn't I?"

"I swear to God, Jack, nobody would blame me if I shot your ass." Roadhawg patted his 1911 model Colt .45.

"Have you ever fired that thing?"

Roadhawg gave him the finger.

About a couple of hundred feet further down, the trail disintegrated into a dusty path where they found a grove of low trees and Jack pulled their truck under a couple of trees. The breeze off the Pacific was chilly and damp, almost foggy, but it kept them cool as they jogged back to Bedford's truck.

"Okay, I see what they've planned," Roadhawg said as they checked out the truck. "They'll land here, close to the truck." He pointed to a large clearing at the end of the runway.

Surveying the area, Jack motioned with his thumb like a hitch-hiker. They decided to hide over on that hill. From that spot, they would be able to see everything. Roadhawg watched the sky to the south as they started toward their intended hiding spot.

Once there, Jack gave a sigh of relief, and then shivered. What the hell? Not now. Come on. Why am I shivering, for God's sake?

CHAPTER THIRTY-EIGHT

Bolo Point lay north of Kadena on the west side of Okinawa overlooking the Pacific. Deserted and serene as it was that early in the morning, Jack felt the cold begin to cramp his feet as he and Roadhawg waited.

"Hey, how about an 'atta boy' for me, Roadhawg? I mean, are we here freezing our nuts off with time to spare."

Ignoring Jack, Roadhawg said, "The drop zone is just as Pog described it, near an abandoned landing strip. Do you think they can see our truck?" Roadhawg looked in the direction of the truck.

"Hell, no. And even if they do, what can they do? Abort the whole shebang?"

"Yeah, that's most likely the case. I just worry."

"Well, worry about something else."

"Damn it, Jack," Roadhawg's teeth began to chatter, "This is so loosey-goosey. And we could've at least brought a jacket. I've got the shivers so bad it ain't funny. And I'll tell you, that damn breeze off the ocean doesn't help."

"When we were in country the first time, I'd sometimes get the adrenaline shakes before some of the hops. But this bone-freezing breeze is the worst ever." Jack looked at his watch. "They should've picked up the payroll and been at Futema by now. I hope everything goes smooth there."

"No shit." Jack watched Roadhawg hug himself, trying to keep warm. "But I'm really worried about Pog getting off their bird okay. I'm even more worried about the possibility of the mystery guy shooting the Air Force Guards."

Minutes seemed to stretch on. Small talk and joking around dominated their endless wait.

"All right, Jackson, you're the perpetual weatherman. Tell me what we got."

"High thin overcast at ten thousand feet or so, obscuring the sun, temp fifty-eight to sixty, wind light to variable out of the west, keeping the humidity high."

"Jack, I swear you've got a career as a network weatherman. But, seriously, what are we so nervous about? Everything so far is working out good. And did we ever luck out that Bill had a storage space for rent at Hamby last night for us to stash the money."

"Here's what I'm afraid of. We might screw up and not get the money," Jack said. "Or we'll get caught with it and have to use these damn forty-fives we're packin'. I mean, we cooked it up last night and here we sit. But lettin' everyone down scares me the most."

Neither of them spoke for a long time.

"Shit, way over there." Roadhawg pointed to the incoming helo. "That's one of our birds trailing smoke. As long as they don't see us, in a few minutes we'll be busy getting the money into those duffel bags."

"Lord, I hope they already broke the locks on the payroll boxes like Pog said. I can't begin to imagine having to shoot this .45 to get them open."

Jack and Roadhawg watched in silence as the big helo approached the drop zone. It landed close to Bedford's hidden truck. The three men in flight suits started carrying off the payroll boxes, putting them into their truck.

Jack nudged Roadhawg because he recognized Sergeant

Johnson, the crew chief, and Tanner, but the third guy in a flight suit remained a mystery, while Hosier and Bedford monitored the controls of the helo. They finished in less than five minutes. The blades labored and made more noise as the bird lifted and headed off to the northwest. When the helo was about a mile out and they were clear, Jack ran to their truck and drove it to Bedford's hidden pickup.

Roadhawg remained by Bedford's truck, and had filled one of their parachute duffel bags they'd brought. But Jack could see Roadhawg was having trouble getting the money into the bags.

"You hold the duffel bag open," Jack chattered, "and I'll empty the boxes."

"Shit, I knew it would be a lot of money." Roadhawg grasped several bundles of money. "There's a shit pot of fives and tens. Take the Franklins and Grants first for this bag."

Jack laughed. "We're really doin' it. Hey, let me know when it gets too heavy. We've got plenty of these duffel bags. Come on. . .hurry, man."

"Damn it, Jack, I am hurrying." Roadhawg lifted the GI duffel. "That's probably sixty, seventy pounds. Let's start another. You're moving slower than smoke off of cold dog crap. Come on, step on it."

"Me, hurry? What about you? If you're putting too much into the bags, we're goin' have trouble just getting them to our truck." Jack zipped the bag shut and hustled toward their truck.

"Man, I'll have it filled by the time you get your slow ass back. Hell, I'm filling this one solo while you're farting off carrying it to the truck."

Roadhawg grabbed his bag and ran to the truck, the weight slowing him down. He had trouble getting the tailgate down. Jack had filled another duffel by the time Roadhawg ran back.

"How much time have we used up?" Roadhawg said,

out of breath, as he grabbed another duffel bag.

"Two minutes since they took off. Shit, we've only got eight to ten minutes left."

"We haven't even made a dent in it, yet." Roadhawg grabbed two filled bags and ran to their truck.

They transferred the cash in silence. Facing each other, they kept checking each other's back to make sure nobody came up on them.

"What the hell's that?" Roadhawg said.

A dust trail gave way to a small pickup truck as it came around the corner toward the water.

Jack strained his eyes. "Keep busy. Looks like some locals. I see a bunch of fishing poles in the back." Jack smiled and waved toward them from behind the truck. "Shit, they can't see what we're doing behind here, can they? Are they stopping?"

"No, I don't think so. Keep moving, you nosy bastards," Roadhawg said through clenched teeth. He walked toward them, waving his arm for them to pass.

Jack also waved as they drove past. "Roadhawg, get back over here. We don't have much time left."

"God, I almost lost it. Those bastards scared the shit outta me. I don't think I'd ever make an inside man." Roadhawg belched.

They'd bagged most all the big bills, but there were three to four times as much of the twenties and tens. Jack shoveled bundles of those smaller bills into the duffel. Then he hustled to the truck and returned. He worried about the time they had left.

"We'll keep at it until we see him heading inbound," Jack said. "Then we have to haul ass."

"What's our time count?"

Jack checked his watch and calculated they were at eleven minutes. But they still had a lot of fives and tens left to go.

Jack wiped his brow, throwing bundle after bundle into

his duffel. "When we see the bird coming, we stop and beat feet. Okay?" He peered into the distance. "I Think I see the bird low on the horizon. There's too much to leave. Hurry, man. We can do it."

"I agree," Roadhawg said out of breath as he kept filling the duffels.

Jack could tell Roadhawg had picked up the pace as he zipped his bag, dashed to the truck, and threw it in. He stumbled and fell flat on his face, then rushed back to help Jack. "I know we're going to laugh about this someday."

Jack threw in the last of the bundles of tens and twenties. "At least I hope we do."

"I'll feel a whole lot better when we lock this stuff up and turn this truck back in. Man, he's about five miles out. Hurry."

Jack struggled to carry the overfilled duffel bag to the truck. He turned around to see what was keeping Roadhawg, and then grinned and shook his head. "What the hell are you doin'?"

"Little Joe has been burstin' at the seams. Thought I'd piss all over the change we left that asshole Tanner. Lemme shake the dew off my lily, and let's haul ass." Roadhawg zipped his pants and jumped in.

Once in the driver's seat, Jack hit the starter. It turned over but didn't fire off. Jack looked at Roadhawg.

"Start, you dumb bastard." Jack cranked the ignition switch. The diesel lit off with a huge belch of black smoke. "Shit," he said as they sped off. He'd forgotten about the glow plugs needing a second or two to warm up before the diesel would start. It had scared the living shit out of him.

"Ha. I never hand any doubt that this baby wouldn't start." Roadhawg pointed his index finger at Jack.

They both laughed and cut up as they disappeared around the turn in the road as the `53 closed to about two miles. It kept moving in and climbing to gain enough altitude for the unknown guy to parachute out.

When Jack and Roadhawg were a mile away. Roadhawg glanced out his window. "There's a chute opening. The sad part is that helo will fly for about two hours with the trim control on. And there goes a perfectly good helicopter into the drink."

"Nawh, what's really sad is we can't see the expression on that asshole's face when he discovers all they've got left is a lot of pissed-on fives."

Jack relaxed as he pulled out onto the highway and proceeded toward Hamby and the storage sheds behind the marina bar. At last, Jack felt relieved as he was waved onto the base at Hamby. "A turn or two and we'll be safely there," he said aloud.

The only car parked in front of the bar was an MP vehicle with the driver's door open.

"Oh, shit," Roadhawg said as they slowed down and drove into the parking lot.

CHAPTER THIRTY-NINE

Jack and Roadhawg froze at the sight of the military police car.

"Listen, if they were waiting for us, they'd have already surrounded us," Jack said. "What the hell is going on?"

"Here he comes out of the place," Roadhawg said. "Looks like the guy's got a coffee to go."

Jack started the truck. "Well, I about shit my drawers. Let's get this unloaded, and get the truck outta Dodge."

Jack drove to the storage unit and backed up to the roll-up door. They looked at each other.

If they catch us with the money right now, our excuse is . . .

"Roadhawg, here's our story. We just got it from that thieving bastard Bedford and didn't know what to do with it. You know, like who to turn it in to. We were just storing it here until we could find out." Jack got out of the truck.

About a minute into the unloading, Roadhawg said, "Aw, go to hell. Here comes that MP. Now they've got us red-handed."

"Ah-h-h, jeez. He's still a ways off. Hurry, let's get the bags in there."

"Gawd damn son of a bitch, now he's heading down to the boat loading ramp. Jeez, he's going to talk to some idiot down there."

Jack dragged two bags into the shed. "Lord, he ain't even looking this way. Hurry, man."

They got the last of the duffel bags into the storage shed without being noticed.

When they'd finished, Jack pulled down the door. Jack said he was relieved it was over. He and Roadhawg nodded as they climbed into the truck. Jack drove out the gate at Camp Hamby and said, "Well, Roadhawg, mission accomplished."

"Jack, I have to take another piss."

Jack strode into the ready room and smiled. Several men still lingered at their desks. Alibis. He glanced at Roadhawg.

"Showtime," Roadhawg bragged.

"Hey, Burton," Jack called.

Dan was busy. He didn't look up but waved his hand.

Roadhawg followed. "It's about eleven-thirty. You ready for lunch?"

"Lunch, my ass. It's crazy around here and I quit. They can all go to hell." He looked up at Jack and Roadhawg. "Guess you guys haven't heard the news, have you?"

"Heard what?" Jack said.

"Bedford and the payroll flight went missing. We just got a call from him on Iwo Shima. He, Hosier, Tanner, and the crew chief are okay, but some guy stole the payroll. Everyone is jumping through their asshole trying to get the details. Nobody knows much for sure right now. But somebody took the money run."

"What? You gotta be kiddin' me," Roadhawg exclaimed. "Seriously? Does that mean the eagle ain't shitting today? We ain't getting paid?"

"By God, unless you're fartin' twenty-dollar bills, nobody's getting paid today."

Jack shook his head. "Unbelievable. Somebody took the money run?"

"Well," Roadhawg said, "if I ain't getting paid, I quit, too. I'm not doing doodly squat. Let 'em kick me out before October third. I. . .Don't. . .Care."

Jack folded his arms over his chest. As Dan stood to leave he said, "By God, That's too rich. Those morons total the S-2, and now they let someone steal the payroll."

CHAPTER FORTY

About a week to the day after the heist, an official investigation was in full swing. The Navy's Criminal Investigation Division (CID) arrived to question those involved and follow up on all the allegations.

Jack sat in the hallway at the group headquarters building. The investigators had already questioned Dan, who was waiting outside in his new wagon. The Roadhawg was in the hot seat at the moment. Jack's thoughts were scattered between thinking how much he missed Ellen and his well-prepared answers.

I'm tired of this waiting. I'm tired of having to sweat about what the investigators know or think they know. They have Bedford within an inch of his life from being caught, and here they're harassing us. He surveyed his surroundings. The solitary bulb provided scant light against the shade of puke green on the walls. The dingy hallway hadn't been painted since the Marine Corps took over the base back in the early '50s. A clerk sat in front of the makeshift office spaces.

"Captain Higgins, sir," the clerk smiled as he opened the door and brought Jack back to the present. "Commander

Friedman is ready for you, now. This way, sir." The clerk motioned for Jack to enter the office.

Jack followed the clerk's lead to a room off to the right. He sat down in front of a small field desk in the only chair provided.

So, this is the big-time-deal investigation, millions lost, and they're operating out of a dump. He was thankful for the window. The sunlight streaming in was blinding, though he welcomed it. He rubbed his eyes, adjusting to the light. And where is this hot-shot Navy commander who was ready for me?

Jack could hear voices outside the small room. He recognized Roadhawg's voice, and then he heard the door to his cramped space open.

"Good morning, and remain seated, Captain. My name is Robert Friedman." The commander had not yet looked at Jack as he maneuvered behind the desk and took his seat. "I'm sorry to have kept you waiting so long."

Jack peered across the small desk and scanned the investigator's yellow legal pad with its copious notes.

"Now, let me begin. This is very informal, and if it's okay with you, I go by Bob. Can I call you Jack?"

"Yes, that'll be fine." Trying to get me to let down my guard, Bob?

"As you know, Jack, eight days ago the payroll was taken, and Lieutenant Colonel Bedford is being thoroughly investigated. He's made several. . .well, let me say almost emphatic, insinuations that you, Captain Hegidio, and Captain Burton are somehow involved." He met Jack's eyes. "I know after his gear-up landing that he and you came to blows. And I want to ask you some questions."

"Okay." Ask all you want. What's any of that got to do with the price of tea in china?

"First of all, where were you at the time of the disappearance of last week's payroll flight?"

"I was with Captain Hegidio moving some of our

personal effects in preparation for our permanent change-of-station orders. We have witnesses who'll vouch for that."

"Yes, I've checked that out. Do you have any thoughts about who might have taken the payroll?"

"I do not. Although I have a history of abuse from Lieutenant Colonel Bedford, I do not believe it's best to let my personal feelings get in the way and speculate."

"Do you believe that's why Lieutenant Colonel Bedford is trying to insinuate that you and Captains Burton and Hegidio are guilty accomplices?"

"It is Bob, right?" Jack waited for the head nod. "Well, Bob, I have no clue as to Lieutenant Colonel Bedford's motives." Well put, Jack. No derogatory verbiage. Keep cool.

"Okay, one last item." Friedman glanced at his notes. "Now, Sergeant Pogany was with you on the night of the aircraft accident, and he was on the payroll flight. But then he walked off. Any speculation on any of that?"

"Sergeant Pogany and I served in country together. When we arrived here, he told me he was having problems with a girlfriend back home and couldn't get the Red Cross, the Marine Corps, or anyone else to help him get in touch with her. She disappeared, and I, along with Captains Hegidio and Burton, talked with him to help him out." Jack leaned back in his chair.

"Yes, he's said as much."

"As you already know, that's what we were doing the night Lieutenant Colonel Bedford's aircraft ran into and totaled Captain Burton's private vehicle. . .on purpose."

"Yes, I went over that with Captains Burton and Hegidio this morning. Still, you must admit it's a strange coincidence. I mean. . .with Sergeant Pogany."

"Even stranger is that he felt bad and took himself off the flight. So what is everyone trying to imply?" Answer that one, Bob.

"Oh, nothing, nothing at all. It's just the only premise

Lieutenant Colonel Bedford is mentioning, and we have to follow up on everything." He turned over the yellow pad. "Well, Jack, I guess that's all. If you have any thoughts or insights, here's my card. Please feel free to call at any time." Commander Robert Friedman handed Jack his card.

"Thank you, Bob, I will."

Outside, Dan and the Roadhawg sat listening to the radio in Dan's Pontiac wagon. Jack got in the back seat.

"By, God, nothin'. They got nothin'," Dan blurted out as they drove off. "Jordan spent the most time with me asking about Bedford and Tanner putting themselves down for the flight. I told him that I didn't write the schedule. Major Brown, the ops officer wrote it. Thank God, because I just played dumb on that."

"Easy for you to do, playing dumb," Roadhawg teased.

"Everybody stay with the pat answers? I know he left the door wide open to slam Freddy boy. But we said we'd all take the high road." Jack stretched out in the back seat.

"Yeah, he seemed to want to get me to slam Bedford and Tanner, but I didn't," Roadhawg reflected. "Did he ask you all about Pogy?"

"Of course, and I told him the truth about the girlfriend deal."

"By God, same with me, and all of our stories line up. He's just checking for any loose ends."

"Geez, I was sitting there letting my mind drift," Jack yawned rubbing his brow. "I was thinking about Ellen. But, it's scary how my mind drifts thinking about all that money."

"Me, too." Roadhawg turned to face Jack. "I think about Sue all the time. It seems to be worse the closer we are to getting out of here."

"Home sweet home." Dan pulled into a parking spot outside their rooms at the bachelor officer quarters. "One good thing about being a short-timer. . .no more having to live in the BOQ."

Getting out of the wagon, Jack waved his arm and said, "Be it ever so humble, it beats the last joint. But I still miss the Cave."

"By, God," Dan said. "Who said? It was the best of times. It was the worst of times."

CHAPTER FORTY-ONE

Three days later, a little before dusk, Jack hid behind some boxes in the back of the squadron's canvas-covered pickup, parked behind the hangar on the north side. Pog was having his last meeting with Johnson beside the truck. If needed, Jack would be the credible witness for Pog. Pog leaned against the truck with the canvas tied down, talking with Jack.

"The prick is over five minutes late," Pog said as he looked around.

"He's probably checking out the area. He's got a lot to lose," Jack said just above a whisper.

"Okay, here he comes. I'd love to deck him."

"I know, but cool it." Jack could see Johnson sauntering toward the truck.

"Alright, Johnson. You called the meeting. So what gives?" Pog began.

Johnson stood in his face. "Listen, damn it, you know something. You just didn't walk off the bird and then someone took the payroll from the drop-off. You'd better come clean, or it might get unhealthy for you. Those guys aren't fuckin' around. That's their message."

Pog, who had four inches and forty pounds on him, poked his finger with force into Johnson's chest. "Tell the douche-bag pricks I was back here in the line shack. You know it, and I know it. I just couldn't be part of the deal. And I walked off. Now, I haven't said shit, but if I hear one more bit of shit outta you or those assholes, I'm singin' like a canary." He moved in closer. "And if anything happens to me, I've got it all written down to be opened in the event of. So tell 'em to come on. Now we're through talking. Leave, and don't say another word, or you'll be talking out of the side of your mouth."

Johnson stomped off. Then Pog headed back toward the building.

Jack waited several minutes, snuck out of the truck, and slipped into the hangar.

Driving through the gate at Kadena Air Base the following Sunday, Jack, Roadhawg, and Dan headed to the auto hobby-shop parking lot. Pog emerged from the front door a few minutes later.

"People are getting nervous around here." Pog sighed as he climbed into the back seat. "Could you believe those six extra armed guards on payday?"

Jack laughed. "Thanks to that thieving bastard Bedford."

"By God, Sunday's a good day to meet. Easier to spot a tail. But I think we're all in the clear." Dan surveyed the parking lot, then drove off, heading nowhere in particular.

Pog glanced at his watch. "I've only got an hour. So the flight's still on as planned?"

"Everything's a go for Wednesday. Dan scheduled Roadhawg, you, and me for a boondoggle." Jack pointed toward Pog. "We'll land on an island three hundred and fifty miles east of Okinawa and rendezvous with the others about sixty to seventy miles north and east of there."

"The bitch is that the boat's so far out, and we've got

202

three and-a-half to four hours out and then the same getting back. That means four internal fuel cells," Pog said.

"More than we're supposed to be carryin'." Roadhawg looked out the window.

Pog leaned forward. "I can cover it. The mission calls for three, and I'll load four and never mention it. Maintenance control won't catch it. Shit, they don't know anything like that. But are you sure you've got the phony flight assignment covered?"

Dan nodded his head. "I've got it faked and I'll be at the ops desk all morning." He pointed to Jack and Roadhawg. "You all will follow the mission assignment to fly out to Iwo Kimma. When you get there, the natives won't know squat about pickin' up their backup generator."

Jack chuckled. "We'll just act like another screwed-up mission."

"But they'll remember you were there," Dan added, "and everything was screwed up. That's if Bob Friedman asks. You'll refuel, and everything will be slick."

"That pain in the ass CID guy, Friedman, won't be asking," Roadhawg continued. "So we land there, establish that we were there, and nobody knows anything about anything. We'll just gas up and leave."

Pog smiled through his mustache. "And we'll celebrate when we get back."

"Well, girls," Jack said. "let's celebrate when we depart Switzerland with the money in the bank, not one minute before."

"One last thing," Pog said, holding up his index finger. "I haven't heard squat out of that Richards guy. Everyone backed up my story about that morning?"

"He hasn't bugged us since then, either. So we'll still keep these meetings to a bare minimum. It wouldn't be good to be seen together." Jack glanced from one to the other.

Roadhawg turned toward the back seat. "That's for sure.

I mean, we all gave you a hard time about turning it in if and when they offered a reward. But, in less than six days, the boat will sail off with it, and we'll be home free."

"I get nervous thinking about when we actually move it," Jack said.

"By God, when that time comes, it'll go quick because of all the help. We'll load it on the boat, and Dennis and Luds will immediately sail off into the sunset."

"Here's what's funny." Pog shook his head as Dan pulled up to the hobby shop. "A little less than a month ago, we thought we'd lost it. Now we've got it, and they ain't lookin' at us. And on that note, gents, I need to git. I'll see you all around the squadron."

CHAPTER FORTY-TWO

The cold had worked its way through Jack's preflight gloves as he climbed off the sponson of their helo. He rubbed his hands together, trying to get them warm. It ain't that cold. Why have I got the shakes? Jack didn't know if it was because he worried about making contact with Dennis and Luds, or itd it was the eight-hour single-bird flight over water. Get your head back into the preflight. It'll be fine.

"My side looks okay. How's your side?" Roadhawg said.

"Fine and dandy." Jack tried not to shiver. "Let's get her buttoned up and hit the trail. Three-and-a-half hours-plus, out and back. I'll feel better when we're mission complete."

Pog, followed the two into the helicopter. "Me, too. She looks good, and I've already checked the fuel transfer from all the tanks. I'm ready when you are."

"Let's do it." Roadhawg and Jack walked to the cockpit. "A picture-perfect day for flyin'. Not a cloud in the skies."

A cool breeze from the west had the humidity up and the temperature down. They taxied out toward the runway. After talking to ground control, they were cleared to switch to the tower. The aircraft shook, and the number-one generator light illuminated.

"Kiss my ass," Jack shouted as he reached up to the overhead panel and turned off the malfunctioning generator. When he cycled the turn-on/turn-off switch, nothing happened. They were functioning on a single generator. The bird was down.

Pog sat on the jump seat in the cockpit. "Jack, the circuit breaker is on your side. Try cycling it."

Jack looked for the circuit breaker among the seventy to eighty others.

"Guys, if it stays off the line, we're technically a no-go." Roadhawg frowned and hit the dash board with his fist.

"We can't head back and get another bird. It'll take too long to get the fuel." Pog stared straight ahead.

"I've got it," Jack said. "Okay, make sure the switch is in the off position. Here we go." He pulled the circuit breaker.

Pog waited about ten seconds and gave Jack a thumbs up. Jack pushed the circuit breaker back in, and Pog turned the generator back on. The airframe shook as the number-one generator came back to life.

"Shit, we don't need that," Jack said.

"Hell, let's get goin' and pray we don't lose the number-one generator over the water." Roadhawg turned to Jack. "Switch me up to tower." After the radio hummed the channel change, Roadhawg said, "Futema Tower. Yankee Hotel, one two, holding short for takeoff."

"Roger, Yankee Hotel, one two, you're cleared to take off. Maintain runway heading." The controller in the tower cleared them. "Climb and maintain two thousand, squawk four three four seven, contact Kadena departure on two eighty-four point four." He also told them to monitor the guard frequency that every aircraft monitored for emergency broadcast.

"Roger, tower. We're rolling, switching, and squawking." Roadhawg taxied out to the runway. The huge helo lifted, departed into the rising sun, and at 2,000 feet, they settled into the view of the vast Pacific.

After a couple of hours of the normal CH-53 vibrations, they relaxed in their element, and continued to monitor their fuel and the number-one generator.

"Alright, Pog, how's the fuel situation?" Jack said well over two hours later.

"We're doing better than advertised. I've got a little left in the third tank. So, I've just topped off the main tanks. How long have we been outbound?"

Jack turned to face Pog as he sat down on the jump seat in the cockpit. "Two hours and twelve minutes, exactly. And by my calculations, we're less than an hour and a half from contact."

"I'll say one thing about hanging over the water this long," Roadhawg said. "It sure is lonely out here. Miles and miles of nothing."

"Well, sweetheart, you and Jack have it written all over your faces," Pog said. "After Dennis and Ludwig get the message to abort the original plan and come on into Okinawa, we'll all be relieved." He got up and left the cockpit for the tenth time since they'd taken off, muttering about checking the fuel again.

Jack said, as if in thought, "The abort and sail on to Okinawa is the only message we're sending. And that's the only time we're going to spend on the radio. No 'how are you' and whatnot."

"At least," Roadhawg agreed as he flew the bird, "that part of the plan is intact." Pog came back into the cockpit and sat on the jump seat. "Well, gents, we've just emptied one more internal fuel tank in the last forty-five minutes. We've got two internals left, and the mains are topped off. Here's the pisser. The number-two tank's empty light just illuminated on my control box. I checked it, and it's full. It just had me jumpin'. Three should have shown empty, not two."

"That's okay. We're getting great fuel mileage," Roadhawg noted.

"Hey, just exactly where is that Iwo Kimma island?" Pog looked outside.

Nodding over his shoulder, Jack said, "About ten miles over there. If you're ready, I'll start the climb."

"You're clear, my side. As a matter of fact, there ain't nothing on my side," Roadhawg glanced out his side window.

Jack switched the UHF radio to the preset channel on the PRC-90 radio. He pressed the transmit trigger and said, "Blue, Blue, this is green, over."

After about ten seconds, he looked at Roadhawg, saying, "Well, I'll try it again. I hope they're up and have the radio set to transmit and receive."

"That's two of us." Roadhawg sighed, shaking his head.

"Make it three," Pog added.

"Blue, blue, this is green, over," Jack transmitted.

"Green, this is blue. We have you five by."

Jack smiled as he recognized Lud's voice. He'd just acknowledged he had the aircraft loud and clear. Then he began to say, "Green, exercise plan white, over. I repeat. Exercise plan white, over."

Silence.

"Ah-h-h, roger, understand, plan white."

They smiled at each other in the cockpit when they recognized Dennis.

"Correct, plan white. Green out," Jack finished as they heard the mic double-click for "okay."

"I'll bet they're wondering, what the shit," Roadhawg said, smiling. "But when Dennis came on, they knew somethin' was up. They're probably thinking something awful has happened, and in reality it couldn't be better."

Pog gave him a nod and a smile.

"Well, Jackson," Roadhawg pointed at Jack, "how's about you seein' if you can find this here island Iwo whatever. You've got the controls." He held up his hands after Jack took the controls.

"Alright, girls, about four hundred miles back home and we're done."

Pog and Roadhawg nodded, but within ten minutes, the emergency panel flashed again, and the aircraft shook as the generator dropped off the line.

CHAPTER FORTY-THREE

The number-one generator stayed illuminated. Jack went right to the circuit breaker this time, and cycled it. Pog had already turned the generator switch to the off position on the overhead panel. Nothing happened when he turned it back on.

"Well, shit," Jack said.

"We don't need this right now. How far to the island?"

"About fifteen to twenty minutes," Jack said as Roadhawg tried to plot the distance.

"Thank God the island has an ADF station, or we'd be up shit creek." Roadhawg shook his head.

"When we get there, let's don't shut `er down. I'll take a look and see if it's something simple, like a loose connection." Pog rubbed his head. "We don't want to fly the four hours to Futema without the number one generator. If we lost the number-two generator, we'd be flying with only the magnetic compass and no gauges or instruments."

"Yeah, I don't like shutting her down, either." Jack worried they'd lose everything as soon as the rotor rpm's dropped below 92%. They could use the rotor brake, but they'd be without any electrical.

"Let's fire the auxiliary power plant. The APP does drive the number-one generator. Maybe it'll kick it in," Roadhawg said.

When they fired off the APP, the light went out. Four minutes later, they spotted the island. Everything checked out normal in the air. Once on the ground, they decided to leave the APP running and haul ass for the barn after they confirmed with the locals that there was no equipment to pick up. They made contact for their cover story, took on fuel, and decided to head for the base.

Jack felt relieved because Lud's boat had changed course and now sailed for Okinawa.

With the auxiliary power plant still running, and the number-one generator functioning, they performed a normal start, run-up, take-off, and climb-out to four thousand feet.

"I'm all for leaving the auxiliary power plant running. I know it makes no sense the APP's making it run while the rotor RPM's at one hundred percent." Jack shook his head.

Pog pointed to the number-two engine's exhaust-gas temperature gauge. "Well, APP's exhaust is running into the intake on the number-two engine, and it's making the exhaust temp run a little bit higher. But I mean, it's not hurting anything."

The extra fuel wasn't a factor, and the main engine was running okay, so they all agreed to leave the APP on.

After an hour, Jack got on the radio again. "Kadena Approach, this is Yankee Hotel one two. We're a single H fifty-three on your zero nine three radial at approximately one hundred twenty-six miles out at eight thousand. We'd like radar following. We're experiencing electrical difficulties, over."

"Ah-h-h, roger Yankee Hotel one two. Please squawk four three two three. Over."

Roadhawg set the number on the IFF radio so the

controller could identify them. After a moment, Kadena came back. Ellen was on the radio. "Yankee Hotel one two, we have you on radar contact, on the zero nine three radial at one hundred twenty-three at eight thousand. Are you requesting direct vectors to Futema? State your electrical difficulties. Over."

"That's affirmative, Kadena. We'd like direct vectors to Futema. We're experiencing trouble with our number-one generator. It's currently functioning normally, but it's dropped off the line a couple of times." Jack didn't want her to worry.

"Roger, Yankee Hotel one two. Fly heading two seven one direct to Futema."

"Roger, Kadena. Turning to heading two seven one, maintaining eight thousand."

The next thirty minutes passed by without incident. The auxiliary power plant was consuming a little more fuel than they'd counted on, and the exhaust kept flowing into the intake, making the number two engine run a little bit hotter and consume more fuel.

"I don't know about you girls, but I could do without this generator shit." Roadhawg laughed. "And if this is my last flight in a Marine Corps helicopter, that'd be mighty fine with me, too."

"I'll amen that," Jack said.

"Wimps. A little generator dropping off the line, and you two girls wanna hike your skirt up and quit." Pog rubbed his eyes as if to wipe away tears.

Jack grinned. "Say what you want, but we're still a long way out."

The bird shook when the bad generator acted up again. They nursed the big helo all the way back to Okinawa. When they arrived, they taxied into their parking place where Dan was waiting.

CHAPTER FORTY-FOUR

Three days later, Jack paced his room, waiting for Dennis to call. When the phone rang, he rushed to answer it.

"Your ship's come in," Dennis said.

"Everything's fine." Jack answered.

"Understand. See you soon."

Jack slipped out of the room and went to Dan's where he gave Dan a thumbs up. Dan put his finger to his lips. As the stereo played, "Me and Bobby McGee," he whispered, "Don't say a word. By God, ears are everywhere. Go get the Roadhawg, and I'll meet you all down by the end of the building."

Jack ran up to Roadhawg's room. He tossed an empty beer in the trash.

"Let's go," Jack mouthed as he motioned with both thumbs out, a signal to pull the chocks. The Roadhawg nodded, and they left without making a sound. Dan had his wagon waiting.

"Guys," Roadhawg said as they got in, "I know we've got to be super careful, but I haven't heard or seen anything that would make me suspect something was going on, except the NCID."

"By, God, the NCID interviewing you girls ain't a coincidence." Dan frowned, returning the gate guard's salute as they drove off the base. "I still don't trust ol' Jordan any more than I trust that bastard Bedford or Petey boy."

Roadhawg sat back. "I've heard rumors about them putting listening devices in rooms and tapping the phones, but I think we're being a little paranoid."

Dan concentrated on the rearview mirror. "Awh, damn it, we just might have a tail. Ha, I've got news for those boys."

He drove onto the base at Kadena. When he approached the turn for the O Club, he turned right from the left lane, cutting across the right-turn-only lane. "Nobody followed, but they could think we're going to the club and swing around. Hang on, we ain't finished, yet." Dan cut the steering wheel, made a U-turn in front of the club, and got into the right turn lane. "Well, that's better. I don't see anyone familiar hanging a U-turn and heading back, so let's git."

"Just to be on the safe side," Roadhawg said, looking behind them, "let's still leave this at the BX and switch to Jack's wagon."

They had left Jack's Impala at the BX as insurance. With one eye on the parking lot ahead and the other glued to the rearview mirror, Dan pulled in front of the BX and parked.

Jack stepped out and walked toward the commissary. He never looked at Roadhawg as he headed into the BX. Dan went to the outdoor garden shop. The plan was for him to make his way into the commissary.

With no sign of anyone following him, Jack picked up a couple dozen eggs, a mess of sausages, potatoes, and four tins of biscuits. Now, for some evening snacks. Next into his basket went chips, dip, and sliced deli meats. He was admiring a bottle of merlot when Commander Friedman appeared.

"Ah-h-h, Captain Higgins," Bob Friedman said, standing next to Jack. "A fine wine, indeed."

"Yes." Jack managed to say.

"Oh, excuse me, Honey," Friedman said, handing a bottle of Chardonnay to his wife. "Let me introduce you to Marine Corps Captain Higgins."

"Pleased to meet you, ma'am," Jack said. Holy shit, what's he going to say about everything in my basket? Jack shook Mrs. Friedman's hand. A good defense is a good offense. He smiled. "Late-evening shopping and no crowds." Jack relaxed a bit.

Taking her husband's arm, she said, "That's my thought exactly."

"Well, Commander, it's good seeing you, again. I'm going to let you two finish and be on my way. Evening, ma'am." Jack nodded toward Mrs. Friedman.

"He seems like a nice guy," Jack heard Mrs. Friedman say to her husband as Jack walked away.

Yes, he is, and I almost shit my drawers. Jack paid for the items, and with arms full, he surveyed the parking lot.

Okay, they're both in the Impala wagon. Jack signaled by rubbing his chin. Yeah, yeah, something's not right. Pick me up in the back of the base theatre, he thought as he entered the rear exit of the BX.

Okay, I've been in here for at least five minutes and no sign of anyone following me. He was sure Friedman had just been shopping, though it still scared him. If he could get to the pick-up point, then he'd be out of there. Here goes nothing, he thought, as he walked out the front door of the BX.

When he rounded the corner of the theater, two concerned Marines sat in the car waiting for him.

Jack approached the wagon and got in. He said, "Friedman and his wife were just in the commissary. Let's git while the gitting's good."

Once on the road, Roadhawg said to Dan, "Come on,

and get your slow ass in gear. I can't wait to tell Luds and Dennis the deal. They'll be surprised to hell and back."

Jack said, "I about died when I ran into Friedman. I got a sick-to-my stomach feeling that we ain't in the clear."

"I've got the same bad feeling," Roadhawg said.

"Jack, here's the deal. Friedman and his wife couldn't be following us, because they'd already done all that shopping. I take it as a coincidence. That's all."

They drove east toward White Beach Naval Base. Once there, they took their time as they surveyed the surroundings.

Dan motioned toward the boat. "I say let's get out and walk down there. I can't wait to tell Dennis and Luds that we got it. You know, they're thinkin' something went haywire and we're empty handed."

"Let's go," Jack said, looking around once more.

The guys climbed aboard. Jack opened the hatch to get the ladder to the cabin and ducked his head to descend. Sitting around the cabin were Dennis and Luds with lost looks on their faces.

"Surprise. By God, we got it," Dan said. "And the MPs ain't looking at us."

Dennis looked up at them. "What the hell?"

CHAPTER FORTY-FIVE

"Don't say a single word until I get us tied up out in the bay," Luds said as he climbed up the ladder to move the boat away from the dock.

"John wants to anchor about thirty yards off shore, just to be on the safe side." Dennis pointed out the window toward the open water.

After Luds shut down the motor and tied up to a buoy, he came back down into the cabin.

"By God, girls." Dan rubbed his hands together. "We got the whole shooting match. Bedford stole it the payday before our payday, and we stole it from him."

"What? You've gotta be kidding me," Dennis said.

Jack related the entire story. When he got to the end of the bagging episode, both Luds and Dennis laughed. "Roadhawg, you actually pissed on the left over money?"

"Have a cold one," Roadhawg said breaking out the cold beer they'd brought. "And, hell, yes, I pissed all over it."

"What made you do that?" Luds said.

He grinned. "It felt like I was pissin' on Bedford."

"So," Luds said, "you all stashed the money, hoping for

a reward, and have never counted or touched it since?"

"That's right." Jack held up his beer in a toast.

Dennis appeared to relax. "Tomorrow we'll go out after dinner. Then when it gets dark, we'll empty the storage locker, head back here, pull the anchor, and sail off. I can't believe it. If we can do that, we're practically home free."

"Jesus, Joseph, and Mary," Luds said from his chair at the dinette. "I would never in a million years have thought it'd end like this. Shit, we got the money, and they aren't chasing us. But it sounds like they're on Freddy boy like white on rice. This is just too sweet. I wish I could go gig him about it."

"Guys," Dennis said, "I think you've played it perfectly, especially by not saying a peep about Bedford. It sounds like he's trying to put Pogy and you all together, but he can't."

"So," Luds mulled, "tomorrow we put on the disguises and go get the money."

Jack said, "Yep, simple as that,"

Roadhawg opened a new Budweiser. "What'd you all think when you got the message 'exercise white'?"

"We knew something happened, but we had no clue." Luds blinked his eyes.

"We never even. . .for a little bit, thought you were sitting on the money, scot-free," Dennis finished. "Shit fire, this is just too good to be true."

"We were worried about phones being tapped and thought it best to go along, normal as possible," Dan said.

"Well, we're all good now." Luds shook his head.

"We oughta be safe enough staying on board tonight, even if they're looking for us" Jack looked at Luds and Dennis. "Screw `em."

"By God, I guess we'll all be solo. Nancy, Sue, and Ellen have duty tonight. So this'll be just like back in sixty-eight. Shootin' the breeze out here and nursing a Bud or two."

The next morning, Jack fixed a huge country breakfast from items he'd bought at his late-night shopping encounter with Navy Commander Jordan. They caught up on all the news, swapping stories about sailing to Okinawa and liberating the money run, again and again. Just like old times watching TV in the Cave. Life was good. He felt at home watching the whole gang together again.

By late afternoon, they decided to head to Hamby.

Jack followed Luds up on deck.

He cast off the line and said, "I don't see any CID."

Luds motored back to the slip at the dock. Jack cleated the big boat, then walked to the Impala and up the hill to look around. A moment later, he gave the cramped "millionaires" the double thumbs up, and they left the boat, heading to the car.

As Jack squeezed into his new set of wheels, he looked over his shoulder. The hair on the back of his neck stood straight up. A government-issued sedan sat well outside the White Beach gate, watching.

CHAPTER FORTY-SIX

Jack's fears were relieved when the sedan didn't move. They drove to Kadena Air Base's BX. Luds and Dennis had never met Pog, but Jack knew the meeting would go well. The five of them stood around the station wagon, waiting for Pog to arrive. The sky displayed an array of beams that broke through the orange clouds above the dark-blue Pacific. In the background, several jet aircraft took off, their engines making it almost impossible to talk.

Pog came walking up behind Jack.

Dan said, "By God, looky what the cat drug up," as he got out.

"John, Dennis," Jack said, pointing to them, "this is crew chief extraordinaire, Sergeant Charles Pogany."

Roadhawg put his arm around Pog. "But we call him douche bag, Pogy, Pog, anything that comes to mind."

"We've heard all about you." Dennis winked, extending his hand.

"Don't believe them. You know officers lie a lot," Pog shot back making the guys laugh.

"Glad to finally meet you, Pogy. You're right when it comes to these guys," shaking Pog's hand. "I go by Luds,

Ludwig or John. Doesn't matter to me."

"Okay, Luds. Well, here's the deal." Pog nodded his head, getting serious. "I was inside watching for tails or anything suspicious. But I saw nothing out of the ordinary."

"Man, you had me worried," Jack said. "We've been waiting for a few minutes."

Roadhawg walked over to the two of them. "Hey, I was thinkin', Pog, we've got enough hands here to move a mountain. So just to be extra safe, we could move the stuff. I mean, we aren't trying to leave you out, but as soon as we get it back and on board the boat, Dennis and Luds are gone."

"You sure you won't need any help? I'd be glad to stay, but I think you're right about separating."

Jack put his arm around Pog. "Thanks, man, but head back and keep the eyes that might be watchin' satisfied that you're just hanging out on a Friday night."

Dan looked at his watch. "By God, it's six-fifteen. Bill should be gone by now, and if there's anybody there, they won't know us from Adam. So we should be cool to show these two apes the wonderful view and atmosphere of the Hamby Diner."

"Pog," Dennis said, "it's been a pleasure meeting you, and I look forward to seeing you in. . .you know where." He finished with a hand shake and smile.

Luds extended a hand. "Same here, Pog."

"All righty." Jack rubbed his hands together. "Let's make like britches and split."

Pog walked back inside the BX, and the rest of them got in the wagon. They headed to the diner at Hamby.

Jack felt a sudden chill.

Driving onto the base at Hamby and seeing everything was normal made Jack feel a little better. He just wished he could get rid of the bad feeling in his gut. He'd be glad when the money was on the boat and they were out of sight.

They got out of the Impala and walked into the almost-deserted diner.

"You guys get teary-eyed over this dump?" Luds teased.

"Shut up, moron." Roadhawg said taking off his black sock hat. "Look at the view. It's something else."

Dennis stared out at the Pacific, the sun just above the water turning it to a brilliant gold.

"Luds, Dennis, see how crowded it is. This is where we did all our planning in the very end booth." Dan waved at Bill and, continued as they walked toward the booth. His grey sweats fit the marina look. "Now follow me to this side of the room, and I'll show you the storage area."

"Hey, guys, quit lookin'. Walk away and head back over to the other side. . .now." Jack whispered.

After they sat down, Roadhawg leaned toward the middle of the table. "What the hell? You look like you just saw a ghost. What is it?"

"I think I saw someone." Jack tapped his index finger on the table and looked around, "like the NCID out there sitting in a car and watching the storage lockers and the diner. Short hair, rumpled suits, you can spot them a mile away. They're in the black government-issued Dodge, just about fifty yards up that little hill, with a commanding view of all the storage lockers."

Then to Dan he said, "Walk out front and act like you left something in the wagon. Don't let them know you see them. Then tell me what you think."

Dan took his time as he walked to the wagon, stretched, opened the tailgate, fiddled around like he'd picked something up, and walked back. When he returned, he looked pale as a sheet. He pulled off his black sweatshirt and threw it in his chair. He walked around readjusting the long sleeved t-shirt several times. "Jack, damn it. You're right. Those guys got binoculars watching something over here. I say we get the hell outta here."

Jack shook his head in disbelief. "Okay, if they're tailing

us, we're in deep shit, and you all need to hit the trail, or should I say the sail?" He looked at the guys.

"If they weren't tailing us here, why are they watching the storage?" Luds said

"I know they didn't follow us here. They might have our license tags, but I doubt it.," Roadhawg said.

"Jeez, so if they didn't follow us here. What gives?" Jack mumbled something about all the bad luck. His anger flashed when he broke his beer bottle throwing it into a trash can.

"It just doesn't fit or make sense." Dennis said. "We don't have enough pieces to this puzzle to get a clear picture just yet."

"Let's stay with what we do know." Jack turned to the others. "They're watching something here, not us or they'd already have arrested us. "We can't risk taking the bags while they're watching."

Dennis looked around and then closed his eyes. He reminded them they should get back to the boat as soon as possible. He got up, depending on his cane more than usual, as he paced. Jack could see the pained expression.

"If we're followed, I think I can lose them at Kadena." Dan said, "and then we'll beat feet for the boat."

Ludwig stood and told them he thought it'd be safe to talk on the boat. And maybe they could make some sense out of all of this. He agreed on leaving right then. Luds didn't want to stick around and take any risk of getting caught. Dennis reminded him of a long sail back, empty handed. You could've heard a pin drop, as they all looked at Jack.

"Listen, they're waiting to see if someone takes it. That's evident. Now it's over. Either way, we can't risk it, and it's time to make like horse turds and hit the trail." Jack put his head in his hands.

"What the hell?" Dan said, "What happy ass played that song?"

Ray Charles on the Rockola, was singing, "Hit the Road, Jack."

CHAPTER FORTY-SEVEN

Jack and the others watched for tails, but no cars followed the wagon. Once on the boat, Ludwig cast off and motored out to one of the moorings. Seated in the galley below, they waited for him to tie off the boat. In the silence, Jack heard the light warm summer breeze catching the sail bags and banging the lanyards against the main sail boom. The hollow aluminum sound would have been soothing under other circumstances, but now everything caught his attention.

"If you wrote a script, nobody would believe it," Ludwig said as he sat down.

Roadhawg frowned. "First we plan it, then that bastard Bedford beats us to it."

Jack shook his head. "Then we take it and hide it."

"You guys sail all the way over here," Dan said, sighing, "and we're like ten minutes from loading it up, and they're watchin' the shed."

"Listen," Dennis interrupted. "We agreed we're not taking any stupid, unnecessary chances, no bloodshed, and so far we've stuck by that." He leaned forward in his seat. "We know this, they're watching. It's over. Time to fold the tent. Come on. We're not in jail, and it's been a fantastic adventure of a lifetime."

Luds looked up. "Let's not sail tonight. We'll wait until tomorrow and grab a couple of things we might need and be off. By mid-October we should make Hawaii. Dennis, do you want to fly back?"

"Hell, no. Do you think I'd let you have all that fun alone?" Dennis winked at Luds.

Everyone laughed.

"Dennis, seriously, I'll be fine, but it's hard to swallow it right now."

"We're in this together, brother," Dennis said. "So tomorrow we set sail for Iwo Jima."

Luds nodded his head. "And from there, Hawaii."

The next morning, Dennis and Luds prepared the boat to leave while Jack, Dan, and Roadhawg headed to Kadena, where the other wagon was parked. Jack drove his Impala solo. By the time Dan and The Roadhawg got to Hamby, Dan's new wagon clicked and ticked as the engine cooled down in the chilly morning air. Jack stood outside waiting.

They walked in and sat down at their window table.

"Hey, look at you two sick-looking bastards. I say we have our standing Sunday lunch like normal. Then we can drown ourselves in self-pity, if that's what you want." Jack looked up and stretched. "But take a gander at that beautiful sky. The temp is about a perfect sixty-eight, so let's celebrate."

"All right, then, Mr. Weatherman," Roadhawg said. "I'm bummed because we've had it, lost it, had it again only to lose it. And I've still got both of you miserable bastards."

"He's right. We need to celebrate." Jack broke out in a grin. "A shot of Jack Daniel's just might be the cure."

With their backs to the bar, they enjoyed the view, but after several rounds, their spirits, unlike the weather, remained clear to partly cloudy.

"What the hell?" Bill said looking outside.

Jack turned around to see flashing lights from the patrol cars surrounding the storage area. "What's going on?"

"It's got to be the money," Dan whispered.

Roadhawg's eyes opened wide. "If it's our storage shed, our goose is cooked."

"They don't suspect us just yet, Roadhawg, or they'd already have us in custody." Jack stood to get a better view. "Guys, if this is it, we stick with our story. We only used the storage shed for a day or two and don't know anything about what's in there."

"Yeah, we used gloves when we handled the money and the bags," Roadhawg said. "So they can't find any prints."

"By God, that bastard Bedford most likely planted it there." Dan grinned.

Jack walked over to get a better view. He couldn't see which locker the cops were looking in."

"Hell's fire. Let's go out there and see what's going on."

"Hey, Bill," Roadhawg hollered. "What's going on?"

Bill turned and jogged over to the aviators.

"Guys, they say they found the stolen payroll in one of the sheds."

"No shit." Jack gasped.

Dan put his hands on his hips. "By God, well I'll be."

"You boys want anything? I want to go check it out."

Roadhawg looked at Jack, then Dan. "We're good, but let us know what you find out."

Bill nodded and rushed out. They watched him talking with a couple of guys standing on the periphery. A moment later, he returned.

"Here's the scoop," Bill said. "That Marine colonel rents a shed a couple of months ago. He opens it up this morning, and all hell breaks loose. They were waiting on the guy."

"You've got to be shitting me," Jack said.

"Get this. He says he got word there was something

planted in his locker and he'd better check it out. He's claiming he knows nothing. They got him red-handed. I think it's that lieutenant colonel who has a hard-on for you all."

Roadhawg turned a lighter shade of shock.

Dan stood with his mouth open.

Jack shook his head. "Are you sure?"

"Got it right here," Bill whispered, looking around to make sure nobody was listening. He held up the rental agreement. "Says right here. Bedford, F. A. He was screaming and hollering that he was set up. I say. . .bullshit, he was coming to take the money and run."

"By God, it couldn't happen to a nicer back-stabbin' lifer of a prick."

Bill looked around, making sure the place was empty. "I heard the Navy types say it's only the small bills, nothing over a five spot."

"I'll be damned," Roadhawg said.

Jack wasted no time as he tossed down his drink. "Well, ah, Bill, we'll come back later when it quiets down. Looks like too much excitement for this country boy. Come on, guys, let's blow."

They hurried out to Dan's wagon and piled in.

"Shit, shit," Jack yelled, beating the back of the front seat. "Let's haul ass over to White Beach and try to catch Luds and Dennis before they sail. The cops weren't watching out for us. It was Bedford."

"I'll truly be damned. Ain't it kind of insulting to us that he even picked the same storage units?"

"Piss," Roadhawg hollered. "I can't believe this. Had it all planned, lost it, had it, lost it, and now we've still got it safe and sound in our storage shed. Un-fuckin'-believable."

"Roadhawg, you're beginning to sound like a stuck record. Danny boy, slow down," Jack said. "If Luds and Dennis are gone, which they most likely are, we've got to come up with a new plan. . .pronto."

Close to one o'clock, they hurried to White Beach, hoping Luds and Dennis hadn't sailed, but the odds were slim. Along the way they tried to come up with a few alternate plans, shaky at best. Driving down the hill to the marina, they saw the boat was nowhere in sight.

Dan parked on the upper parking lot, which gave him a grand view of the marina and the Pacific stretching to the east as far as the eye could see.

Jack got out and shaded his brow with his hand. Roadhawg stayed in the car.

Nobody spoke. Jack got back in the car. Dan started it up but sat for a moment or two.

"Let's head back to the base," Jack said through gritted teeth. "There's got to be a silver lining in this here cloud that we're just not seein'."

Dan put the wagon in drive and headed toward Hamby.

When they arrived, most of the patrol cars were gone. The threesome sat down at their table and began kicking around thoughts and ideas.

"Well, Jackson and Mr. Burton," Roadhawg announced, "I don't like the idea of shipping it back with our furniture."

"I don't want to take it out, bury it, and come back later for a little at a time, either. And I sure as hell don't like putting it in packages and mailing it," Dan said.

"I've been thinkin'," Jack said, scratching his head. "It's a long shot at best, but what about this?"

CHAPTER FORTY-EIGHT

When Jack finished talking, the three sat mulling things over.

"Let me see if I've got this straight, Jack," Dan looked straight ahead. "We get a bird first launch, day after tomorrow. We help Pog load the bird with the money tomorrow night. Then Tuesday we fly out. We know Luds's departure route. We'll see if we can find him and drop it aboard and fly back."

Jack pushed back in his seat. "That would be the plan, yeah."

Dan drove in silence, as they headed for Futema. "Your thinking is good about doing it Tuesday. Tomorrow's flight schedule is already posted. I'd run too much of a risk to try adding an aircraft on in the morning."

Roadhawg shook his head.

"What?" Jack said. "What're you thinking?"

"Hell, I mean it's got some merit, gets the money off the island and safely to John. If we can find them out there in that hell of a big ocean."

"Long odds at best," Dan added. "I'm thinking. . .big ocean, little boat. And what'll we do when you don't find them? It's too risky to fly back with the money still on board."

"Plus, Jack," Roadhawg said, "two days is two hundred and twenty to fifty miles out."

"Hey, if we have two internal fuel tanks, that would give us an hour and a half on the flight out, an hour to look, and an hour and a half back." Jack more than grinned his half McQueen smile

"And if we don't find them?"

"Well, we fly back to the grunt's million square mile Northern Training Area, stash the money there, hot-pump if we're low on fuel, and come back without the dough. I mean, no grunt's gonna be out in the boonies skylarking around. Then we come back in a day or so and try to figure something out." Jack looked at each of them.

Dan sighed. "By God, it's got a lot of holes in it, but the NTA covers a whole lot of desolate landing areas."

"It's the best we've come up with," Roadhawg said from the back seat. "But I still think it's a big risk taking the money out there. How about dropping Dennis and Ludwig a note and have them sail back? That way we don't have to move the money."

Jack looked at his Mickey Mouse. "We're supposed to meet Pog any time now. Maybe he'll have a thought or two."

"Yeah, let's head back to Hamby," Dan said.

They arrived at Hamby and walked to their usual table.

Jack raised his hand to get Bill's attention. "I wonder what's keeping Pog?"

Pog approached the table, two steps in back of Jack. "In fact, I'm right behind you, sweetheart." Pog took an empty chair beside Jack and laughed. "Guys, did you hear about Bedford?"

"Hell, yeah," Jack said. "I wonder what he'll do to try and squirm outta this one."

Bill walked over with four Budweisers. "Good to see

something normal today." He set the beers down. "They finally cleaned out that storage over there. Took down the tape and left."

"So everything's quiet and peaceful now?"

"Since about an hour ago. Are the women coming for lunch?" Bill said.

Jack nodded. "That'd be a yes, and I for one can't wait."

Bill headed off to the kitchen.

"How did loading the, you know what, go?" Pog rubbed his thigh.

Jack asked if Pog wanted the good news or the bad? Pog said he wanted the good news, and Jack told him the guys had sailed that morning.

Then he went into detail about the fiasco the evening before with the CID watching the storage units. Dan told Pog the guys thought the CID types were watching for them. Jack could see from Pog's expression—he realized the money was still sitting in the storage unit.

Jack, Dan, and Roadhawg brought Pog up to date on their best flimsy plan.

"Just flying out and dropping Luds and Dennis a note sucks. . .if we don't find them," Jack said. "That leaves a huge problem with moving the money." He reminded Pog that they'd have to get a military truck so they could stash it in the NTA. They just won't let a privately owned vehicle in the training areas."

"Guys," Pog said, "I'm for taking the money out to the boat and hiding it up in the NTA if we can't find them. Sounds to me like it's our best and only shot."

"Risky as hell," Roadhawg said, "if we get caught with the money. Shit, we'd be busted with no alibi, no flimsy explanation. Nothing."

"By God, we're clear as can be right now, but one little slip-up and, like Roadhawg said, we're up to our asses in alligators. So we either let it sit or go." Dan downed the last of his Bud.

They all nodded yes.

Looking at the parking lot, Dan mumbled, "Okay, here come the women."

"Aw, damn it, we've got to figure this out." With his elbows on the table, Roadhawg put his head in his hands.

CHAPTER FORTY-NINE

Jack felt the weight of the world lift from his shoulders when he saw Ellen. But she wasn't the smiling gal he was used to.

"Honey," she said grasping his hand. "Could we go take a walk?"

"Guys, we'll be right back." They headed toward the door. "What gives?" he asked after they stepped outside.

"Let's go down to the marina so we won't be interrupted."

The breeze off the water was chilly, and the salt water smell permeated the air. Seagulls squaked and hovered into the wind, and the dock bumped and groaned as a slight wave action moved all around the marina making the masts bob up and down.

They walked without talking. He felt more than the coldness from her hand. Once on the docks, they sat on a small bench, and she let go of his hand. "Jack, how do feel about us?"

"Baby, you're the only thing in my life that gives me peace."

"How do you explain the last three days?"

"I know I've been a little out of pocket, but. . ."

"A little?" She wiped the corner of her eye and turned her head.

"Honey, I've been. . ." he paused, hung up on the half lie.

"Usually you call and talk to me when I'm on duty."

He reached for her hand. "I've just been tied up with the guys."

"Jack, if you want out, if you need space. . ."

"No way, El. Not now or ever."

"I tried your room all night, and no answer."

"Look, we had a party with some guys from our first tour."

"And you couldn't call?"

"There wasn't a phone." He wished he hadn't said that.

"How convenient. How would you feel if I disappeared for three days and I told you there wasn't a phone?"

"Okay, look. Honey, look at me."

She did as a tear welled up in her eye.

A lump formed in his throat. "Ellen, I love you with all my heart. Please don't cry. I've been trying to juggle the guys, stuff about getting out, and falling incredibly in love with you."

"And that's why you can't call me for over three days?"

"I screwed up."

She asked if he'd told the guys that they were getting married, and did they even know?"

He was slow to answer then told her he thought so, but truthfully he wasn't sure if he had. He knew as soon as he said it how awful it sounded.

He tried to recover by saying he'd go in right then and tell the whole world how much he loved her and that they were getting married. He swore to God, as his witness, he loved her more than anything in the world.

She said she didn't want him to have to feel like he had to tell anyone.

Jack reassured her he wanted to, but sounded like he was being forced to. "Ellen, please listen to me." Jack took her in his arms. "I wouldn't let anything come between us. I've just been, I don't know, way, way side-tracked. But it's not what you think."

"Then tell me what's been going on."

"It has to do with Bedford and nothing to do with us." He stood back a little, looked past her, placed his hands behind his head, and exhaled enough to scare a seagull off the dock.

"Let me tell you what I know. Bedford tries to kill you. Then he has the payroll stolen from his aircraft, and then he gets caught right over there with some of it." She pointed to the storage-shed area.

"Yes."

"And you want to tell me you know nothing else about any of it?"

He tried to gather his thoughts for the answer, on what he would be drawing a fine line, he knew.

"There's more to it than that. We'd like to lynch the bastard. But it hasn't a damn thing to do with me falling out of control in love with you. Okay?"

"Jack, falling in love, getting married, and planning the rest of our lives shouldn't be this stressful for you."

"Damn, it's not."

"Last chance. Tell me what's bothering you if it's not our relationship."

"Recently, there's been a boat load of shit that's come up, revolving around Bedford and our first tour that we've had to handle."

"And it's so hush-hush that you can't even share it with me?" She glared at him.

"El, come on, I just told you. The stuff is going to blow over in a couple of days, you'll see." He knelt down and held her face with both hands. He felt the interrogation subsiding.

"And you can't walk in there and tell them that we're getting married?"

"Hell, yes, I can. Come on."

He took her hand and then regretted what he'd just committed to.

"I don't want you to do it because I made you. And that's exactly how it sounds."

"Let me start over." He forged ahead. "Ellen, I want to marry you as soon as we get out of the military. Will you spend the rest of our lives with me? I want you more than anything on this earth."

"Yes, if you can act excited about it. . .like you love me and I'm the most important thing to you."

"Come on, Honey. We're announcing it." He took her in his arms. They kissed with the romantic Pacific setting as a backdrop. All of a sudden, Jack felt chills, and it wasn't from the breeze.

Ellen smiled and said, "Okay."

Arm in arm, they walked back to the diner. Jack tried to compose his thoughts. He knew what he had to do, and he more than anticipated the reactions. They'll all say it's too close, and keep your mouth shut, and why now?

Jack held the door open for Ellen. He wished he'd waited a couple of days to make his announcement.

"Hey, they're back," Roadhawg said as he stood and pulled a chair out for Ellen.

With his hand on her shoulder, Jack said, "Hey, I've got a little announcement that I want to share with you all."

"Oh, no" Roadhawg smirked, "Somebody's eating for two."

Everyone laughed. But Jack was deep in thought, choosing his words. He took Ellen's hand.

"Here's the deal." Jack knelt to one knee beside Ellen, and at eye level he looked at her. "All my life I've waited for the right one, the one who would take me just as I am. Someone I love with all my soul. Ellen has just said that she'll marry me."

"Congratulations," Pog said as he stood. "Is it kosher to kiss the betrothed, now?"

Sue and Nancy laughed at his teasing, but Dan looked like he'd seen a ghost. Jack caught it and gave Dan a slight nod.

"Well, we're all happy as hell," Roadhawg said, but he looked shocked. "Let me buy the next round." He headed toward the bar.

The girls gathered around Ellen, hugging and talking. Jack stood as Dan glanced toward Roadhawg at the bar. Jack followed him there.

Dan whispered, "Yes, I'm happy for you two, but your timing couldn't be worse. What in the hell?"

"I know," Jack whispered back, "but I haven't told her anything."

"We've got more plates spinning than we can handle, and you add a gazillion more, Jack."

"Trust me, damn it. She's everything to me, and I'd die for you guys. In two days, it'll be over, one way or the other."

"And if it turns out bad?" Dan walked a couple of steps down the deserted bar and threw his hands up, not looking at Jack.

Jack hurried and stood in front of Dan. "Then come visit me in the fucking brig. Damn it, Dan, why can't you be happy for me?"

"Listen, Jack, I'm one hundred percent for you. But I'm not letting anything get between us. Especially now."

"Well, good for you. I'm doing the best I can. And if you can't see that or go along with that, then kiss my ass."

"You need to listen to yourself, Bud."

Bill walked from the storage area and saluted toward Jack. "Hey, drinks on the house to the newly engaged," he said, grinning.

"By God, today is a mighty fine day. Greatly

appreciated, Bill." Dan pointed his finger like a gun at Bill.

Then Dan glared at Jack and held his thumb and fore-finger slightly apart.

"What?"

Dan looked around and then back to Jack's face. He held his fingers close in front of Jack's nose. "We're this close to pulling it off, and you're this close to blowing it for all of us. That's what."

CHAPTER FIFTY

Jack and Dan walked back to the tables, where Ellen, Sue, and Nancy had finished their first screwdrivers, and were waiting on their seconds. After the guys caught up with the celebration, Bill brought them club sandwiches cut in small triangles, and BLTs.

"Hey, this is my treat. It's way past lunch, and I thought this might hit the spot." Bill placed the food on the table and took the empties.

"Well, thanks. That's really nice of you, Bill," Jack said.

The celebration continued as the sun began to move into their view of the west. The mood had mellowed out, and the women were making plans to attend a late afternoon meeting back at the air traffic control center. They gathered their purses, getting ready to leave. Ellen stood, keys in hand. She put her other hand on Jack's shoulder. "Since we've missed the last few dinners, how about spending tonight at my place, Jack?"

Dan glared at Jack and then closed his eyes.

Jack ignored him. "Honey, give me a bit to finish some stuff here with the guys, and I'll be over."

After taking a sip of his beer, Pog said, "Now that the

girls are gone, what's the plan if we have to stash our cash in the NTA? That's a lot of money to hide."

Dan interrupted. "By God, first things first. Jack. Are we on the same page?"

Jack drummed his fingers on the table, then took a swig of beer. "Hundred percent," he shot back.

"Well, that's good to know." Dan folded his arms. "We need to go to the PX and get twenty or so one-hundred foot ropes to lower the bags on to John's boat."

"Next," Roadhawg said, looking at Jack. He exaggerated a nod to Dan. "We'll need some of those camouflaged net coverings because we sure as hell ain't going to have the time to dig a hole and bury it."

Jack stared out the window, still drumming his fingers. "Yeah, we'll pick out that remote landing zone, I think it's number fifteen. . . you know, the one out by the water with an access dirt road that runs to it. Plus, the grunts never use it because it's too near the water."

"I agree," Roadhawg said. "I like that zone."

"I think it might be easier to load the bags into one of the wagons rather than get the duty truck to move it." Pog glanced around the table. "So we're on for tomorrow night?"

"It's startin' to look that way." Dan stared at his beer bottle. "And as far as the schedule goes, I see no problem getting you all on for Tuesday. Shit, I wish we could add it on for tomorrow. Every minute Luds and Dennis are getting farther away," Dan said, leaning back in his chair.

Jack looked at each one of them. He told them it was going to be a little dicey, because if they got caught with the money now—they'd have no alibi, no excuse. Nothing.

The Roadhawg added the weak excuse that waiting for a reward wouldn't be believable at all once they embarked on their new plan. He pursed his lips. "We didn't steal it from the military. We liberated it from those thieving sons of bitches, and that's the truth."

Jack shook his head. "But once we head out, we're guilty of something serious."

"Yeah, it's kinda hard to say we had it, couldn't decide what to do with it, and then decided to take it. I think they'd want to put us in Leavenworth so we could make big rocks into little rocks for a very long time." Pog toyed with his empty bottle.

"Damn it, Pogy has hit the nail smack dab on the head. Once we go down this path, we're committed. So here's what I think," Jack said. "Let's say for the sake of argument, we get caught. Roadhawg and Pog and me." He pointed at Dan. "You play it cool and disavow any knowledge. Tell 'em you had no clue what was going on. They can't prove doodley shit. You're clean as a whistle."

Roadhawg raised his eyebrows. "I don't get what that does for us."

"Hold on. I'm getting to that," Jack said. "Here's the plan B of all plan Bs."

Dan leaned forward. "You finally got my attention."

Jack smirked at Dan. "Let's pretend we get caught with no excuse. Our shit's hanging in the breeze. What do we have going for us?"

"Nothing. Absolutely zilch." Roadhawg emptied his beer.

"So here's what I'm thinking," Jack said.

The plan was to take some of the large bills out of the storage locker that night and the next day mail them in small packages to Georgia, Dan's dad or his grandpa.

Pog told them mailing the money would be too dangerous.

Jack said it might be, but by mailing it themselves, the recipients wouldn't have a clue what was in the packages. The important thing would be to send it in packages weighing less than fifteen pounds to avoid suspicion.

"So what's really cooking, Jackson?" Roadhawg said.

Jack could tell more explanation was needed. "Dan flies

helicopters. That way it'd give Danny boy a little stash to spring our ass out of Leavenworth or wherever the hell they'll put us. And it'd give us a little to disappear on and start over."

"Jackson. . .Joseph, I don't like you all taking the heat. . .but I think you're on to something."

"We could mail boxes from the exchanges at Kadena, Sukeran, and Naha," Roadhawg said starting to grin. "Send them to different people. Pass the boxes off as uniforms and whatnot that we're sending home ahead of our release from active duty."

"What did we say. . .a million in Franklins weighed about twenty-two-and-a-half pounds?" Pog said. "So how much were you thinking about, Jack?"

"Close to three mil would be sixty-eight pounds. Put it in eight boxes, so they'd weigh a little over eight pounds plus seven pounds of uniforms, and we're set. We have a good chance to cut and run if we get caught."

"By God, Jackson, they'd have a hard time proving I was in on it if they catch you guys. I'll call Dad and Grandpa tomorrow and tell them I'm sending uniforms and just put the boxes away in the barn." At last Dan broke into a grin.

"How would you let them know not to open them?" Pog held his palm up.

"Easy as pie. I'd warn them, under no circumstances, should they let anyone know about the packages or where they hid them."

"Do you think they'd be okay with that?" Jack said.

"Yeah, my Dad and Grandpa will be cool with that. They know my disillusionment about getting out and all. And Georgia will keep quiet and play dumb."

Jack looked around the table at each of his friends. "So I take it we're agreed on plan B?".

"I'd drink to that," Roadhawg said, holding up his beer bottle, "but I got a problem."

CHAPTER FIFTY-ONE

Roadhawg's "problem" was a strained bladder.

Jack left and headed to Ellen's. She answered with the lights off. He stepped inside.

"Baby, what have you got on your mind?" He held her close.

"Something," she said and took his hand, leading him to the candlelit bedroom.

"My timing is lousy, but Honey, could we talk for a little bit?" Start real general. Don't get specific.

"I can't talk you out of talking?" She kissed his neck and started to unbutton his shirt.

"Yes. You know you can, but I need to ask you something."

She sat down and patted the space next to her on the turned-back Murphy bed. "What do you want to talk about?"

"Okay, you know they caught Bedford with some of the payroll. And. . ."

Her eyes narrowed. "Yes." She told him she thought, if someone found some of the payroll and was waiting for the reward, she couldn't see anything wrong with that. And she reminded him that no reward had been offered.

Jack remained silent. Ellen looked at him, then looked away as she rolled her hair round her fingers. She went on to say she thought that those persons should keep the money, especially for all the rotten things the service had done to certain people. She smiled at him. "It serves the military right."

Jack had to leave at 10:30 to meet Roadhawg for a couple of hours.

She turned his face to kiss him, "And, Jack, be real careful." Jack realized for the first time, Ellen knew more than he'd suspected.

When Jack knocked on Roadhawg's door, he was dressed and waiting. Jack drove the two of them through the gate at Hamby and up to the vantage point where the NCID guys had been watching Bedford's storage unit.

"Shit, I'm about to grow an ulcer," Roadhawg said.

"This is worse than waiting for Bedford to show up when we first took the stuff."

"Well, my man, I think it's time to do the deed. You got the flashlight?"

"Yeah, and I gotta piss like an Arabian race-horse." Roadhawg opened the door.

"Hurry up and get that Vienna sausage drained."

"Vienna sausage my ass, more like a giant anaconda." Roadhawg laughed.

When he got back in the car, they drove down to the storage sheds. Jack parked parallel to the shed's rollup door with the back of the wagon in the middle of the soon-to-be opening.

Jack worked the combination while Roadhawg shined the flashlight for Jack.

"Shit, come on, open," Jack whispered. He yanked on the lock several times until it gave way. "Let's slide this door up only a couple of feet as quiet as we can. Then we'll crawl in and pull it back down."

Once inside, they found a couple of the B-4 military parachute duffel bags with large bills.

Roadhawg looked inside an open bag with stacks of hundreds. "Shit. How do we know how much is in there?"

Jack held up a couple of bundles. "Man, ten of `em is a hundred grand. We'll make thirty stacks of ten, and then we'll haul ass. Come on. It'll go quick."

They counted and packed, and after a short time, the flashlight began to dim.

"Shit. I forgot to bring extra batteries," Jack said.

After about ten minutes they were almost done. Twenty-eight stacks of hundreds, ten bundles in each stack equaled two million eight hundred thousand. Jack started putting fifteen of the stacks into one bag while Roadhawg dug around looking for twenty more bundles of hundreds. It took a while longer than either of them expected. Jack zipped and snapped shut each bag.

"Alright. Let's grab a bag and get the hell out of here. Lift up the door." Jack noticed Roadhawg seemed to be fiddling around with the slide-up door.

"Ah, shit," Roadhawg said. "I can't get the door up."

Jack put his bag down. "Here, let me help you."

"Damn, it's stuck." Roadhawg struggled. "We're both pushing up. It ain't budging."

The flashlight dimmed to a faint amber.

"Give me a break," Jack moaned. "I think we're stuck in here."

CHAPTER FIFTY-TWO

Once Jack realized they were stuck in the storage unit he became worried about the light dimming. He had Roadhawg turn it off. It made no sense to either one of them why the door wasn't opening. The immediate concern centered around the Impala wagon sitting out in front of the unit. It would attract the attention of the night security guard.

Roadhawg thought they could say they were stuck inside when the door rolled shut. Jack worried about all the bags. With the remaining battery life, they hustled sipping and stacking the bags in some sort of order. They both sat there not saying a word.

Only the brisk sea breeze could be heard as they sat in silence. The coolness in the storage shed felt like a freezer. Jack wrapped his arms around himself.

"Joe," Jack said pointing to the back wall, "Give me a couple of seconds of the dying flashlight here on this wall."

"What?" Roadhawg turned on the light for a few seconds. Then switched it off.

"Okay. Yeah, man, that might work."

"What might work?"

Jack blew into his hands and rubbed them together. "The inside here has two-by-four studs with plywood paneling nailed on the outside."

"Okay. And so what?" Roadhawg said.

"I think, if we can kick the bottom corner hard enough, it might come loose. If it does, we just might get the outside paneling loose enough to pry it back so I can crawl out."

"Well, hell, let me get to kicking." Roadhawg started moving the bags.

They both put their backs on the floor and their feet at the bottom of the back corner of the plywood panel.

Jack gave the whispered count to three, and they both kicked at the same time for all they were worth. After three kicks they stopped. Jack looked to see if some of the nails had come loose. Roadhawg had to shine the light close because the dim light was failing. Jack thought he felt the siding give a bit.

Roadhawg counted and they both kicked. The noise was loud. For a brief moment, Roadhawg switched on the light.

It looked like the wall hadn't moved all that much, so they kicked it again and again. After the third kick, Jack thought he felt the panel vibrate.

"Hey, hold it." Jack switched on the amber light. He saw a half-inch of separation between the floor plate and the plywood.

"Yee haw," Roadhawg shouted.

"Come on, man. Hold it down. We're making enough racket. This time you kick up the wall stud. I'll move over and kick near the floor plate."

"Okay, I'm ready." Roadhawg began to laugh.

At last, the plywood began to separate from the studs. The more they worked, the larger the gap became at the bottom corner.

A couple more minutes and Jack had enough room to crawl out.

"Roadhawg, hand me that damned flashlight. I'm going

around front to see what's screwed up."

He walked to the end of the storage buildings and stopped. Lights from a car were approaching from up the hill. Jack hurried to the front of their storage unit. He discovered the hasp had fallen down on the latch, so he unfastened it and lifted the door a couple of feet.

"Roadhawg," Jack whispered. "Hurry. A car's coming."

Roadhawg stuffed the two duffel bags through and rolled out. He threw them into the wagon. Jack lowered the shed door and locked it.

Roadhawg started the wagon and put it in gear.

Jack jumped in. "Don't turn on the lights."

"Hey, it looks like some civilian car going down to the docks." Roadhawg sighed in relief.

"Let me run around back and hammer those nails back." Reaching for the toolbox, Jack noticed the car park in front of the diner.

"Try to hammer quietly."

"Yeah, right." Jack got out of the car and disappeared around the building.

In less than five minutes Jack shot around the corner of the building and into the wagon. Roadhawg drove off without turning on the Impala's lights.

Once out the gate at Hamby, the two got to snickering, talking about the whole mess.

"Hey, Roadhawg, when we get back, I want to see if Danny's mellowed out."

"Might be a good idea. He's bent way out of shape."

"No kidding?" Jack rolled his eyes. "He thinks my timing with Ellen is putting us at risk. Honest, I haven't told her diddly, but I will before we get married."

"Jackson, my man, Ellen isn't brain dead. Sure as shit, she's got some idea."

"Yeah, she does, but I ain't talked, and I want to smooth things out with Dan."

They drove up to their BOQ, each of them carried a bag

to Jack's room, and hid them in the closet. Then knocked on Dan's door.

Dan answered. Jack told him they needed to get out of the room and take a ride. Dan grabbed some clothes and met them at the car. He had brought some cold ones and handed one to Jack one and to Roadhawg.

"By God, let me get this straight. The batteries died, then you were locked in and had to kick the shit out of the ass end of the shed so Jack could snake out?"

"Man, you wouldn't think it was so funny if it'd been you." Roadhawg gave him the finger.

"Unbelievable. We oughta write a book about it. But it'd have to be fiction because nobody would believe this shit." Dan laughed.

"Danny, are we cool now?" Jack said.

"Yeah. It's just that I'll feel better when the stuff you guys got tonight is in the mail."

"Now, can the two of you kiss and make up?" Roadhawg said.

"I'm all good," Dan said.

"So am I."

Jack dropped them off out back at the BOQ and headed to Ellen's. He let himself in with the key she'd given him. As he slipped into bed, she rolled over and kissed him.

"Do you trust me enough, now?" she said.

They talked about getting out. Ellen wanted to get married in Hawaii—at Bellows, no less—in late October. They agreed to live in Southern California on Balboa Island in Newport Harbor. It would be close to her work, and Jack could continue his education.

The time passed until Jack noticed her clock.

"Lord, Ellen," Jack said, checking Mickey. "It's almost six. I've got to pick up the guys before the seven o'clock AOM."

"Hurry. I'll share the shower with you."

At 6:20, Jack left Ellen's to pick up Dan and Roadhawg

at the Q. They needed to make an appearance at the all-officer meeting. Jack and Roadhawg departed as soon as the meeting was over. They went to the PX at Futema and bought eight, fifteen-by-fifteen-by-fifteen-inch shipping boxes and brown wrapping paper, then headed to Roadhawg's room.

"Line each of the bottoms with some of these uniform pants and shirts," Jack pointed as he laid out the clothes. "Then we need to put in thirty-seven to thirty-eight bundles on top of the clothes. After that we'll line the top with more pants and stuff."

"Shouldn't we at least weigh one to make sure we stay under fifteen pounds?'

"Yeah, you keep packing, and I'll take this one up to our post office, and if it's good, I'll mail it." Jack put Dan's dad's address on the box and a fictitious name and return address.

After he parked in front of the post office, Jack took a deep breath before taking the box inside. He felt relieved because there was no line as he approached the military postal clerk. "Hey, I'm shipping home some of my uniforms. Does this stay under the fifteen pounds?"

The clerk slid the package on the scales. "Yes, sir. Fourteen pounds, two ounces. Do you want to insure it?"

"Sure, why not?" Jack almost laughed as he handed the clerk a twenty. He pocketed the change and hurried out.

"Man, it went smooth as silk," he said, bounding into Roadhawg's room. He had prepared two more boxes, ready to seal. "How much did it weigh?" He finished putting clothing on the top of the money.

"Right at fourteen pounds. So we're way cool."

"Let's get this stuff done. It makes me nervous being here with. . ." Roadhawg pointed to the bags of money.

After working for the better part of a half hour, Jack finished the final touches on the last box.

Roadhawg put his hands on his hips. "All right, Jackson,

let's skedaddle."

"A couple of trips to the wagon should do it," Jack said as they walked out.

Once inside, Jack relaxed. "First stop, the post office at Kadena."

When they arrived, Roadhawg said, "Okay, I'll take a couple and send them to one address, and you do the same with the other address." Roadhawg hustled out of the car. "Here goes something we said we wouldn't do."

Jack followed, going around back to open the tailgate. "I think we'll be fine. If they were watching us, we'd already be sitting somewhere where we don't want to be."

After a few minutes, Jack found Roadhawg waiting outside the BX post office.

"Jeez. What took you so long?" Roadhawg said.

"I insured it." Jack laughed. "They said it'd be safer."

"Are you serious? You don't believe that, do you?"

"Hell, no. I'm kidding you. Let's get over to Camp Sukeran, and we'll get the other three off from there."

By eleven that morning, the eight boxes were in the mail, and they headed back to the squadron. After posting Tuesday's flight schedule, Dan was ready to take the rest of the day off. Jack and Roadhawg had an 0700 take-off for a three-hour flight.

CHAPTER FIFTY-THREE

Sitting on the engine cover on the top of the aircraft, Jack squirmed and waited and waited. The sun was peeking out from between the clouds behind the hangar with a spectacular display, but he was not enjoying the sunrise at the moment. Luck holding out, my ass, Jack thought. Here we finally got the money loaded and the two internal fuel tanks, and now the bird is down on the preflight.

Pog was hustling, getting the tools to see if he could fix the problem.

"Guys, I'm sorry I missed it. I was hurrying, trying to sneak the two internal tanks on board, making sure nobody came inside, and I just missed it. This raggedy piece of shit ain't my bird, and the H links are out of limits. Let me have ten minutes, and we'll be ready to see if the shims will work."

"If they don't," Jack thought out loud, "I mean it'll be a little rough in the air, but I don't think it'll be a safety-of-flight issue."

"Not this early on." Roadhawg said as Jack and Pog stood on the top of the bird. Pog hustled to loosened the lower H link bolt. "But I'd rather fix it than say piss on it and go. I just worry what else is screwed up on this pile of junk that we don't know about."

"Come on, girls, where's your 'can do' spirit?" Roadhawg flipped them the bird.

"You can blow it out your ass, Roadhawg. That's where it is." Pog laughed.

Jack grumbled, then slugged Roadhawg's arm. "Don't tempt him. He had beans last night."

Roadhawg got a strained look. "And I could play reveille for you whiners if you'd like."

"Awh, Jeez. I've just about got this thing put back together, and you had to go and do that. Man, Roadhawg, something crawled up your ass and died. Jack, can't you do something?"

"Yeah, I had some Hamby beans last night. Just give me a second."

Pog cotter-keyed the bolt and said, "Officers and gentlemen, my ass."

"Pog, you're a genius. It feels tighter than a fifty-five-year-old virgin." Jack shook the tightened H links.

"All right, girls, let's see if this pig will light off, and then let's get the truck outta Dodge." Roadhawg hustled down off the big bird.

"Technically, this could be our last flight in the Marine Corps," Jack said as they taxied for takeoff. "Let's have a ball."

Once in the sky, they took a due-east heading of 090, and things settled down.

"We're short about nine of the hundred-foot ropes that you all bought to lower the bags down to the boat," Pog said over the intercom after about ten minutes over the water.

"Man, that's all they had at the BX at Kadena and all the other PXs we hit." Jack looked at Pog sitting on the jump seat in the cockpit. "Hey, can you pack the money from some of the lighter bags into the others?"

"It'll take some time, and I guess we won't need to be looking for another hour or so. Oh, yeah, the fuel transferred just fine. So we're in the green. Our luck's still good."

Yeah, sure. Just look at that overcast. Probably three thousand feet, and the weather's supposed to deteriorate the farther east we go.

"So our plan is still to fly by, make a visual contact and signal Luds not to use the radio?" Pog stuck his head into the cockpit and said before he sat back down on the jump seat.

"Yeah, we don't want ears hearing anything," Roadhawg said. "I know we'll be most likely out of everybody's range, but still."

"Guys, I gotta tell you that so far I feel good. The night before last, you guys taking the money out of the shed still makes me laugh, but it's all turned out good so far. And then last night when I was getting all of it out to the bird and nobody asked me a thing. We got lucky. I mean that was a shit load of bags," Pog bragged.

In an hour, they climbed to a little over four thousand feet. On a clear day that would give them about forty miles of visibility, but the weather wasn't cooperating.

"Pogy, what's the fuel state?" Roadhawg said.

"We've got a little over half of an internal left, so figure an hour and fifteen to the base, and that'll leave us a good hour and fifteen to find them."

The plan was for Jack and Roadhawg to look forward and to their side, and for Pog to look out each side from the back of the helo. After fifty minutes, the concern level had risen, and intercom chatter was nonexistent as they strained and concentrated on any anomaly on the dark blue, almost gray, white-capped Pacific.

"We've run five-minute legs and two-minute turns to keep heading further east," Jack said. "Anyone have a suggestion?"

They knew they were heading for Iwo Jima which was due east, give or take, as the crow flies, with a 093 heading out of Kadena. Now they'd flown that radial out for the time they'd allotted. Roadhawg checked his calculations on his knee pad. Pog checked the fuel in the internal tanks, again.

Jack rubbed his forehead. "I hate to think about having to call it off. We've still got about twenty to twenty-five minutes, and that'd be cutting it close."

"Here's my two cents' worth," Pog said. "Let's fly for seven more minutes, and if we don't find them, we go stash the stuff."

"Sounds as good as anything," Jack said. He turned the big bird to the 093 heading, and they continued to search the dark-blue Pacific.

"Hey. . .I thought I saw something," Pog shouted. "Shit, it's gotta be them. I swear, it's a sailboat at our three o'clock about a couple miles out heading about zero seven zero."

Roadhawg stared hard out the right side. "I don't see a thing. Keep your eye on it and turn me into it."

"Keep turning farther right," Pog said.

"I don't see a thing," Jack said.

"Oh, hell, yes." A smile spread across Roadhawg's face. "I see it. It's got to be them."

"I don't have them," Jack sat up trying to look out the right side window.

"It's them. Shit. It's them." Roadhawg yelled and clapped his hands.

"I'll be getting the first bag with the note ready. Ramp coming level," Pog said.

The helo descended to make a low pass at less than fifty feet. Luds and Dennis stood on the deck and waved. Jack, from his side, gave the no radio signal to Dennis who acknowledged.

Roadhawg slowed to almost a hover.

"Steady, man." Jack said motioning for Luds to drop the sails.

"He's got it. I see him dropping the main-sail," Pog said as they started to circle.

"Yeah, I see that now," Roadhawg said. "Okay, Jack, you got the bird. I'm heading back to help Pog lower the bags." He climbed out of the cockpit and headed into the cabin to plug his helmet into a long cord so he could monitor and talk on the ICS. Jack took his time as he hovered the helo above the aft of the sailboat.

"The boat's coming under the nose," Jack said.

"Roger, we got it in sight," Pog relayed to Jack. "Steady, slow, hold. Hold. We're lowering the first bag. Hold. Back five. That's good. Load about ten feet off the deck. Hold. Whew. Lud's got it. The first rope is dropped. You're drifting aft. Slide to your right ten. Hold, next bag's being lowered. Hold. Ten more feet. Roadhawg, hold yours off the side. Good. Now Luds has it."

"Guys, I'm hovering into a cross wind. This bird is wallowing around like nobody's business. They're still under sail, moving one direction and the wind's trying to blow us in another. And that damned main mast can't be a couple of feet below us, rolling up and down with the waves. Let me bring it around and hover with our nose over the boat's stern. That way I'll have a visual reference."

Jack brought the bird around, nose to stern at the other end of the boat.

"Jack, we're starting to lower the ropes again," Roadhawg yelled. "Shit, Pog, how much did you put in this one? It weighs a ton."

Jack brought the nose up a touch to stop the forward drift. That caused Roadhawg to stumble back toward the edge of the ramp. He grabbed the overhead, but his grip slipped loose on the bag.

"Oh, shit. I just dropped it in the ocean. Shit, it sank. Damn it, it sank clean outta sight. Lud's trying to get the rope. I mean, it went straight down and deep."

CHAPTER FIFTY-FOUR

"Guys, I'm looking forward into a million miles of ocean. I can't see shit back there. Talk to me. What's going on?" Jack pleaded from the cockpit.

"Hey, Roadhawg, there it is. It just popped up about thirty feet behind the boat. What the hell is Ludwig doing?" Pog shouted from the back of the ramp.

"He's got a grappling hook, trying to snag it," Roadhawg said and began stomping his feet.

"Screw it, boys, We're five minutes past our time. We don't have that much gas for Ludwig to screw around. Get the rest of them down. I don't care if you drop them on him. We're going to be low on fuel as it is. Hurry."

They started lowering two more bags. Dennis had the line and was pulling the floating bag in.

The Roadhawg talked above the noise from the aft of the helo. "Way to go, Dennis. He's hauling them in like nobody's business, Jack. There's the rest of the rope," Roadhawg said as Dennis got the bag on board.

"Hold steady," Pog said. "Mine's swinging, Jack. Okay, now he's snagged it. I'm letting out the rope. Rope is away, bag on the deck. Nine more to go."

"I know I don't have to tell you," Jack said as he held the helicopter over the boat. "We're way over our time."

When Dennis and Luds got the last bag on deck, Jack departed as Pog waved good-bye and Roadhawg ran to the cockpit. He slid into his seat. "How's the fuel?"

"Pog, are you sure the internals are empty?" Jack didn't answer Roadhawg.

"Yeah," Pogy mumbled as he entered the cockpit and sat on the jump seat. "Guys, they're dryer than a popcorn fart."

"If the internal tanks are empty," Jack said, "I figure we've got over an hour and forty to the base, and we've only got about an hour and thirty of fuel left."

All eyes were on the fuel gauges.

"Guys, we're not going to make Futema. There's not enough fuel left," Jack said as he tapped the fuel gauges while Pog turned around and left the cockpit, not saying a word.

The three of them sat in silence while the massive T-64 engines seemed to scream even louder, all the while drinking precious fuel.

"Bullshit. Let's slow it down and fly the max endurance airspeed. We gotta milk ten more minutes outta the tanks or we're going to make a liquid landing." Jack looked from Pog to Roadhawg.

"From the boat's flag, if it helps us any, we've got a quartering tailwind. Kadena's a couple of miles closer, but how do we explain that we're out of fuel and had to refuel there? Plus, we're going to be late on our chock time back at Futema. I don't see any good options here." Roadhawg shook his head and looked out the side window.

"I've pumped every ounce out of the internals," Pog added as he joined the two pilots again in the cockpit and sat down on the jump seat.

"Hey, Roadhawg, how about this? We fly max endurance, and drop down to ten to fifteen feet off the

261

water. We'd be in ground effect and save power."

"What are you talking about?" Pog said.

"Shit, yeah." Roadhawg came to life. "Pog, within a rotor's length of the surface we pick up ground effect and it requires less power. You know, like when we hover in ground effect. If we could climb high enough, we'd get better fuel efficiency, but the overcast limits that. Come on, Jack, let's start skippin' across the waves."

Jack leveled off at about fifteen feet. The windscreen picked up salt water spray, and, sure enough, about five percent less power was required.

Jack hated doing that to a bird—because of salt water ingestion and spray all over everything, He knew they didn't have much choice, and shook his head.

Roadhawg reminded Jack and Pog that if they couldn't get Kadena's navigational signal, and if they couldn't get the Kadena TACAN, they'd probably be flying off the most direct course, and they realized that'd be wasting more fuel.

Their conversation ended with Jack saying if they were lucky enough to make land, they could set the helo down and have Pog break loose an engine fuel line. Then it would be easy to say they discovered the bird was losing fuel and had to put it down as soon as they reached dry land. He realized he was grasping at straws.

"It'd cause a bunch of questions to be asked, but I'll be glad to see the terra firma. We'll go with that, if and when we make land." Roadhawg shook his head and rubbed his chin.

The next hour dragged by. Their usual banter was gone as they flew in silence.

Jack new Roadhawg was nervous, because he rubbed his chin again, then said, "Okay, girls, we're getting seriously low on fuel and no land in sight."

"Well, thanks, Roadhawg, you had to jinx it. There's the low-fuel light." Pog pointed out the glaring yellow panel light. Just then, Pog pointed over Roadhawgs shoulder straight ahead.

"Hey, hey, look there, I think I see it. Yes, it's land in the horizon . . . I think." The Roadhawg also pointed straight ahead.

Jack said, "Might just be low clouds."

"Shit, yes, its land." Pog yelled. "And look, the TACAN is locking on to Kadena."

"The distance is not locking on because we're too low." Jack stared at the gauge.

Roadhawg babied the controls. "Boys, I think we're about straight on course for Futema. The distance-measuring equipment is trying to spin around to tell us how far."

"I never thought seeing this piece-of-shit island would look so beautiful," Pog said, rubbing his hands together as he turned and left the cockpit.

"Amen, but the bad news is, the DME has us forty-three miles to Kadena, and we have less than twenty minutes of fuel. At two miles a minute, we're still short." Jack looked at Roadhawg.

"We could make White Beach." Roadhawg pointed at the land in front of them. "And try to pull the leaky-fuel-line routine."

"I hate doing that. We'd still be in trouble for running that short. Plus, all the questions they'd raise, like, why didn't we come home sooner?"

Pog chuckled. "I'll take anything short of landing in the water." Again, he spun around and returned to the cabin.

"Let's make land first. I think if we come a little more to the left we'll be heading straight for White Beach." Jack pointed in that direction.

Pog returned to the cockpit after a few minutes. "I scavenged the pumps in the tanks to make sure I got every last drop into the main tanks. They're dry as a bone. How long have the lights been on now?"

"Fourteen minutes." Jack tapped the clock on the

instrument panel. "We've got White Beach about a mile ahead and maybe five minutes of fuel left. Wanna land at White Beach and call it quits or try for Futema?" Jack looked at Roadhawg.

"I don't know. I just the hell don't know. But if we could make Futema, we're home free. If we shut her down at White Beach, we're going to be in deep shit. So, what do you guys say?" He looked from Jack to Pog.

Pog, not looking at either one of them, said, "I say let's go for it."

Jack looked Roadhawg square in the eye. "You're the aircraft commander."

CHAPTER FIFTY-FIVE

"Screw it. We're heading for Futema. Remember. . .no guts, no dead war heroes." Roadhawg cocked his head and grinned at Jack.

"So we'll request spot three. We can fly straight to it, and it's closer to the fuel pits. You're holding 120 knots. Let's keep the gear up until we're on final."

Jack made the radio call when they approached the field boundary. "Futema tower, Yankee fox one two is approaching five miles to the east for landing."

"Ah-h-h, roger, Yankee fox one two, winds are light. You're cleared to land on two four. Call five miles, over."

"Roger, tower, we're five miles. We'd like to land on spot three."

"Yankee fox one two, I have you in sight. Report your gear, and cleared to land on spot three. You have no traffic."

"I'll hold your gear until we're in close," Jack said to the Roadhawg over the intercom.

"Roger that." The fuel gauges showed empty.

When they approached spot three, Roadhawg transitioned to a hover over spot three.

Jack lowered the gear and reported to the tower, "Yankee fox one two has three in the green."

"Roger, Yankee fox one two, cleared to land spot three."

"Shit, girls, I think we're going to make it." Roadhawg flared to land.

About thirty feet in the air and in a huge flare, Jack said, "Oh, shit, we're losin' fuel pressure to number one."

"Roger, we're rocking over, so I'll no-hover land." Roadhawg transitioned to land. He set the fuel-starved bird on the deck, first the two main mounts, and then he feathered the nose gear on the deck, smoother than silk.

"Shit, we did it. We're on the deck," Roadhawg hurried to the fuel pits with only the number-two engine turning. Number one was spooling down.

"Now, if we can make the pits before number two flames out," Pog said.

"Tower switching to ground," Jack reported. Without waiting, he switched to ground control. "Futema ground, Yankee fox one two is spot three to the pits. Close us out, over."

Pog stomped his feet for joy like a little kid as he hit Jack on the shoulder.

"Yee haw," Jack yelled, loud enough to be heard over the noise of the single engine.

"Thank you, Lord," Roadhawg said.

"Roger, Yankee fox one two, you're cleared to the pits, and you're closed out."

"Pull in, and I'll jump out and get the hose pumpin' ASAP." Pog hurried out of the cockpit.

When the bird came to a stop, Pog was already out. Jack watched him sprint to the three-inch fuel line and drag it to the fuel point on the aircraft like it was nothing. Pog gave a thumbs up, turned, shook his fist over his head in celebration, and then shouted over the intercom. "There, damn it. Now, we're pumpin'. Hot damn, we made it. I knew we could make it."

Jack and Roadhawg looked at each other as they both shook their heads.

After about fifteen minutes, they finished refueling. Pogy turned off the pump and disconnected the fuel hose.

They taxied to their line and shut the full bird down.

For the last time, they'd made it home.

"Hey, sirs," Pog said with his mustached smirk.

"What?" Jack answered.

"We just took six hundred and forty-five gallons. If both tanks were dry, we'd take three-eighteen a side. That means we took nine gallons over the limit. Gents, what it means is we ran out in the pits while we were pumping fuel."

"Nobody's lookin' at the fuel logs anyway, and if they do, just say we accidentally pumped some into the internals." Jack began to laugh.

"Yes, sir, that's exactly what I was getting at. I've always said I'd rather be lucky than talented any day." Pog clenched his fist and shook it. "Any day."

They did their post flight inspection, Pog did his post flight inspections. Roadhawg and Jack walked into the maintenance control.

"And now that's it," Jack said as he finished filling out the yellow sheets on the long counter.

"Well, Jackson, what a way to end a career." Roadhawg broke into a smile.

"Joseph, I quit. The Marine Corps got the last bit of me today," Jack said to Captain Hegidio as they walked out of maintenance control. "Let's go get Danny and be done."

Dan waited for them at the entrance to the hangar. "Girls, here they are. We're officially FIIGMO." He shook the release from active duty orders "Ah-h-h, I Got My Orders, if you know what I mean. A week from today, the three of us are homeward bound on the same freedom bird."

They walked to Dan's beige Pontiac wagon.

"Hey, Danny boy," Jack said more than asked. "Admit it? You're gonna miss this wagon, aren't you?"

"Hell, no," Dan smirked, "but I might buy me a six-pack of `em when we get home now that I can afford it."

"Well, ladies, I'm having dinner with the future Mrs. Higgins. What's on your agendas?"

"Nancy's got a little ditty planned for just the two of us." Dan nodded with a smile.

"Sue's borrowed Ellen's car, and she has two days off. So we're heading to those romantic special-service's cabins that you all went to." Roadhawg patted Jack on the shoulder.

"Well, they can kiss my ass if they think I'm showing up tomorrow." Jack looked at his two Marine Corps combat brothers.

"By God, me, too," Dan joined in.

"Hey, I've got to tell you. In a million years, I would've never. . .ever. . .thought it could've been this screwed up, and we'd come out smelling like a rose." Jack did his half Higgins grin.

"Wanna know the best part?" Roadhawg slapped Jack on the back." We didn't screw up like Bedford and Tanner."

Dan drove to the parking lot at the BOQ.

Jack headed straight to his phone and called Ellen. "Hey, we're done," he said.

"I'm dying to hear the whole story."

"And I'm going to tell you all about it."

CHAPTER FIFTY-SIX

Late February the following year

An Oklahoma chill still hung in the air over Grand Lake. The water reflected the rising full moon like a mirror, and the emerald-covered hills leading down to the shore faded into ebony as the sun began to approach the horizon.

The flat deck on the pontoon boat had an open-pit fire in the center. The gang had gathered around the pit, sitting on benches. The wake following the boat broke the surface of the water as Dennis shut off the engines, allowing the boat to slow drift to a peaceful stop.

Jack listened to the scrub oak as it popped and crackled in the fire pit. Breaking the silence, he began, "From the Cave to Dennis's boat." His arm was around Mrs. Higgins. With his other hand he raised a cold bottle of Coors and toasted. "Here's to Dennis and Georgia's new place and to this fine boat of yours. And, here's a toast to the Cave. I've really missed watchin' TV with you all."

Dan chuckled. "By God, let's not forget to have a toast to Bedford and Petey boy."

"I still can't believe the investigators couldn't fully pin it on them. I mean, they caught Bedford in the storage unit,"

Dennis said.

"The note he produced saying he needed to check out the storage shed was bogus." Roadhawg shook his head.

Dan said, "If they'd checked the hand writing, it was probably Petey boy's."

Ellen looked at each of the Marines before she said, "And those two still retired with full pay. That stinks."

"They're out of our life, and I say forget `em." Jack said.

"Me, too, Jack. But I want to say this to each one of you all. Thanks for showin' up." Dennis stood and picked up a small floating pyre made of wood.

Pog said, "I wouldn't have missed it for the world."

Then Dan, Jack, Luds, Roadhawg, Dennis, and Pog together, placed the pyre in the lake, and Dennis set the wood on fire.

As it drifted away from the boat, Jack said, "Here's to Herb and Todd. You guys will never be forgotten."

Dennis turned on a cassette player. "Toddy loved the Beach Boys."

"California Girls" began to play, and the pyre burned brighter. The light from the fire illuminated everyone's face in the darkness as the song ended.

Dennis said, "Herb always wanted the bagpipes."

The Marines stood at attention as The Marine Corps Hymn followed. When the pipes finished, they sat down. Silence remained until the light from the pyre died.

"You'll be with us for all times," Dennis said when the water took the last of the pyre.

"I think they'd be proud of us." Dan raised his bottle. "Here's to us. We did it. And we survived."

"Luck was on our side, but perseverance and the best crew ever didn't hurt none," Jack said. He lifted his bottle. "Thanks to you all."

"Speaking of saying thanks, guys, thank you for. . .well, everything." Now Pog raised his bottle to each of them.

"I don't know about the rest of you, but I'm ready for a

new adventure." Dan grinned.

"Hell, it'll be hard getting Bedford and Petey to take the blame for us again," Jack said. "But it'll be tough to top this one."

"I could use a next one," Dan said. "I gotta admit I've been getting a little restless these last few months."

"Well, I'll be damned. I know how we could make millions of dollars." Jack turned to face the group.

"Well, Jackson, we're all ears," Roadhawg said.

"Invent non-reflective lenses for binoculars." Jack stared hard at the shoreline to the east with the sun on the horizon. His grin disappeared. "I don't want to sound paranoid, but somebody's watching us. I see the reflection off their binoculars. I mean, the sun is reflecting off them big time."

"Where?" Dennis said.

"Don't everyone look at once. See the reflection over there on the east shoreline?"

Roadhawg was looking at the hills. "Hell, yeah, I do, but who'd give a royal rat's ass about us now?"

"I don't know," Jack said, "but I got a feeling, somehow we're not finished with the money run."

ABOUT THE AUTHOR

P.R. Steele flew as a pilot in the CH 53 helicopter for the Marine Corps in Viet Nam, and also the money run on Okinawa. He is retired from the military with 27 years of service on active duty and the reserves. He lives in northern California and enjoys tinkering on his old cars, writing, avoiding work, and honey dos.